AF539687

THE INFECTED

sands press
Brockville, Ontario

THE INFECTED

PERRY PRETE

sands press

sands press

A Division of 3244601 Canada Inc.
300 Central Avenue West
Brockville, Ontario
K6V 5V2

Toll Free 1-800-563-0911 or 613-345-2687
http://www.sandspress.com

ISBN 978-1-990066-07-8

Publisher's Note

This book is a work of fiction. References to real people, events, establishments, organizations, or locales, are intended only to provide as a sense of authenticity, and are used fictitiously. All other characters, and all incidents and dialogue, are drawn from the authors' imaginations and are not to be construed as real.

For information on bulk purchases of this book or any book published by Sands Press, please call 1-800-563-0911.

To book an author for your live event, please call: 1-800-563-0911

Sands Press is a literary publisher interested in new and established authors wishing to develop and market their product. For more information please visit our website at www.sandspress.com.

Day 1

Luzy, France

2:57pm

Meteor strike

Day 7

First human infection reported

Day 365

Known dead: 2 billion

Known infections: 5 billion

Day 915

North America
Somewhere near the Quebec/Vermont Border
Late Summer

Pain.

The first thing that registered was a sensation in his side, something he had never felt or couldn't recall. It was uncomfortable and caused him to take notice. He didn't know how to quantify it—wasn't even sure what the feeling was—but it hurt. He couldn't recall ever having felt this sensation before, the level of discomfort was overwhelming. There was nothing for him to relate it to, no reference, nothing in his brain to say, *This is pain, this is what pain feels like. Record this so that if it happens again, you will know. It hurts, avoid feeling this again.* He wasn't sure why, but he reached down and instinctively covered the area that hurt with his hand. He probed a small wound in his abdomen and felt something wet. His fingers moved around, and he accidently stuck a finger into the wound. His agony increased to new heights and he quickly removed his finger. He wanted to scream but was unable to make a noise. His breathing increased, and he lay immobile, his eyes closed, until the feeling subsided.

Time had no relevance. Did he lie there for a minute, an hour, or days? Like his new-found discomfort, time had no reference for him.

The man lay on his back, opened his eyes and saw—something. There was no way to be sure what it was. The room was dark, whatever he was looking at was black and white, with shades of gray and shadows casting long silhouettes across the surface. A tiny fracture of light broke through something. His mind was filling with stimuli that made no sense to him. Everything happening to him since he woke was new.

The ache he felt hadn't gotten any better, the taste in his mouth was—dry. Uncertain if that was the norm or if there was some other sensation he was supposed to experience, he opened his mouth, moved his tongue around, and grimaced. Again, this was new. Whatever it was in his mouth was bad; he didn't like it. Not remembering ever having tasted anything, he couldn't describe what it was, only that he didn't enjoy it. He spit and a large chunk of bloody flesh hit the floor. He had no idea how that had managed to get into his mouth.

The man felt the need to sit up. He tried, but couldn't. He braced an arm on the floor and pushed, forcing his head up, then his shoulders. There wasn't enough strength to raise the rest of his body. Without realizing what or why, with his free hand he reached behind and steadied himself to sit upright. There was more pain in his hand as he pressed it upon the floor. Looking down, he noticed a small piece of flesh missing from the side of his palm just below his little finger. It stung but he fought against the pain. Sitting up caused his stomach to hurt again.

He paused for a moment. His mind began to process the information, but had nothing other than the first few minutes of experience to use as reference. Like a new computer hard drive, his mind had no operating system, no directives, no references to base decisions upon. He didn't recognize what was happening. He was running on instinct that he didn't understand. His stomach wound began to ache anew; he covered it again with his hand.

Looking around the room, he went back and forth taking in

what information he could that might help him begin to understand what was going on. The pain was still strong, the wetness on his hand getting worse. He pulled his hand away and looked at it. There was something on it, something liquid that moved, then dripped to his lap. It was dark; everything was either black or white or somewhere in between. The substance on his hand was warm, dark, almost black and fluid. He put his hand back over the wound and pressed harder. For some reason it felt better when he did that.

He looked to his left, then scanned to the right. What he saw made no sense to him. There were things around him, things he felt he should recognize or know what they were, but for some reason his mind refused to divulge its secrets, refused to let him in on the horrible secret it was keeping.

That thing on the right that let the light in was square, with ragged material partially covering it. It was bright white in a room that was mostly black. He covered his eyes against the light, stood on weak legs that could barely hold his weight. He felt as if he would fall backwards, steadied himself and walked over to the square, white shape. Pushing the material aside, he moved in close bumping his head on the glass. Stunned, he touched the glass with his bloodied hand leaving a handprint. Puzzled, he tapped the glass with the tip of his index finger. With each tap, a tiny spec of blood was left behind. He studied what he had done, then looked beyond the blood smears.

The bright light burned his eyes; he squinted, having a difficult time adjusting, but eventually he could see what was on the other side. Tall brown things with thick bases and arms with tiny green fingers that fluttered in the wind were everywhere. The area was bathed in white light, almost no darkness anywhere except at the base and between those tall things.

When he turned around, the area he was in was dark. He'd been able to see things before, but since he'd looked out the white square, his eyes had trouble focusing on what he had seen earlier. It took a few minutes, but his eyes adjusted once again. He still didn't understand or comprehend the horror in the cabin.

He looked around. Everything was new to him. He didn't know if what he was seeing was horrible, pleasant or something in between.

The cabin was small, had been modern at one time and was most likely a vacation cottage for a family, but was now littered with bodies and mayhem. It was long and narrow, and from where he stood he could see everything, but couldn't understand any of it. To his left, the only bedroom had the door ripped from its hinges and a lone female body lay on the floor beside the bed. Her throat had been ripped open, bitten, gnawed at, her left arm was missing, and blood pooled around the body. Directly in front of him, the kitchen was still immaculately clean except for the blood splatter against the cabinets and across the refrigerator door. The family dog lay on its side. The dog's abdomen had been ripped open and the bowels trailed out to where he was standing. On the floor beside its mouth rested a small chunk of flesh it had torn from the person responsible for killing his family. He turned his injured hand and compared the missing piece to the one on the floor.

The thought quickly disappeared as he moved to the right; the living room had two chairs that had been toppled in the fight, a flat screen television hung on the wall with a small bullet hole in the bottom left corner. The partial remains of two small children lay in the centre of the carpet, each with injuries similar to the family dog.

He looked at the small hole in the television and looked down at the hole in his abdomen. They were the same. He looked back up to the bullet hole. Walking to the television, he placed one hand over the hole in the screen, the other over his wound. His mind began to make the correlation. In the glossy black screen, for the first time, he saw his own reflection. A stranger was looking back at him, a face he had never seen. He wasn't even sure if he had ever seen another face before. Is this what everyone looked like, was he normal? He didn't know for sure. His skin looked different from those on the floor; his own skin looked darker, rougher; his eyes were solid black. He touched his cheek, felt the coarse texture of the skin, noticing a laceration on the right side. It wasn't wet, no dark blood, and he wondered if that was supposed to be the way he looked. Beside his image, on the floor, he saw the reflection of the two smaller bodies.

He turned to the bodies and knelt beside the children, unsure of what they were. They appeared to be smaller versions of himself, one looked like him, the other looked like the other child but with longer hair and softer features. For some unknown reason, he wanted to reach out and touch them. His hand traced the outline of the boy's face, felt his hair, and marveled at the perfection of the little person. No scar or cuts on the cheeks. The other child was lying on her back, her stomach ripped open with her bowels strewn across the floor. They were both dead, but he wasn't sure why. He poked the body with his finger, gently at first, then harder. There was no response. He attempted the same with the second body and received the same results. He had never seen death before; maybe he had, but he wasn't aware what being alive meant either. Tiny bits of information began to form in his mind, and without realizing it, his mind started to form thoughts. Now, he wanted to know if the world was anything more than the cabin and the surrounding area.

Standing over the two young bodies, he turned to the bright white light emanating from the square in the wall. His mind began to work, wondering where the white light was coming from. He slowly walked towards it and stared outside. As he had done earlier, he reached out and touched the pane and began to push against it. The glass refused to give; he pushed harder. Still, the glass remained intact. Pulling his hand away, multiple ideas continued to form in his head, ideas that meant nothing to him. More information was needed, information he could not get in the cabin.

Holding his injury, he hobbled around the room, wondering how to leave. With his free hand, he pressed against the walls, pushing, and pulling, without success. As he made his way around the cabin, he noticed several smaller holes in the walls like the one in the television and his stomach. Each time he stressed his wound, a fresh wave of pain would pulse through him reminding him what pain was. He made his way to the bedroom and stepped in the dark pool surrounding the large female body. His foot slipped in the half-coagulated mass, but he caught himself before he fell. He crouched down and noticed something odd, the older body looked strikingly familiar to the dead younger female. This made him think; he wondered how two different bodies, one old and one young, could look so similar.

As these new thoughts confused him, he noticed something he hadn't before, and he didn't know what it was. Like the new sensation of pain, now he could smell. He inhaled deeply and the odour of something foul filled his senses. It was the scent of death, the metallic copper smell of spilled blood, and soon the room would be filled with the stench of rotten flesh.

All these new sensations and emotions filled his head causing confusion, but he would soon come to realize what they were.

He touched the open wound on the dead woman where her arm had been. It was cold and looked like his own wound, only larger. Leaning in closer, he sniffed, taking in the smell of the blood pool.

It was unpleasant and left an odd taste in his mouth. He pulled his hand away from his own wound and smelled the blood upon his fingers. It too was the same odour. Were they all the same, the dead and him? They bled; did they also feel the same pain?

His urge to leave the cabin increased. Was it fear? He knew not. He only knew that now was the time to leave. There was another window in the bedroom, and he pounded on the glass panes until they gave way, shattering, sending shards falling to the ground below. He reached through as the broken glass that remained in the frame cut deep through his skin causing more pain. He pulled back, gripping the laceration on his arm, and tried to scream but nothing came out. Was that all he could do? Had he forgotten how to speak, or scream?

He was learning quickly. He pushed the remaining jagged pieces of glass from of the wooden frame. The sharp edges cut his fingers, but he persisted. Grabbing the frame, he squeezed himself through the broken window opening. He landed hard on the ground below, more pain. He stumbled to his feet, barely able to stand upright, he scanned the area around him, looked up towards the blue sky, and for no apparent reason, staggered off in the direction of the woods. The sun hurt his eyes, burning them. He was having difficulty adjusting to the bright sunlight.

He limped through the trees as he protected his stomach wound with one hand, covering his eyes with the other. The terrain was rough as he made his way deeper into the forest and away from the light. He was running on some primal instinct, something he didn't understand but that told him to leave and get away. He followed what he felt inside. The further he went, the larger the trees and the more difficult the underbrush was to navigate, but he persisted. In the dark and moist thicket, he slumped against a tree and slid down, sitting on the damp moss. The pain had increased in his stomach; he didn't really understand why or how this was happening. Something came over him. His eyes grew heavy, his body no longer had the energy to move forward; he thought he would die—like those others that were dead in the cabin. He fought to keep his eyes open, but eventually they closed and stayed closed.

When he woke, darkness surrounded him. There was no way to tell how long he had been sleeping, if that's what it was called. There were no dreams, no nightmares, no rest. He had stopped his journey, sat against a tree and fallen asleep. Now, he looked up, the sun had disappeared from the sky replaced by tiny bits of brilliant light that sparkled in the night. His eyes no longer hurt the way they did when he stared into the bright daylight.

He looked at his hand. It was difficult to see, but he felt the blood had dried to a crusty shell in his palm. His wound still hurt, but not nearly as much as it had before he fell asleep. He still had pain, but this pain was different, it gurgled and made noise. He opened and closed his mouth repeatedly. The metallic taste was gone but he needed something else.

On his hands and knees, he rummaged through the leaves, pushing the brush aside, sniffing the ground until he found wild mushrooms. He pulled them from the earth; without cleaning the dirt and debris, he ate one after the other until they were gone. He continued to brush more earth aside. Leaves rustled as a mouse scurried away. He pounced on the rodent and held it by the tail. The tiny brown field mouse squirmed and spun around attempting to escape its capture. Dangling by its tail, it flung itself onto the finger of the hand that held it and sunk its teeth into the flesh, taking a small bite. He felt nothing as the mouse continued to attempt an escape, taking tiny bites out of its capture's finger. He held the small animal high, looking at it, wondering what it was, and finally just let it drop to the forest floor. It quickly burrowed into the brush and disappeared.

Scavenging for the type of mushrooms that he had eaten earlier, he crawled on his hands and knees until he found more and ate until he was full. His stomach rumbling began to subside, but now he looked for something for his thirst. He continued to crawl on the ground feeling for moisture. He gathered some damp leaves, placed them in his mouth and sucked on them for several seconds, drawing the moisture away, then spiting them out.

Even though the sun had gone down, and darkness had overtaken day, he could still see just as well as in the light except his eyes no longer burned.

He stood and began to walk. With no real destination in mind, he just walked, lumbered between trees, making his way deeper into the forest.

Day 916

It was just after sunrise when Carrie Jordan slowly turned the doorknob to the cabin. She put her shoulder against the door and forced it open, pushing against the debris on the other side. The smell of death and decay was evident the moment she entered. Holding her small caliber pistol in one hand, she pushed the door open wider and scanned the interior, stepping carefully, making certain nothing would reach out from within the carnage. She checked every corner, behind every door, under the furniture, inside the closets and cabinets. Once she felt certain she was alone, she holstered her pistol and knelt beside the two children. Her hand glided over the bodies, cold and rigid, dead. It was obvious it had been some time since they died. Looking around the cabin, she spotted the adult at the other end and went to her side. The injuries were horrific, and Carrie knew her friend was gone. Among the other injuries, all three bodies showed signs of bite marks. She pulled her knife from its sheath and dragged it through the blood. Only the centre of the pool in the deepest section was still moist. The rest was dry and hardening. It had been more than twenty-four hours. She wiped the blade on one of the bodies before replacing it.

Sympathy for the dead had long since been replaced with survival instinct. Carrie found a backpack and dumped the contents to the floor. Her own was old and thread worn, with open seams held together by duct tape. She picked through her old bag, found what she wanted, tossed the items into the new pack then walked about the cabin collecting things that might come in handy. She rummaged through the drawers for flashlights, batteries of any size, anything to help power electronics. There were none, but she did find two butane lighters and several packs of wooden matches. There was also some canned food, bottles of water, dried meat, Advil, and prescription medications, which she stuffed into the pack.

In the bathroom, on the vanity, she found what was left of a bar of soap. Carrie picked up the soap, held it close to her face and inhaled. The fragrance of lavender overwhelmed her senses. For a moment, even with three dead bodies just outside, she thought about taking a bath—a long, relaxing bath—wash her hair, shave her legs and feel like a girl again. Bubbles and smooth legs, how perfect would that be? Perfect, she reasoned, if not for the bodies in the other room. As quickly as the thought came to her, it left. Beside the sink was a pail full of clean water. Carrie lifted the pail and drank what she could. The water was stale and tasted of plastic. She pulled the pail away from her mouth, coughed, then tilted it again. She drank until her stomach was full. With the remaining water, she dunked her hands and used what little was left of the soap to lather up and wash off weeks' worth of dirt and grime. She looked at her clean pink hands with more dirt under her nails then she cared to admit.

From the bathroom, Carrie went to the front door, found a nylon poncho hanging from a nail, rolled it tightly and ran it through the loops of the backpack. In the bedroom closet she retrieved a rifle and almost twenty rounds of ammunition.

Standing over the body of the dead woman, she thought about her friend for a moment then flicked the lighter and lit the curtains on fire. She also lit the curtains in the main room, and the sofa, then stepped out of the cabin without looking back. She heard the crackling and felt the heat as the fire spread. It would certainly attract attention and she had to put some distance between her and cabin quickly. At the end of the lane, she turned back only to make sure the cabin was fully engulfed, then broke into a jog in the direction of the dirt road at the end of the driveway.

Carrie had to meet up with the rest of the group the next day and had a long walk ahead. It was still unseasonably warm for this time of the year. Holding the rifle in front as she ran to the road make it difficult to keep a steady pace. She wasn't used to carrying so much weight for such a long period of time—or being alone; no one liked being alone anymore. Fatigue soon took over and she slowed her pace to a fast walk. Turning around, she saw the fire was now just a tiny glow in the distance. Beads of sweat dripped from her forehead and the tip of the nose. Carrie wanted to stop, but she knew that was a very bad idea in the open.

She kicked the dirt with her boots as she moved along the country road. It was wrong to make noise as she walked but it was something she had done as a girl and it still made her feel young. Except back then, she didn't have to worry about being ambushed. When she had the energy, she broke into a slow jog, moving along as quickly as the load on her back would permit. Listening for any noise coming from the brush along the roadside, she longed for the days when she could listen to music as she walked or worked out. It had been years since she had heard her favourite songs, a podcast, or watched a television show. Not having any distractions was good. She knew she wasn't supposed to be out after dark, but she had to rejoin the group, and soon.

In her mind, she hummed tunes and sang the songs as she remembered them; some of the lyrics most certainly were wrong. She chuckled at her lapses in memory, but it had been so long since she'd heard some of them. Batteries were almost impossible to find anymore, and if any did turn up, they were almost always reserved for flashlights or to power shortwave radios.

The sun broke through the tree canopy and provided some light as Carrie walked alone down the road. Mosquitoes attacked her from all around and bit her exposed skin. She slapped her bare arms, neck, and face, killing the insects by the dozens. Without any insecticides, insects had increased their numbers and had become more aggressive. She retrieved the poncho from the backpack and slid it over her head, pulling the strings tight around her hoodie. Carrie knew the nylon would impede her hearing against possible attack, but the onslaught of mosquitoes made it impossible to walk without covering her skin. She was breaking several key rules of survival:

1. Don't walk alone
2. Don't stay out after dark
3. Always be vigilant

But this wasn't the first time. Over the years, the rules had become more of a guideline. And depending on who you spoke to, they all had their own version.

Several hours into her walk, Carrie realized she would never meet up with her group on time. Looking towards the sun, she estimated it was late afternoon, sometime before six, and knew all too well that there could be anything lurking in the woods just off the road and that she could miss a turn if she hurried. It was best to find a place to rest. She was close to exhaustion and hadn't eaten in almost twenty-four hours. Up ahead, a hulking dead figure lay across the road. The shape was familiar, one that she hadn't seen in months. Carrie swung the rifle from her back and readied it. Her pace slowed as she got closer to the abandoned car, then she stopped and listened. She waited, unmoving, for any sign that the car was a trap and that someone would jump from the woods or just shoot her where she stood.

Once certain she was alone, Carrie knew it was time to rest. A quick inspection found the tires flat, but more importantly, all the windows were intact, and all the doors were still attached and closed. She cupped her hands around her eyes and peered in through the glass. The car was empty. Carrie hoped the doors weren't locked as she pulled on a handle. It opened without resistance, and she was met with a burst of stale air. A second look behind the seats and she felt safe that she was alone. She tossed her backpack onto the passenger seat, climbed in, and quietly closed the door locking them both, then pulled both front seats all the way forward and crawled over to the backseat. Curling up on the floor between the front and back seats, she covered herself with the poncho hiding herself from view. She would be safe from the insects, but if she were attacked, she wouldn't stand a chance. The rifle was on the backseat, the hammer cocked in case she needed it in a hurry.

She retrieved the backpack and found a small can she had taken before setting fire to the cabin. Under the poncho, she couldn't see what it was, and she didn't care. Carrie pulled her Swiss Army Knife from her pant pocket. From experience she knew which tool to open and carefully removed the lid. She recognized the scent of dog food, most likely well beyond the expiry date, but it was food. No one cared about eating dog food, or expired food anymore. It was edible, and the protein and fat were badly needed. Using her fingers, she scooped out the food. Carrie had eaten worse to survive, they all had. At least she didn't have to kill whatever she was eating. Even after all this time, she hated killing to survive. Her belly almost full, she wiped the inside of the can with her finger and licked it clean, then placed the can on the seat beside the rifle. She would bury it in the morning along the roadside.

The only sounds came from insects buzzing around the car and the animals outside—sounds she had grown to hate. Carrie longed for the noise of city life: car horns, tires rolling along the highway, people, lots of people laughing, drinking, dancing, music. She wanted to dance, to listen to loud music, to feel the bass thumping against her chest as she partied in the club, the smell of stale beer and men's cologne. Carrie wanted to dress up, to wear something feminine, something other than boots and pants. More than anything, she wanted a hot shower—no, a bath, a long hot bath with bubbles and a glass of wine, piano music playing softly in the background. She wanted to sleep in a bed without the fear of death every night. She wanted to live, to enjoy living, not just survive. Right now, she wanted to cry. Instead, she began to hum a song. She couldn't remember which one, or from which group; maybe it was a blend of many different songs; it didn't matter anymore. Carrie bolted upright, reached over the seat, and pushed the power button on the radio. There wasn't a key in the ignition, but she did it anyway. The radio didn't light up, music didn't start to play, there was no static, nothing. She fell backwards to the floor and began to weep. She was lonely, scared. Maybe dying was the easy way out. She gripped her pistol and felt the weight of exhaustion overtake her as she fell asleep.

Walking aimlessly all night until the sun was about to rise, he found the need to stop and sleep. He curled up at the base of a tree and buried his face deep in the brush to keep the morning light out. Not knowing why, the urge to hide and rest overcame him. He pulled more leaves and earth around his head to blacken out the light. As he lay still, ground insects began to crawl over his face, yet he felt nothing. They didn't seem to bother him as they moved along over his open eyes, into his mouth. He didn't move. Eventually his mind began to drift off, thinking of nothing, until he saw flashes of the dead people from the cabin. The images didn't frighten him; they didn't cause him any anxiety or any emotion at all. He had been an amoeba, unable to think for himself, just able to survive. Now, these images began to fill his mind, images that made no sense. He was beginning to—would he call it—remember?

He fell asleep as the images played over in his mind. Looking around, he wanted to get up but the pain in his stomach was intense. Running his fingers over the hole, he slipped a finger inside causing the pain to spike. He opened his mouth to scream but heard nothing. It took quite some time for the pain to settle, and the experience took a lot out of him. If he'd known what he was dealing with, he might be able to comprehend what he was experiencing. But he knew nothing. He tried to straighten out, but it caused him pain. Whatever he tried to do caused pain. The pain made him tired.

Closing his eyes, he fell asleep.

Day 917

The heat inside the car was becoming intense as the sun beat down through the trees. Carrie yawned and pulled the poncho to the side as she felt her muscles ache and demand to be stretched after a night of being cramped on the car floor. She slowly peeked her head above the top of the seats, scanned the horizon for anything moving and watched the treeline around the entire perimeter. Almost ten minutes passed before she felt comfortable enough that she was alone. She had slept past sunrise, longer than she wanted to, but alarm clocks, or time for that matter, no longer existed. Looking up into the sky through the windshield, she guessed it was a few hours after sunrise. The night terrors would be sleeping, but danger still lurked in daylight.

She carefully unlocked the door, pushed it open, holding the rifle directly in front of her. Stepping from the car, she continued to watch for signs of any type of movement from the edge of the road. That's where she would be if she was watching the car. Satisfied she was alone; she got out and placed her pack on the roof. Carrie took in a deep breath, longed for a toothbrush and mouthwash, but settled for a bottle of water from her backpack and gulped it down. She tossed the empty back in the pack to refill from a stream if she came upon one.

Now that there was ample light, she went thought the car for anything she could scavenge. She opened the glove box and the trunk, looked under the seats, inspecting any little cubby hole that could hold anything of value or to trade. The car looked as if it had been ransacked multiple times, but she never passed up a chance to find something someone might have missed. She grabbed the back seat and pulled. The seat cushion came up easily and underneath lay two emergency road flares. Carrie smiled. She couldn't believe her luck; no one had bothered to check under the seat cushion. She grabbed both flares— they felt dry and in good condition—then tossed them into the pack. With all her gear ready, Carrie buried her dog food can, flung the pack over her shoulders, readied the rifle, and began to make her way down the country road.

Her stomach rumbled. Was it hunger again, or was it the expired dog food? Carrie had some food in her pack but not enough if she didn't make it back to rejoin the group. Only a few years earlier, she could have used her cell phone to call her friends and tell them where she was. But that was a long time ago, a lifetime ago. Those things didn't exist anymore. Looking towards the treeline, the sun was just cresting the tops of the trees. Birds flew above and squirrels ran across the ground foraging for food. If the squirrels remained on the ground, she was safe. If they ran up the trees and began to shriek their high chirps, it was a warning that a predator was nearby. It was another warning sign that was now just part of life, nature's security system. If she couldn't find food soon, one of the alarm system squirrels would be lunch.

Ryan Bowker ordered the group to break camp, they would leave within the hour. Three of the four other members protested, but Ryan argued that staying in one place was what got people killed.

He was kneeling in the dirt, gathering his effects, stuffing them into his backpack when Steph stepped before him, silently, setting her foot on the corner of his blanket.

"I can't really roll it up with your foot there, now, can I?" His voice was calm, his eyes never looking up at her.

"We're leaving Carrie behind?" Steph lifted her foot.

Ryan stuffed the blanket in his pack, "We've already stayed

longer than we should have. She knew we were supposed to leave at sunrise."

Steph's voice grew louder and sterner. "We've never left anyone behind before. Why now?"

Ryan used a bungy cord to secure his pack and stood. "I never made the rules. We …" He looked around to the others, and twirled his index finger in the air. "We all made the rules and agreed. If someone doesn't make it back by the agreed-upon time, we leave. We don't know what has happened to Carrie or even if something has happened, but we can't take that chance, now can we? You remember what happened the last time we waited?"

Steph lowered her head and nodded.

He put his hand on her shoulder. "Two more hours, then we head out. I'll give her two more hours."

Steph looked up smiling. "Thanks." She wrapped her arms around Ryan and gave him a hug, "We are all family now," she said, and skipped away.

When Steph was out of earshot, Ryan mumbled to himself, "Fuck. This is gonna bite me in the ass. I just know it." He looked to see his younger sister talking to the rest of the group, telling them they were going to wait a little longer for Carrie. Ryan took in a deep breath and let it out slowly, knowing he was putting the group at risk. They had an itinerary they had to adhere to, and this would cause a delay meeting up with the rest of the group in two days.

Ryan pulled a paper map from his pack, unfolded it, placed it on the ground and used stones on either corner to keep it from being blown away in the breeze. There were black marker notes in codes scribbled on the edges of the map. Each tribe had their own code, and the leader of each tribe had to learn at least one other tribe's code. It was designed so that if any one tribe went rogue, they would only have the cypher for one other tribe: low tech security. Not long ago, paper maps were antiquated and obsolete. Now, paper was their only option. Ryan studied the notes, jotted a few of his own and used his finger to do some math in the sand. As he did his calculations in the dirt, another member walked over and stood beside him without saying a word.

Ryan continued his calculations, ignoring the person standing beside him. When he finished, he folded the map, secured it in his pack, then stood before Jarvis Cook. Jarvis had a look of panic, and his body language reflected his mood. He rocked back and forth waiting for Ryan to say something.

The mouse rolled over in the den. Pain flashed along its nerves, flooding its senses. This was a new experience for it. Its muscles twitched and its limbs contracted; its mind was becoming clouded and what few memories it had were gone. It kicked and clawed at the dirt; its tail flicked as it rolled about. Eventually, exhaustion took over and it collapsed. Hours later it woke up—changed—its mind numb, all survival instincts gone; the only things that remained were raw hatred and rage.

It walked down the dark, earthen tunnel, lumbering its way, not knowing where it was headed. It was drawn to the noise ahead. It stopped at a fork, listened to the sounds, and took the tunnel to the left. It scurried along, no destination in mind, no thoughts in its head. As it emerged in a larger chamber, it noticed a small cluster of adult field mice. For no reason, it lunged at the closest mouse, sunk its teeth into the unsuspecting prey's neck and ripped out a chunk of flesh. The mouse let out a low whine as blood squirted from the open wound. The attacker ran at a second mouse, knocking it over and biting the exposed abdomen, tearing at the flesh, releasing its bite then attacking again. Hearing the assault, the other rodents turned, and fled down various tunnels, away from the attacker.

The infected mouse looked up while chewing on the bowels of its victim, watching the other mice disappear, then went back to feasting. Once it finished eating what it wanted from its victim, it slowly walked over to the mouse with the neck wound. The first mouse, on its side and close to death, was still breathing. It looked up at its attacker. If mice had feelings or were able to understand life, it wondered why this was happening.

The attacker opened its mouth wide and bit down hard on the head of its fallen prey. The skull crunched under the powerful jaws. Its teeth dug deep into bone and pulled hard, tearing the head off the dead mouse.

Jarvis had difficulty expressing his concern about waiting another two hours for Carrie without raising his voice. "We are supposed to be meeting up with Scott and his group before nightfall. If we don't leave now, we won't make it."

Ryan stood patiently before Jarvis. "Listen, one thing you don't know is that we always pad the meeting times. Remember when we used to take plane trips and sometimes they would circle the airport for half an hour or so, or they had a headwind and were delayed a bit, they always had reserve fuel. We do the same, if we are supposed to meet at six tonight, we have time. If we have to hustle a bit, we run for a few miles." He politely smiled at Jarvis who didn't look convinced. "Besides, we're low on meat and water. I've already sent Greg and Jen out to hunt and gather whatever they can find. They'll be back soon. As soon as they get back, we're leaving. Is that alright with you?" Jarvis felt a little more comfortable with that answer and nodded in agreement.

Ryan placed his hand on Jarvis' shoulder. "I wouldn't endanger anyone. We have a schedule; we'll meet up with Scott and then we'll continue north. Tell everyone I'm heading out to find a tree and take a dump." He pointed in the direction he was planning on going. "Give me five minutes."

Any time a team member wanted privacy, they had to tell someone where they were going and how much time they were going to be gone. Without saying another word, Jarvis spun on his heel and walked away. Ryan picked up his pack, slung it over his shoulders and slowly walked into the bush.

He found a fallen log, dropped his pants and sat down. He pulled a copy of *Tecnobeat* magazine from his pack and filed through the articles. In his previous life, Ryan had been involved in high-tech, designing software for new electronic devices. Now, he flipped through the magazine, reading articles from faded pages about devices that no longer existed. Even if he happened to come across a used laptop or cellphone, there wasn't anything to power them. All device batteries had long since gone dead. He sighed deeply, longing for those days. After he was done, he rolled up the magazine, placing it carefully back in his pack, then pulled out a roll of toilet paper. As he did, a cellphone fell from his pack to the forest floor. He carefully picked it up, holding it before him, brushing off the dirt. He pressed the power button, knowing full well it wouldn't turn on. Ryan wanted that phone to have just enough power to turn on one more time so he could open the photo app and see the face of his girlfriend. He held the button down; nothing happened. "Please," he whispered. The phone battery hadn't worked in years. He held the power down for another minute, but nothing happened. "Fuck technology." He dropped the phone into his pack.

Jen and Greg returned with several plastic milk jugs filled with cool stream water, and half dozen dead birds hung upside down from their poles. In a cloth carrier, they had brought back fresh eggs,

"Breakfast in thirty minutes."

Ryan rejoined the group, smiling at the morning's haul. "That's amazing guys. How did you get all this so quick?"

Greg was ready to tell his story when Jen began to talk over him. "Greg found this field, open, beautiful. The birds were nesting on the ground, and we snuck up on them. It was a like a grocery store, isle after isle of birds and eggs.

Jen turned to Ryan, "You okay? Your eyes are red."

He rubbed at them, wiping away the wetness. "Allergies. Miss the days when we could buy Benadryl."

Carrie walked along the road; her pace just short of a power walk. She had been watching the sun make its way across the sky and guessed the time, 11:30. She looked at her watch, a cheap one she "acquired" from one of the homes they had come across years earlier. It was a wind-up watch, no batteries. Carrie made certain she wound the watch every few days, 11:42. "Close enough," she said softly to herself, knowing no one could hear her. It had become a game she played with herself, learn to tell time by looking at the sun and stars.

She knew she was late. She was supposed to have met with Ryan at dawn. The group had most certainly broken camp, but she knew where they were going. She had discussed this with Ryan before attempting to meet with her aunt. Instead of a family visit, she'd had to burn her aunt and cousins and the family cottage to the ground when she'd found them murdered. Death had become commonplace; so common, she didn't feel sad or shed a tear. Carrie almost envied them. Their pain and suffering were over, hers would continue for God knows how long. Sometimes she wanted everything to end and thought about killing herself almost every day. Maybe not every day, but unquestionably every night.

Luckily, Carrie didn't need a map; she had an amazing ability to find her way around. If she had been somewhere, anywhere, once, she could find her way back. And, she had travelled these roads several times as a child. As she made her way, a familiar sound caught her attention; she paused for a moment, listened and knew what it was. She broke into a full run, breaking through the brush, pushing the branches aside, some slapping her across the face, others sticking her in the bare skin. She stopped in the clearing before a small, fast running creek with water collecting in a shallow pool. She dropped her backpack and rifle and fell to her knees, sticking her face in the clear water. She drank until her belly was full and couldn't take any more. The water was cold, fresh, and delicious. Falling back on the grass, it was a slice of heaven in a world filled with evil. Rolling on the grass, her stomach made a long-forgotten sound of fullness as the water sloughed back and forth inside her. Eyes closed; she had a half-smile of contentment. She lay in the tall grass with the morning sun beating down on her damp face, wanting to fall asleep, and forget. Instead, she got on all fours, pulled several empty containers from her pack, and filled them with fresh water. The added weight would slow her down but having access to cold fresh water was a luxury she could not pass up.

At the water's edge, she spied a frog staring at her. It was large, green, and would give her enough protein to last the day and probably the next day as well. She stopped, looked at the frog and remembered her bedroom as a child. Porcelain frogs, frog stickers, fluffy stuffed frogs, they all adorned her room and now she longed for the large green plush frog doll she slept with. Carrie pointed a finger at the eyes in the water, "Today is your lucky day my friend. Hide when someone comes by to drink from your home and stay alive or the next time you may get roasted."

Just above the water's edge where the frog kept his lookout,

Carrie spied a small bush with red berries. Her spirits soared; her pulse quickened as she stood, steadied herself and jumped across to the opposite bank. Kneeling, she gently cradled the raspberry bush, carefully turning over the branch then pulling berries free and placing them between her lips. She closed her eyes and let the berries fall into her mouth, they were sweet and juicy and delicious.

Carrie turned to the frog in the pond who still hadn't moved, "Oh my God. I had forgotten how good these taste. It's been so long." She pulled one more raspberry free and tossed it into the water. Again, the bullfrog didn't move, it's eyes never leaving Carrie. The berry floated and bobbed not far from the frog. "My way of paying for the berries I'm taking from your home." The berry settled along the bank, lodged in the wet grass. "Not a berry eater, huh? Well, I am. This is the sweetest thing I've had in a long time." She sat down and continued to pick the raspberries off the bush. "I appreciate you letting me eat and drink here. You're a mighty fine host. I don't suppose you get many visitors along this way." Carrie looked over her shoulders, first right then left, "It's beautiful here. Maybe when all this is over, I'll come back and build a cabin right over there," she pointed to a large clearing. "The living room windows will face south, and I can stop by every morning and chat with you when I gather my water and raspberries."

She knew talking to a frog bordered on insanity but having an opportunity to have a casual conversation was too good to not take advantage of.

She popped another handful of berries in her mouth, closed her eyes and let the juices flow as she squished the fruit, "This is heaven; it really is." With her mouth still full, she introduced herself to her host, "I'm Carrie. And you are?"

The frog continued to stare at her, never moving, wary of her presence.

"I hate those cliché names; you know when they use names like Froggy or Kermit. Although, I have to admit, I loved Kermit. You don't look like a Kermit. How 'bout Mulder? He was in my favourite show growing up. If I call you Mulder, I can never think of you as dinner." She filled her mouth with berries again, "I loved—I mean, loved—Mulder. He was so, I don't know, cute." Carrie laughed as she savoured the berries and looked at Mulder in the water. "Well Mulder, I'm so pleased to meet you. I hope you and I will become close friends and get to know each other really well."

The remaining ripe raspberries on the bush were giving way to smaller berries that needed a few more days to mature. Carrie ate another handful, thanked her host again, then decided it was time to leave.

She placed the full bottles of water in her pack. The aroma of the lavender soap rose up to from the bottom and she briefly considered taking a bath in the stream. "I would never muck your home Mulder. Even though I would love a bath. I can always find another place to clean up." Carrie leaned forward, stuck her face in the water one more time and drank as much as she could until she felt she would burst. She turned back to the eyes in the water. "I want to see you next time I stop by for a drink Mr. Mulder." Hydrated and with a full stomach, she gathered up her gear and made her way back to the road. It would be difficult to keep the pace she'd had before stopping for a drink, but she hadn't felt this full in a long time, even if it was just water and berries. An odd thought came to her. *For the first time in a long time, my pee wouldn't be yellow, but clear.* She smiled. The little things in life.

The fox stood motionless at the base of a tree watching the fallen leaves on the forest floor rustle as the mouse scurried beneath them. The mouse poked its head above the leaves then ducked back under the foliage. It moved about back and forth, pushed its nose in the dirt, then raised its head again.

The fox slowed it's breathing, never moving, only its eyes followed the rustle of leaves hiding her prey. She hadn't eaten since the day before and her empty stomach ached with hunger. A mouse wasn't a meal, but it was better than going hungry looking for larger prey like squirrels.

The movement under the leaves stopped. The fox lowered its head to just the top of the leaves and opened her jaws, ready to strike. As she was about to pounce, she felt a sharp pain on her back and yelped loudly. Turning to see what was causing the pain, she noticed another mouse had attacked her and dug its teeth into her skin. The fox spun around in tight circles, attempting to toss the tiny attacker from her back. Failing to rid herself of the aggressive mouse, she rolled over onto her back, another instinctive move to lose the attacker. When she righted herself, the mouse was still holding on tightly with its bite. The pain from the attack increased causing the fox to contort herself so she could kill the mouse which was now riding on her back like a cowboy breaking a horse. The fox's teeth dug deep into the aggressor then pulled hard. Unable to hold its grip on her skin, the mouse let go and decided to attack the face of the fox. It bit the lip, tearing into the flesh, ripping out a small chunk of skin.

Although the fox had sunk its teeth through the body of the attacking mouse, the little rodent never let up on the assault. It was close to death, yet it spit the skin from its mouth and attacked the fox again and again until it died. The fox didn't bother to eat the kill. Instead she lay down, pain searing through her, blood dripping from her lip. She whimpered for a few minutes then felt something new as her nerves began to feel like fire roaring though her body.

He rolled over in the brush unable to rest. He couldn't recall if he had ever had this problem before. Did he sleep; was he supposed to sleep? Was it that he couldn't remember, or that everything was new and he didn't have a programed response.

There was an irritant in one of his eyes, so he blinked repeatedly to remove it. Debris fell from his shoulders and back as he sat up. He leaned against the tree and rubbed his eyes. Looking at his fingers, he noticed tiny bugs crawling over his hands. His mind registered something new, something he had never noticed before. As he rolled his hand back and forth, staring at it, he noticed a small circle of colour had formed on his index finger. Looking at the rest of his hand, the rest of his skin was a solid shade of gray, no variation, no deviation. Pulling his sleeve up, the colour of his skin remained constant.

He looked beyond his arm to the forest, and again he was amazed by what he saw. The sun had not yet set, the light bothered his eyes, but it showed him something that he'd never noticed before. There was a hint of new colour, the leaves on the trees cast a hue, a colour that didn't have a name. There was never any colour in his world before today, only shades of gray. In fact, he couldn't recall anything before yesterday, yet he clearly remembered everything he'd done on that day: waking up in the cabin, fighting to find a way out, walking through the night, and waking up here. He remembered everything, but nothing before that.

His world had been night; during the day, he'd buried himself in the dirt away from the sunlight. It was instinct; not done because he wanted to, but because he was coded that way. Standing up, he fumbled slightly and braced himself, then stood tall and stretched. His joints cracked, and he felt a sharp pain in his abdomen. He remembered the wound. He slid his hand down; there was tenderness where the hole had been, but it was better today. Pulling his hand away, he noticed something again; his hand had a small amount of wetness on it that yesterday was black, but today it was something different. There was a colour to it, not like the colour of the patch on his finger or the colour of the leaves on the trees, it was darker. He looked up past the treeline and directly into the sun. The light burned his eyes so badly, he shut them quickly, dropping to his knees. He fumbled about, put his head down and pulled loose dirt and leaves around his head to block out the light. Pain coursed through his head as tiny bursts of light popped in his eyes. Eventually they stopped, and he rested.

The main road broke into a fork. Carrie stopped, dropped her gear, and decided to rest. The area around the intersection was a large clearing with the overgrowth of trees and bush at least fifty feet from the road's edge. If anyone or anything tried to approach, she would hear them or see them before they got too close. She sat on her pack, took off her boots and socks, then rubbed her feet. "What I wouldn't give for a mountain bike," she said to herself, half expecting a response from some unknown bystander. Mulder's stream was too narrow for a bath, but it would have felt good to soak her feet after she filled the water bottles. Time didn't allow for such indulgences. Carrie could feel fatigue begin to take hold and knew if she stopped for much longer, she would most certainly fall asleep. She donned her boots, took a sip of water, lifted the gear in place and kept to the road on the left.

Along the way, cars, trucks, and other vehicles littered the road and shoulders. Over the years, all the vehicles had been scavenged for any useable parts. The doors were open, the trunk and hood were up, and the gas caps were open. Anything and everything that could be used for survival was gone: gas for fuel; mirrors to help start fires or use as communications devices; batteries for power; tools that could be used as weapons. Fabric torn from the seats could be used as a fire starter or clothing and anything mechanical that had a use was pulled from the wreck. There was little reason to go through these heaps of metal, they no longer had any value to anyone.

Less than an hour later, Carrie came upon a deserted camp. She knew the group had a schedule to follow and would leave without her, and it was her own fault she was late. It was high ground, an excellent vantage point all around; easy to defend. She walked to the fire pit, placed her hand over the embers and felt the warmth. She turned over the rocks from around the pit until she spotted what she was looking for, a tiny arrow showing the direction the group had taken. She smiled, scrubbed the dirt to erase the arrow, and headed in the direction the message indicated.

Carrie kept a strong pace as she made her way to the meeting point. She wasn't far behind and wanted to alert Ryan to her position. She glanced up at the sun hanging low in the sky, estimated the time and knew she might have to pick up the pace. She unslung the rifle from her shoulder, checked the magazine, fired one shot into the air, counted to ten, then fired a second. She counted to ten and heard a single shot in the distance. Over the years, they had all developed the skill of narrowing where the gunshots were coming from and how far the other shooter was.

From the sound of the gunshot, Carrie knew she was on the right road and estimated her group was only a few miles ahead. If she kept a steady pace, she hoped to meet up with them by sundown. The last thing she wanted to do was spend another night alone and unprotected. She pulled one of the water bottles from her pack, took a long slow drink, capped the bottle, and replaced it. Even though the water was no longer cool, it was still the best water she had tasted in a long time.

Most of the time, the water they drank was brown with sediment at the bottom of the bottle. When they were forced to start drinking lake or stream water, many became ill after clean water became a luxury. They drank what they could when they found it. Not long after the event, Carrie came upon an abandoned Coca-Cola delivery truck. Much of the load had been scavenged, but she found a few dozen cans that had rolled under the vehicle and had been missed. The cans were still intact, and she drank the sweet, carbonated pop until she burped and her belly was bloated. That was the last time she recalled drinking something sweet. The simple taste of sweetness had been replaced with bland foods, no salt, no pepper, no spices, no sugar.

Carrie felt refreshed enough to break into a jog despite the weight of her pack. A mile or two at this pace and she certainly would meet up with her group by sundown. Carrying the rifle in both hands, the gun rocking back and forth in cadence with her stride, she felt like a soldier, heavy equipment pack and a rifle bobbing side to side. A few years back, all this would have been a dream, she chuckled, a dream, more like a nightmare. Sweat formed first on her brow, then dripped steadily off the end of her nose and down the centre of her back. Her shirt had become moist and her breathing laboured, but she fought against it. She could no more bear another night alone in the woods than she could killing Mulder the frog.

She thought back to her plush frog in her bedroom. A clean house, a bedroom, a bed with fresh sheets. She longed for those things, but they were things that belonged in a different world. Carrie was from a different world, one that believed in families and comfort and things like beds and plush toys.

Well into her run, even over the sound of her breathing, Carrie heard a branch snap in the woods. It was faint, but she heard it, distinct and familiar. A sound she had heard many times before. She didn't bother to turn around; instead, Carrie kept her pace. Her heartrate and breathing increased. Between breaths, she heard the sound again coming from the same area. Stopping for a moment, she turned and held her breath. A few moments later she heard another branch fracture under the weight of something large. It was coming from the edge of the road to her right. Whatever it was, it had no intention of hiding its presence. It was definitely large—a bear, a deer or moose, perhaps even human. The sun was setting and the overgrowth along the road edge was mired in darkness. She waited for whatever it was to show itself as it crept closer.

Fear spread through her in an instant, and she knew that to remain still was foolish. Carrie turned and broke into a full run. She held the rifle at the ready, turning around every few moments to see if whatever it was had shown itself. It was difficult to see anything in the murky darkness, but nothing had broken through the brush.

It had been a long time since Carrie had been this afraid of the unknown, but at that moment she felt alone, scared, and vulnerable. She decided not to turn around, but she did stop, if only for a moment. She held her breath, waiting for whatever it was to make itself known. The sound of footfalls in the grass had increased; whatever it was, it was not remaining still; it was following her. The hairs on the back of her neck tingled, sending tiny lightning shocks down her spine. Taking in a deep breath, she bolted down the road, refusing to look back.

Her boots pounded on the gravel. The pack she carried made her feel as if she was being weighed down by hundreds of pounds. Carrie wanted to shed the pack but knew she needed the fresh water, food, and survival gear inside. She could run much faster without the weight, but could she make it back to the group without the equipment.

Not far ahead, Carrie spotted a thick group of trees that would provide protection against attack. In one movement, she slid on the gravel then rolled between the trees. She cocked the hammer back, aimed the barrel down the road, looked through the sight, and gently placed her finger around the trigger. Holding her breath again, Carrie listened for sounds of any kind.

Branches broke, grass crunched, but nothing showed itself; then the sound eventually stopped. For several minutes, Carrie waited for whatever was making the noise to move closer. There was nothing but silence. Sweat rolled down her forehead, beads stinging her eyes making her blink uncontrollably. She wanted to wipe her eyes but was scared the very moment she took her hand from the gun something would attack. After several minutes she chanced it and wiped the sweat free from her eyes.

With clear vision, she trained her eyes to where the mysterious noises had come from, but now there was nothing but the sound of crickets. Carrie held her breath one more time and stared down the barrel into the murky grass. Squinting to focus, she was positive she saw the tall grass move. Her index finger folded around the trigger and began to apply pressure. As she waited for whatever was in the grass to show itself, the movement ceased.

It's getting ready to pounce, she told herself. She waited. Time passed and Carrie remained motionless. There had been too many times in the past when she gave up early only to be surprised that one of them would attempt a surprise attack. She watched as the shadows spread themselves across the road and the grass became nothing more than a large black mass, making it impossible to see if whatever was hiding was even there any longer. Eventually, the entire area became mired in darkness. She could no longer see any detail in the area from which she believed it was staring at her from. It would be easier for her to sneak away, if only she could avoid making any noise.

Her trigger finger relaxed; her thumb pulled back on the hammer and let it return to its resting position. The hammer made a soft clicking sound as it moved. Releasing her grip, she placed her palm flat on the ground, slowly applying more pressure, letting the dirt and grass settle under her hand. Pushing herself up, Carrie's gaze never left the spot where she was still certain whatever it was lay in wait.

Placing one knee under her torso, Carrie was able to stand without making any noise, her eyes never losing their focus. She placed one foot behind her, the toe of her shoe on the ground, repeating the motions she had done with her hand. Her foot slowly rolling back letting the soil beneath her shoe settle as she applied more weight.

She did this several times, each step calculated and slow to complete. Eventually, she felt comfortable there was enough distance between her and the stalker to make a run for it. She stood motionless, silent, waiting for movement from the grass or any sound at all.

Carrie slung the rifle over her shoulder, secured everything she had on her back, then turned and ran. As she did, her stalker sprang from the grass and gave chase. Dirt and grass crunched behind her. Carrie knew better than to look back. She could lose her footing, run into a tree, or fall. Instead, she took in a deep breath and quickened her pace. Instinctively, Carrie felt her stalker was gaining ground on her. The water, guns and supplies had added more weight that she would normally carry, and she again had a fleeting thought about shedding the gear to lighten her load. Instead, she found her pistol, pulled back on the hammer, planted her feet, slid in the dirt, turned, and pointed the gun into the darkness. From past experience, she knew a pistol was better for close combat.

Her chest heaved. Panting, Carrie tried to catch her breath as she waved the pistol from side to side, sweeping the area for anything that was following her. It was too dark to see anything more than a few feet in front of her. If she did spot anything, her stalker would be on her before she could get off a shot. She waited in the darkness for whatever it was to show itself. There were only the sounds of the leaves as they brushed against each other in the soft, evening breeze and crickets sending out their call. She could hear nothing else, nothing at all.

The chase had been too short for whatever it was to give up. Carrie knew with her gear she could easily be outrun. It still had to be out there, waiting for the right moment. Maybe it was small, she thought, too small to make an outright attack, and needed to attack from behind.

Carrie blindly stepped back, one pace at a time, her pistol still moving side to side. Her outstretched arms had begun to weaken, the gun slowly lowered, as she was unable to keep her arm straight. She decided to hold the pistol in the other hand, letting the blood flow again to her fingers. Carrie flexed her fingers, then relaxed them, repeating this as she continued to move slowly deeper into the woods.

Her mouth was dry, pasty, her upper lip stuck to her teeth. If she weren't so scared, she would take a sip of the stream water from her bottle. Even warm, it would be refreshing. With her left hand, she reached for the water bottle, found it and attempted to flip up the flexible straw. Carrie fumbled with the lid, silently cursing the tight flip top that she thought was so great when she took it from the abandoned dollar store. Not wanting to lose her water bottle, she made certain it was placed back in the pocket of the backpack without taking a drink.

Carrie continued her slow backwards pace until the heel of her boot stuck something. She carefully backed up even more and felt the trunk of a tree against her pack. With her free hand, she felt the base and knew the tree was large and would support her weight. Reaching up to find a branch, Carrie felt nothing but the evening air. Instead, she made her way around to the other side to put the tree between her and her stalker, her eyes never leaving the sight at the end of the pistol. With the tree acting as a shield, Carrie felt she had the time to see if there was a low hanging branch, she could grab to pull herself up. A quick glance made her smile.

The pistol went to her left hand; she reached up, took hold of the limb, and pulled hard. It held. Carrie knew the steps she would have to take to climb the tree as quickly as possible: holster the gun, grab the limb with both hands, pulling herself up using her feet to help propel her, and scramble up the tree as far as she could without looking back.

She counted down in her head from three, hoping this would give her the courage and strength to save herself. *Three.* Pause. *Two.* Before she could get to one, her stalker sprang from the grass and ran toward her. A dog, feral now—but possibly at one point it could have been a family pet. Lips pulled back, teeth bared, it jumped at Carrie. In a panic, she pulled the trigger. The dog didn't yelp. She'd missed her mark. She fell backward, landing on the ground as she blindly pulled the trigger, firing the remaining five rounds, her free arm protecting her face. The dog landed on top of her. She expected it to start biting; instead, the weight of the dog was limp across her body.

Carrie began to scream wildly, pushing and kicking the body of the dog off her. It rolled lifeless to the ground. She kicked the body several times to make certain it was dead. Finally, she took in a deep breath, thumbed the cylinder release and flipped the gun to the left, letting the empty cartridges spill from the barrel to the ground. Pulling a handful of bullets from her pack, years of practice helped her to quickly reload the .38 calibre pistol.

She stood, panting, adjusted the pack on her back, then used her foot to tap the body of the dog once again. Her heart still pounding, Carrie knew full well dogs now ran in packs, and unless this was a loner there would be more to follow shortly. It was safer to climb a tree than risk walking alone in the dark. She picked up the dog's hind leg and dragged it to the edge of the clearing. Scavengers would be by throughout the night; she was certain of it. Carrie didn't want to attract attention to herself if they caught her scent. Once the carcass was displayed in the open without any obstruction of trees or thickets, it wouldn't take long before others came to feast on the fresh kill.

Carrie rushed back into the woods. She found a suitable tree to rest in for the night, holstered her gun, grabbed the lowest branch, and pulled herself up. The backpack kept getting caught on the overgrowth. She braced herself between a large branch and the trunk, pulled the pack off, retrieved a few items for the night, then wrapped the straps around the highest branch she could reach. Exhausted, she climbed up as far as she could, in the darkness, found a fork between two large branches and settled in snuggly. She secured her legs, torso, and chest firmly to the tree with the rope she had in the backpack so she wouldn't fall out when she fell asleep. It wouldn't be as comfortable as the back seat of the car, but it would be safer than sleeping on the ground alone. She closed her eyes, and let her mind drift off to Mulder the frog and the serene creek with fresh water and berries. It wasn't long before she was asleep.

He pulled himself up from his covering, and once again the recent sensation of pain coursed through him. He reached around and rubbed his lower back, his fingers digging deep into the stiff muscle. It soon felt better. Putting his head back, he let out a soft whimper. The noise startled him. He wasn't aware he could make that sound. He felt the area on his stomach where the hole was and ran his finger around the edge. The pain was still there, but now it was barely noticeable, and the bleeding had stopped. He ignored the wound, looked about, then made his way through the trees.

His mind was once again filled with strange images and thoughts. If he had been more aware of who and what he was, he would have realized the images were memories from long ago. Now, the memories were foreign; strange images of places and objects that he couldn't recall or even recognize what they represented.

He shook those new images from his head and felt that pang in his stomach, hunger. He needed food. He had only walked a few feet beyond the treeline, and he noticed the sun was low in the sky with bands of orange, red and yellow streaming across the horizon, melding with the clouds. Colours, he was noticing colours once again. He marveled at how beautiful the sky was, no longer seeing just shades of grey. He stood motionless, staring at the sunset, wondering what it was that caused those colours and how he could have missed seeing them before.

It was only then he realized something he hadn't done before; he was considering time. Staring into the sky, he began to wonder about a lot of things, but the sounds made by his empty stomach won out. He walked along the treeline hoping he could find something to eat soon. Moving slowly, he sniffed the air hoping to catch a whiff of something in the area. Nothing. He scanned the area, looking for movement in the grass or in the trees. As he approached, the crickets went silent, alerting the animals that a predator was nearby. He carefully lowered himself to his knees, remaining motionless for minutes on end. Eventually, the crickets would begin again to chatter. Even then, he wouldn't move. Something new occurred to him; he noticed he was having a more difficult time seeing in the dark and had to squint to see the movements around him.

He continued to listen closely as the crickets chirped. Cupping his hand, he focused on the sounds, then slammed down upon an insect. Picking it up, he popped it into his mouth. He chewed once or twice, then swallowed. It wasn't enough to fill his stomach; he repeated the process over and over again. His belly barely noticed a dozen or more insects.

The remaining crickets stopped their chirping as he stood and made his way through the tall grass. He heard rustling as tiny rodents ran for cover. To him, the sound of rodents in the brush was nothing more than a potential meal. He fell to his knees and began to grab at the sounds in the dark. He slapped to the right, then left, wherever the sounds went; he haphazardly cupped whatever was making the noise. Finally, he felt something under his hand. Whatever it was, it scratched and dug at the dirt attempting to escape. He slowly closed his hand around the prey until it was unable to move. Squeezing it tightly, it was now completely trapped. Holding his cupped hand close, he pulled his thumb back slightly to reveal a tiny field mouse. He was about to toss it into his mouth and eat it whole when the thought suddenly seemed repugnant to him. He could barely see the tiny rodent in the dim light, trapped in his hand, it's face staring back at him with no clue of what had almost occurred.

He loosened his grip, the mouse took advantage of the moment, jumped to the ground and disappeared in the grass.

From Carrie's perch high in the tree, she could hear scavengers attacking the carcass of the dog she had killed earlier. She felt uneasy about being so close to them, but she didn't want to be caught by another hungry predator dragging the carcass any further. The sounds of the animals fighting over scraps of meat frightened her. The smaller animals yelped as larger one's bit or snapped at them if they tried to eat before their turn. Carrie heard bone breaking and flesh being ripped from the body echoing in the trees, making her stomach turn. She pulled on the knots, checking them to make sure they wouldn't give way in the middle of the night. She questioned herself, wondering if she should have climbed higher. Could the dogs, or wolves, or whatever they were climb up and attack her as she slept. Maybe it was something other than a dog or a wolf. "No!" she told herself, what she was worried about didn't make any sounds and she knew they couldn't climb trees.

Eventually, the sounds of the feeding frenzy waned until Carrie could not longer hear the scavengers at all. She stared into the cloudless night sky through the branches, their leaves remaining perfectly calm, to the moon surrounded by thousands of stars. Despite how the Earth had changed, the moon and the sky hadn't changed a bit. She recalled looking up at the moon with her father when they spent time at the summer cottage. The stars were exactly as she remembered. She pointed at them with her index finger and traced the patterns in the sky the way her father had taught her. Carrie had forgotten the names of the constellations, but the patterns her father had shown her repeatedly until she had perfected them, never left her. Over the years, Carrie promised herself she wouldn't dwell on the memory of her family. It re-opened a wound she wanted healed. A wound that went deeper each time she thought of them.

Feeling exhaustion taking hold, her compulsion made her double check the knots, tugging them; they hadn't changed since the last time, but she didn't want to fall if she rolled later in the night. Before she could think of her father again she fell fast asleep, her chin resting on her chest.

Waking several hours later, Carrie heard a noise she was familiar with. She rubbed her eyes, quietly yawned, then scanned the ground through the leaves in the direction of the sounds. There was enough moonlight to illuminate the open area where she'd left the dead dog. Carrie had seen similar sights in the past; yet, regardless of how many times she had seen it, the mere thought repulsed her. All she could make out was a shadowy, lone figure in the dusk. The figure, a male she suspected from the way it stood, was wearing whatever was left of a suit, the tattered edges hanging freely. It was hunched over the carcass, pulling, tearing, then eating whatever it ripped from the body. It made loud smacking sounds as it chewed and gnawed on a bone. It dropped the bone and went back to pulling at another part of the carcass. Not being able to pull anything free with its fingers, it reached in with its mouth and bit at the exposed ribs. It chewed and pulled away small chunks of raw flesh, then went back for more. The figure continued to feed for almost half an hour before it stood and simply walked away.

Carrie shifted and strained to see the carcass. The body had been ripped open and devoured in the short time since she'd killed it. It was difficult to see, but even the skeleton had been broken apart and picked clean of flesh. She swallowed hard to keep what little food was in her stomach in place.

She tilted her head back, cracked her neck, and tried to relax and get more sleep before the sun rose. She knew that she had fallen behind and would have to make up more distance just to catch up. Carrie hoped they had left a message for her to find where they were headed. Now was not the time to think of such things. Now was the time to sleep, recharge and make sure she survived the night.

He stumbled through the woods, placing his hands on the trees for support to prevent him from falling. Recalling the little creature he couldn't eat, and set free despite the fact he was hungry, he shook his head; he couldn't understand why he'd done that. What would happen if he didn't eat? His stomach made noises. He had painful cramps when he didn't eat enough, but he didn't feel weak if he did find something to eat. Instinctively, he just knew he had to eat.

He paused for a moment, noticing how bright the forest was. He looked up through the leaves to see the large white ball in the sky. There was another brighter ball in the sky that would come up over the edge of the forest making the darkness give way to light, which hurt his eyes and made him want to bury himself to avoid the light.

He wondered what would happen if he stayed out after the bright ball in the sky came out and the darkness gave way to light. Continuing to make his way deeper into the woods, again he wondered. He couldn't recall why he'd started to question things—what happened to make him wonder about the balls in the sky, and the changes from the dark to light, and the way his stomach made noise?

He stepped through the trees into a clearing and stopped. Farther up the overgrown path, he heard bones snapping and something feeding. He stood, silent, his hand propped up against a tree as he turned towards the sounds and watched the lone figure hunched over the carcass of something dead, biting into it and ripping away its flesh. Whatever was feeding, it was something that looked exactly like him: thin, longer hair, and wore what was left of its clothing. It didn't take long before it had finished its feast, letting out a soft grunt, then stood and walked away.

He waited until it was out of sight, then made his way to where the other one had been feeding and stood over the remains of the dead animal. He didn't care what it had been, he just looked at it. Limbs had been torn free of the main body, the skin had been peeled free from the skeleton, the skull was gone. He casually looked around for it, but it was nowhere to be found. He turned his attention back to the animal; whatever it once was, it had been a meal to many. Even in the darkness, his eyes were able to see soft hues of colours. Colours that he never noticed before. The flesh that remained on the bones was a darker shade of red, tiny strands of white ran through the flesh, and the bones were also white. The dog's fur was brown with black sections blending into the night.

While trying to understand what he was seeing that same odd feeling came over him; he was feeling something for the dead beast. It was the same feeling he had for the tiny creature he'd held in his hand. Shaking it off, he was about to move on when he heard rustling in the trees. He turned towards the noise; seeing nothing he dismissed it. Then he heard it again. He looked around, then up. High in the tree, he noticed something balancing between the branches, its head resting on the trunk, both arms dangling down. Staring at the figure in the tree, he could make out that it resembled himself and the thing that was feeding earlier on the dead animal. Then an image flashed though his mind, a memory. Whatever was up in the tree looked like the thing that had been on the floor in the cabin, like him but different. Those images of the bodies in the cabin frightened him. Closing his eyes, he forced the images away.

He walked slowly around the base of the tree, his eyes never losing sight of the thing sleeping in its branches. Studying the figure, he was now certain it was like the body on the cabin floor. The two looked like him but were somehow different. Stopping, he looked at his hands, turning them over, then back up at the figure in the tree, its hands dangling loose. The pink hands looked so much smaller than his, softer almost, they looked delicate. He looked at his own hands, his skin grey and leathery; his fingers were longer, the joints bony, his nails long, dirty and broken. The small patch of pink on the back of his hand had grown considerably since the last time he took notice. Forgetting about the thing in the tree, he scratched at the pink spot; the skin felt smoother, softer. The spot didn't go away, regardless of how hard he scratched. Continuing to scratch the spot with his broken, sharp nail, he quickly drew blood and noticed something new again; the same red fluid he noticed around the dead animal was oozing from the scratch on his hand.

He wondered about the red fluid on his hand that matched the red fluid coming from the dead animal, that thing that was feasting on the dead animal that looked just like him, the other one up in the tree that looked similar but different, the bodies in the cabin, new colours, and the balls in the sky. His mind was suddenly flooded with images and thoughts. The images, too many for his primitive mind to process, caused a burning sensation shooting from side to side in his head. He placed his hands over his ears, but the pain only increased. All attempts to stop the pain failed. If he could have screamed, he would have.

With his eyes closed, he fumbled back onto the path and into the woods. He wanted to bury his head in the dirt like he had when he would sleep. Blindly walking from the path past the treeline, he collapsed to his knees.

Day 918

The sun came up directly facing Carrie, blinding her as she woke. The warmth was welcoming. She had been chilly throughout the night and came to with her hands tucked in her pockets. Her neck was stiff, her entire body ached. Carrie longed for the days of Advil and coffee. She stretched, forcing out the kinks in her muscles. Looking down where she'd left the dead dog, she saw the carnage that had occurred overnight. There wasn't much left of the body. If she hadn't known it was a dog, she wouldn't have been able to identify it. There were so many flies and other insects feeding on whatever was left, they buzzed around, bumping into each other, eating and laying their eggs anywhere they could.

She turned her attention back to watching the sun rise a little further into the morning sky. Carrie thought it must be around six-thirty, but honestly, no one cared about time anymore or even what day of the week it was. The only thing that people cared about was survival and storing enough food to get through the winters.

She wiggled and pulled against her bonds to loosen her muscles. She freed the restraints around her feet, collected the ropes and stuffed them in her pack. She pointed her toes straight forward making her ankles crack and tightened her calf muscles. Once her legs felt like moving, she let them drape over the edge of the large branch that had supported her overnight.

Carrie continued to scan the area to see if other animals or anything else might still be lurking close by, enticed by her legs swinging from the branch. She watched the treeline, the tall grass, and the area directly beneath her for any signs of danger.

Until the sun was up high and the chill from the previous night replaced with the day's warmth, it would still be dangerous for her. Once she was free and all her gear stored away in her pack, Carrie dropped the bag to the ground and waited for a few moments. Nothing. Not a sound or movement from anything in the area. She felt comfortable enough to lower herself slowly to the ground. She gripped the branch, lowered herself down, swung for a moment, then leaped from the tree. She hoisted the gear over shoulder and walked to the corpse. Looking over the dead dog, she wondered if there was any meat worth cooking for breakfast. The scavengers had picked the body clean of most of the flesh. Insects had taken over the rest. Around the body, she noticed three shoe prints and one bare foot print. There had been two of them there overnight and one was walking around wearing only one shoe. She wondered if the two were together or separate. More than likely, they were not together. They usually travelled alone or in larger packs. The thought that she was so close to two of them sent shivers down her spine, the hairs on her arm stood up. Two of them had been only feet away from where she slept. If she'd had anything in her stomach, she would have vomited.

Carrie gulped air several times to calm the nausea, then realized if she had thought of it, she could have cut a chunk of meat from the dog's body and kept it over night high up in the tree with her. Although the scent would have drawn the animals to her. Besides, she hadn't had time to cook the meat before she had to retreat into the tree, and she wasn't certain if the dog was infected or not. To be safe, they had to cook the meat almost to the point of not being edible. But it was still food, and right now Carrie was hungry. Since the dog had already been exposed to animals and infected scavengers, she didn't want to risk eating anything that she could scrape off the bones.

She looked up toward the rising sun. Her plan was still to reunite with her friends, and she was falling further and further behind. If they stuck to the plan, her friends wouldn't be waiting for her, and Carrie was getting worried she might never catch up.

Carrie finished the rest of the berries she had collected the day before and more than a litre of water. She was hydrated, and her stomach wasn't full but was satisfied for now. Shortly she would be hungry again. She needed protein or it would only be a matter of time before she started getting weaker. She decided at this point anything edible could be breakfast, lunch or dinner.

With her pack secured, she took to the path that only a few years ago had been a dirt road. Carrie held her gun high; the feeling she wasn't alone was strong. If fear had a smell, she was smelling it.

Shortly into her walk, Carrie noticed footprints in the soft sand, the left wearing a shoe, the right barefoot. It must be the same scavenger who had eaten thanks to her leaving the dog out. The right toes dragged as it walked and most of the weight was on the outer aspect of the foot. Was it carrying something or injured?

As she followed the prints, Carrie caught herself looking down at them instead of keeping her eyes up. She hadn't anticipated attacks from other animals as she walked in the open. Rookie mistake. She still wanted to hunt something; anything would do.

The sun climbed higher in the sky. "Nine or nine-thirty," she told herself and chuckled. A few years ago, at nine, she would have been walking to her desk, fresh, hot coffee from Starbucks in hand, something sweet that really was coffee in name only. She would sit down, power up her laptop and read the emails that came in the night before from overseas suppliers. She would delete most, forward some to other departments and answer a few. It would be almost ten before she actually started to do any real work. Her job was social media for a publisher; no stress; she got to surf the net for a living. Keeping the company's Facebook, Twitter and Instagram accounts current, discussing upcoming releases, helping the authors and planning their posts, tweets and pictures one week ahead of time was easy. Carrie always had all of her posts prepped weeks in advance. Only if something important came up would she bump a day's or a week's posts.

Every day at lunch she would meet one of her girlfriends, and on Friday or Saturday night she would be out hitting the clubs—no responsibilities, no long-term relationships, no commitments. One of her biggest regrets was not having followed through with a long-term relationship. There had been one guy.

But none of those things existed anymore. Coffee shops, night clubs, restaurants, having a normal relationship, they were all foreign to her now. The only thing that mattered was survival.

Her mind was in a fog. When she looked down, the shoe/barefoot prints had disappeared. Carrie spun around and ran back along the path until she found the prints in the dirt. They veered off into the grass by a group of trees. She silently unclipped her pack and let it softly drop to the ground. With the hammer cocked on the gun, she held it directly in front of her. Following the trampled grass, she placed her feet where the scavenger had walked earlier. Each step was calculated and meticulous. The tracks took her into the woods where the tree canopy shaded the ground from the sun. The temperature dropped considerably the further she went in. It became increasingly difficult to follow the tracks except for the barefoot imprint which left its telltale toes deep in the ground.

Carrie knew exactly what she was looking for as she paused, aimed the gun low towards the ground and looked for the exposed lower section of the one-shoed scavenger. She followed the sights of the gun barrel as she swept it back and forth across her field of vision. Going deeper than she wanted, she argued with herself that if she had come this far, what were a few more feet. Then she caught sight of what she was after.

She let the gun lead her to the mound sticking out of the ground. The shoulders, back, pelvis and lower limbs, with one bare foot, were visible. Only the head was buried. Standing to it's left, she hauled off and kicked it in the ribs. Nothing! It didn't move. Or it didn't register the pain. With everything she could muster, she swung her leg back and kicked it again in the same spot. Again, nothing. She raised her foot and dropped it hard on the lower left leg. The bone cracked with a gut-wrenching sound. It didn't move. The gun still pointed at where the head would be underground, she walked around and broke the bones in the right lower leg. This time she stomped on the right leg twice. The bones broke through the grey skin. Even in the dusky forest, the white bones were in stark contrast to the skin tone. There wasn't any blood.

This is what she had been taught to do. It would never walk again, but it could still crawl. She was breathing heavily; Carrie wasn't sure if she was winded or just angry. She hated them. Not them, but what they represented. She raised her foot again and brought it down hard on the right arm. The sound of the bones breaking almost made her vomit. When she pulled her foot away, the lower arm was angled as if it had a second elbow. The arm made almost a perfect "Z" with a hand at the end.

Carrie walked around to the other side and broke the left arm in much the same way. Still, it lay there, with its head buried in the ground, unaware it was now a quadriplegic; two broken legs, two broken arms, and no way to get around.

They didn't feel pain she'd been told. For all Carrie knew, it would cut off its legs at the knees and hobble around looking for food. She wanted this thing dead, not handicapped.

The only sure way to kill it was a bullet to the head. You had to blow its brains all over the place. But she had also been taught not to waste bullets. She holstered the gun and decided on another option.

Carrie looked around the forest until she found a large, thick branch. She swung it like an axe against a tree to make sure it wouldn't break. After several more attempts, she knew it was strong enough.

Back at the "infected," she grabbed it by the feet and pulled. The bone ends ground against each other as she pulled. Leaning back, she placed one foot back and pulled harder. Eventually, it began to free itself from being buried. As soon as the head was freed from the earthen grave, it awoke. It went to reach out, to roll over, and both arms flailed as it attempted to braced itself. Carrie lost her grip and stumbled as it rolled. She fell backwards, landing on her rear. Out of habit, she panicked and wanted to run, but instead, she took control of herself and watched. It was unable to right itself, push itself up or do much of anything. As it rolled back and forth, the two broken arms flopped about like wet rags on the end of a stick.

Carrie got up, for once standing in front of one of them with no fear, only hatred. She stepped in closer, swung her leg and kicked it on the side of the head. If it could have screamed, it would have. But it didn't. She raised the club high over her head and looked down at it. It showed no fear, no idea of what was about to happen. The club came down hard and connected. There was a sickening sound as it penetrated the skull and broke it open.

She pulled back and raised the club high. The infected was still moving on the ground; unaware it should be dead. She swung the club again, and again, and again, smashing it into its skull. She continued until her arms hurt and she was out of breath. Her grip was tight on the club, but now it was firmly embedded in the bones inside the skull. When Carrie pulled, the thing's head raised off the ground. She released her grip. Either she didn't want to or couldn't muster any more energy to continue the onslaught. It was gone. Fortunately, the club covered most of its face. Carrie didn't want to see what she had done to it.

All emotions exhausted, she stood there panting—drained of all her rage.

"Fuck you," she said, her words barely audible. "It was worth it to save a bullet." She wiped the sweat from her face with the back of her sleeve then spit on the body. As she walked past, she tapped the club, but the creature wasn't moving.

Walking out of the woods into the sunlight, Carrie could feel her muscles burning. It had been a long time since she had done anything like that, and it was apparent she was woefully out of shape. Picking up her pack, she flung it over her shoulders and was about to holster her gun when some rustling at the edge of the clearing caught her attention. She slowly turned with her gun at the ready and pointed forward. Looking past the barrel, she spotted a flock of half a dozen wild turkeys less than twenty feel away. They were making there way out of the woods to feed in the open grassy area.

Her stomach began to rumble at the thought of a turkey dinner. Carrie raised the gun, but at this distance she would most likely miss hitting any of them. She was happy she had saved a bullet now that she could use it to help get a meal. Slowly lowering herself down below the level of the grass she kept her sights focused on the flock. They continued to graze and move about in the clearing. The birds turned and made their way further away from where she lay hidden.

After years of hunting wild turkeys, Carrie knew the birds were big, could run fast, and were not great at flight. But they made good eating. She watched them move as a group, back and forth across the field. After several minutes, she decided to crawl closer to the edge of the clearing where she could get a better shot.

Carrie unclipped her pack and let it slide to the ground as she crept along in the grass. The gun was held out in front, ready to pull the trigger when she got close enough. When she got to the edge of the grass, she looked over the flock to see which one would make the easiest target. With a steady hand, she pointed the gun at the largest of the birds, aimed and pulled the trigger. Without exception, all the birds took to the air. Carrie had missed her mark. She knelt, took aim once more, and pulled the trigger pointing at the mass of birds in flight. For a moment nothing happened, then one fell from the flock to the ground.

Proud of her marksmanship, Carrie walked over to the dead turkey, and stood over it. The other birds had already flown off. She felt a sense of shame as she stared at the dead bird; killing an innocent animal was still difficult for her—unlike the feeling of accomplishment for what she had done only a few minutes earlier to the body in the woods.

She scooped up the bird by the feet. It was lighter than she expected, only a young bird, but she would still eat well.

It took more than two hours to dig the fire pit, line it with rocks and get the wood coals hot enough to cook. In the meantime, she plucked the bird, gutted it, and cut it into quarters for faster cooking.

When the smallest piece was ready, she devoured the turkey breast—skin, and flesh—as the rest of the bird cooked over the open fire. It had been a long time since Carrie had had a hot turkey meal. As she took another bite, she dreamed of her favourite sides: mashed potatoes, cranberries, and stuffing. Finishing the leg, she tossed the bones, retrieved the rest of the meat from the spit, then found some clean shirts to wrap the meat in before filling her pack.

She kicked dirt over the coals, smothering them before making her way to the road. The sun was directly overhead. She had barely walked a few miles since waking. It had been a productive day, however. With a full stomach she kept a fast pace that she knew she wouldn't be able to keep if she were hungry. It was getting darker earlier now that fall was around the corner. Each night, the air felt a little crisper. If Carrie wanted to make it north before the cold weather arrived, she would have to double her efforts.

There were also fewer infected the further north you went. The infected didn't fair well in the cold, with many perishing in the winter months. Because of the lack of food and their inability to think and find shelter, they froze with their heads buried in the ground. Then the animals would find their frozen corpses and eat them. For some reason, no one knew why, some animals would get infected from eating the diseased, while others seemed to be immune. More often than not, the infected animals died off quickly when they got sick.

The argument had been made several times to stay up north year-round to avoid any of the infected. But the lack of a stable food source and the constant cold made the decision to migrate in the fall easier. Only those who could tolerate the cold and knew how to survive in such a harsh climate didn't ever have to deal with the infected. At times like this, Carrie wished she had been Canadian living far up north. For her, the decision to travel north and remain as far as possible from the infected was an easy choice.

Carrie watched the sun carefully, knowing full well she didn't have any place to bed down and not looking forward to another night strapped high up in a tree—safe but amazingly uncomfortable.

Sipping the last of the fresh water, she made note of one more thing on her checklist to look for as she made her way to rejoin the group.

Carrie thought again about traveling north. No more killing. Hunting wasn't killing, she rationalized; it was survival. So was killing the infected to avoid being killed. That, too, was survival. She played both pro and con, arguing with herself as a way to pass the time. It was something she did when she was bored. It was an awful feeling. The first time she'd had to kill an animal for food, she cried for hours, refusing to eat the life she had just taken. Carrie said she would rather starve than kill again. That argument lasted only a few days, until hunger won the fight without so much as a counter argument. Still, she thought, as long as there was remorse each time she was forced to kill to survive, she wouldn't lose her humanity. And in this uncertain time, humanity was rare.

Then, without warning, he popped into her head. Noah. Damn, not again. Carrie hated it when he made his presence known. Somehow, he must have been hiding close by, lurking behind some other unrelated memory, and decided to make a visit without asking permission. Noah wasn't just a guy; he was the guy for Carrie. In every sense of the word. If there were two people made to be together, it was them. Everything they did was special: love, fighting, sex. Everything was over the top. They did nothing ordinary.

Her pace slowed momentarily as she fought to keep him away. Whenever she thought about him, remembered him, depression wasn't far off. Carrie couldn't do this to herself again. She tried to think of work, when she used to work, then she would slide back to a memory of Noah.

Carrie finished the last of the fresh stream water, then broke into a slow jog to keep her mind occupied with something, anything. She tried to remember where she was supposed to meet and what the signals were. She went through the seconds it took for a gun shot to travel and estimate how far off it was. It worked for a short time until

Noah slid back into her thoughts and made things worse.

"Hi. Remember me?" Noah's voice resonated in Carrie's mind.

"Of course, I remember you. How could I forget?" Carrie was breathing heavy. The pack bounced on her back. She fought to tighten the straps as she ran.

"Well, you haven't thought about me in a long time. I was beginning to think you didn't care," he said softly.

"I never stopped caring. I just can't let myself think about you. You are, were, part of the past. You're not around anymore."

"I'm around as long as you think of me."

Carrie was having the same argument with Noah that she had every time she remembered him. Her heart was beating faster as she quickened her pace and thought of him.

"You left when I needed you most."

Noah took her hand, "You say that, but it's not like I had a choice in the matter."

"Why didn't you come back?" Carrie was screaming in her mind.

"We both know the answer is a mystery. You don't know what happened to me and neither do I. If I could've made it back to you, I would have. I never wanted to leave you."

"Then why didn't you come after me if you survived?"

"Everyone was scattered, no one was where they thought they should be. Did you end up where you wanted?" Noah asked. It was the same discussion they'd had countless times and never resolved.

"I needed you. You said you would never leave me. You never came back. I can't trust you. I can't trust anyone except myself. I only have myself."

Noah's voice was soft and reassuring, "You can't do everything on your own. Everyone needs help. Don't be so proud that you can't or won't accept help from someone because of vanity."

"You never came back after you said you would never leave. I couldn't trust anyone after that except myself," Carrie screamed inside her head. She countered every one of Noah's comments with the same response.

"You were like that before. You haven't changed. You know, I love everything about you, even that stubborn, pig-headed attitude of yours. Stop being so, so, you. There's nothing wrong with accepting help sometimes. No one can do everything on their own."

Inside Carrie's head, she and Noah continued their imaginary disagreement, each going back and forth trying to prove their point. It always ended the same way. Even though it was Carrie's fantasy conversation, she could never win the argument.

Carrie stopped running and placed her hands on her knees, breathing heavily. Her damp bangs hung low, covering her face. She hated that Noah never came back, but now she wanted him more than ever. She stood and flipped her hair back, still breathing deeply. Looking overhead, she saw that it was now mid-afternoon. She pulled the last of the water bottles from her bag; she knew it was empty but hoped a few drops remained.

She held the empty bottle high with her tongue out. Nothing. She sighed heavily, closed the cap, and placed the bottle back in her bag. Carrie wasn't far from the place where she was supposed to meet the group days earlier.

"Another time, Noah," Carrie said aloud to no one in particular. "Maybe next time we can finish this conversation."

In the afternoon sun, as Carrie held her head back with her eyes closed and took in the warmth of the day, she could hear the insects buzzing about overhead. She took in a few deep breaths and tried to forget about Noah. Carrie had been trying to forget about him for a long time and nothing really worked. He always seemed to manage to pop back into her head without warning. Now she hoped he would stay away, not for good, but at least until she was back with the group.

Carrie pulled a turkey leg wrapped in a red T-shirt from her pack, took one large bite, then put the meat back in her bag. In this heat, the meat would spoil quickly; she estimated she had until the next day before the meat would be bad. With one final deep breath, she shifted the pack on her back and began to make her way south on the path. Carrie had plenty of energy, she had eaten well and only needed more water for hydration. She kept a steady pace and expected to make it to the meeting point soon.

The sun was strong as dark clouds began to move in from the west. Carrie continued watch the clouds as she made her way along the path. First the leaves began to rustle more briskly; the birds disappeared from the sky, then the sun was blocked from view by thick clouds. She could feel the temperature drop, causing goosebumps on her bare arms. She looked up and squinted into the wind as it picked up. Carrie scanned the area, looking for shelter. Rain was going to be coming down soon. She pulled the poncho from her pack and readied her water bottles to be refilled with fresh rainwater. Fumbling at the bottom of the pack, she found the old plastic funnel she used to help collect rain.

Carrie located a tight gathering of trees that might provide some shelter from the coming downpour and squeezed in at the base. All her water bottles were collected, the lids removed and tossed back in the pack. She dug several small holes in the ground with her hands and placed a bottle in each, then packed the loose earth around. She put the funnel into the largest bottle first, and when that bottle was filled, move it to the next, and so on.

Hopefully the rain would last long enough to fill them all, but not so long that it would cause more delays getting back to the group. Carrie leaned against a tree, pulled her legs in tight, pulled the poncho down to her feet, then wrapped her arms around them. The wind picked up, leaves and debris began to roll across the forest floor before her. She closed her eyes, leaned her head back against the tree and let her mind wander. Before the rain arrived, Carrie had fallen asleep.

The howling wind and rain slapped her face, waking Carrie up from her nap. She looked out from her perch to see the downpour just beyond the treeline. Her first bottle was already full and spilling over the top of the funnel. She reached out, removed the funnel from the first bottle and placed it in the second, then pulled the first bottle from the mud that held it in place. Instead of cleaning it and replacing the lid, she gulped half its contents then stuck it in the mud again. Carrie wiped her mouth with the back of her hand as she moved further back around the tree, away from the rain.

She looked up into the sky to see the black clouds continue to jockey for position high above. Carrie watched from under the trees as the sky grew darker and more ominous. She was in for a long wait before the rain would let up enough to make her way to her friends. With her eyes closed once again, she heard the sound of raindrops splashing in the mud puddles.

The methodical sound of the rain as it landed in the puddles forming in the earth reminded her of nights in her childhood bedroom when she would curl up under the covers listening to drops against the windowsill. It was those times when most young girls think about things like marriage and family and children. She would fantasize about who she would meet, where she would work, what she would do, how her children would look. Carrie smiled under her poncho, they were warm memories of days long gone, but still made her feel young and innocent.

With her legs pulled in tightly, watching the steady downpour, Carrie's eyes grew heavy and let her mind wander through her memories, eventually drifting off to sleep.

It was dusk when he woke up. He wiped the dirt from his eyes and scanned the area around him. It had rained hard while he rested, and it continued to sprinkle lightly. His clothes were wet, hanging heavily off his frame. It never once occurred to him to remove his clothing. He never understood what the garments he wore were. To him they were no different than the fur on the animals in the forest or the feathers on the birds. This was the first time he noticed his clothes were different somehow from the animals and more like those of the bodies in the cabin.

He tugged at the suit jacket on one side, feeling it pull on the opposite shoulder. The jacket was frayed at the bottom, the lining hung freely from the inside. This was the first time he'd noticed that there was some sort of extra material on either side of the bottom of the jacket. Uncertain what they were, he patted down the outside of his jacket and felt something high on the left side. He tried unsuccessfully several times to retrieve whatever was hidden inside. Pulling on the lapel, he noticed there were pockets inside the jacket. It took a few more attempts before he was able to pull a wallet from the inner breast pocket.

He wondered how long this thing had been there. Not knowing what it was, he turned it over several times, sniffed it then bit it. It tasted dry and bitter; unlike anything he had tasted before. It wasn't edible. He continued to flip it over and it unfolded causing something loose to fall to the ground. The small piece of paper landed in a shallow pool of water. Puzzled, he looked at it, then picked up a photograph of two people he had never seen before.

Rain continued to fall, and a few drops landed on the picture.

The drop distorted the image of the girl and man beneath. With his thumb, he brushed away the water until the image was clear once again. He stared at the people in the image and wondered who they might be. There was a sense of familiarity, but he couldn't access the right memory.

Raindrops continued to dot the photograph, distorting the images once again. He wiped the water clear, then went to replace the photo in the wallet when it slipped from his hand, landing beside a puddle. He picked it up and saw his reflection, then glanced back at the photograph. The man in the photo looked like him but different. Even in the dim light, he could see the man had pink skin like the patch on his hand, but his face was smooth, his hair was shorter, and he was smiling. In the water, he could see his own hair was longer, falling freely around his face. The faces looked the same—but different. He looked at the photo again and tried to emulate the smile, but all he could muster was a poor imitation. He looked at himself; his teeth were brown with a thick crust covering them. The man in the photograph had perfectly white teeth and a full, broad smile. He tried again, and this time his smile was an exact duplicate of the man in the photo—could they be one and the same? Who was the girl standing so close to him and smiling too? There were flashes of familiarity too brief to understand.

He picked up the photograph and cradled it, wiping off the water and dirt before returning it to the safety of the wallet and the inner pocket. He wanted to recall who those people were. Their appearance was so vastly different from who he was now, he wanted to know why he was different.

He stood unmoving a few minutes, attempting to process the new emotions and memories he was experiencing. Turning around, he noticed the path and made his way towards it. He attempted several times to smile. It was unnatural and forced, but he kept practicing; walking along the path, he would look at a tree and smile. Not quite certain what a smile was, the more he did it the easier it became. It gave him a funny feeling, something he had never felt before. Something else that was new.

Stopping in a clearing, he looked up to the dark sky, tilted his head back, opened his mouth and took in what water he could. The moisture felt good. He did something spontaneously, without realizing it. He smiled.

Carrie woke up under the trees, as panic send lightning through her. It was dark, she was exposed, unprotected and vulnerable. She scanned the area around her for movement, or any sound at all. Nothing except the sound of rain. It had slowed but continued to drizzle. She quickly gathered up her water bottles and funnel, secured the tops before cramming them in the backpack, and made her way deeper into the woods.

Each step was planned to avoid making sounds.

It would be difficult to find a proper perch high in the trees at this time of night. Carrie couldn't use a flashlight; it would attract them like moths to a flame. In this new world, there was no light at night. Everyone knew that any light would draw them closer. She missed the days of streetlights and not being afraid.

"Honey, make sure you come in as soon as the streetlights come on," Carrie's mother yelled from the kitchen. "Dinner will be on the table waiting for you."

Carrie turned to her mother, "We have the same discussion every single night. I know I have to be home as soon as the streetlights come on. Why don't you give me a cell phone like every other kid so you can just call me?"

Carrie's mother wiped her hand with the dish cloth, walked to her daughter and knelt low, "Technology is great and makes our lives easier. If I have to call you when it gets dark, you won't take any responsibility for your own actions. If you act when the streetlights come on and you come home, you get a nice hot meal and get to sit with your family and talk while you eat. If you don't, then your meal will be left out, cold and dried up and you eat alone. We will always be a family and family dinner is so important. I want you to want to be here for dinner for as long as you can. Live beyond technology, it is a servant to you, not the other way around. I won't always be there to call you when the streetlights come on, so you need to learn to rely on only one person …" She touched Carrie on the chest over the heart with her index finger. "You."

"Fuck, what I wouldn't give for my mother to call me when it got dark or for the streetlights to remind me to come home," she mumbled to herself. Carrie touched the same spot where her mother had touched her decades ago. She kept a steady pace, making her way deep into the woods. She knew exactly what she was looking for and wouldn't stop until she found them.

The deeper she made her way into the woods, the less dense the woods became, exactly what she was looking for. The larger the trees, the thicker the overhead canopy; the smaller trees were unable to take hold and grow along the forest floor. Carrie stopped and looked above, allowing her eyes to settle in the darkness. To her right, a medium sized tree with enough low branches to assist in her climb. Everyone knew *they* couldn't climb.

It didn't take long before she was secured in the tree, her pack tied above her head. Her stomach rumbled loudly as she bit into a large chunk of turkey meat. In the morning, she would finish whatever was left to give her the energy she would need to catch up with her friends. She ripped at the meat, tearing another large chunk, wishing she had some spices to enhance the meal—or a side dish—any of the standbys like cranberry sauce and mashed potatoes with gravy. Carrie smiled, laughing at herself thinking of more childhood memories. She swallowed, took another bite, and tasted the cranberry sauce and side dishes in her mind.

She stuffed the bones into her jacket so they wouldn't fall to the ground overnight. She pulled the hood up over her head, tied the drawstring, closed her eyes, and let her body go numb with a full belly. Her eyelids grew heavy and her mind grew cloudy as sleep overcame her one again.

The clouds had broken and given way to a clear sky with stars and a half moon, its white light partially illuminating the area before him. He had walked for hours, only stopping to feed on beetles and other insects as he made his way along the path. Thoughts of the people in the photograph never left him as he walked. He was filling himself on insects he found under tree bark as he made his way towards—what?

There was another realization. All this time, he never quite understood where he was walking to. Something instinctively drove him to walk—somewhere. He didn't know if he was walking away from something or to something.

With his bony grey fingers and long jagged nails, he dug into the tree and pulled out more insects. From between two pieces of bark, he hauled out caterpillars and tossed them into his mouth. Standing at the tree, he continued to rip bark away from the trunk finding dozens of dark caterpillars with a gold stripe down their backs. He would catch them, then eat and repeat until there weren't any insects left on the tree.

Making his way out of the bush, he was again walking south with no clear destination in mind. The woods opened to a small clearing.

Like birds flying south for the winter, was it evolution, instinct, or just plain nature? Was it nature that made him, or man? He stopped for a moment, unsure why he was suddenly having trouble seeing the trees. This had never happened before. He never had trouble with his vision at night. He squinted, then rubbed his eyes, but it didn't do any good. Things were still blurry and dark. Squinting helped slightly but, like his skin colour, his vision was changing.

He continued to wonder about that photo he'd found in the wallet—two things he didn't know even existed until a short while ago—or know what they were. If he was the same person from the photo, why was he now so different?

Carrie woke up in a panic. She turned in her sleep and might have fallen out of the tree, if not for the ropes securing her to the trunk. She reached out and took hold of the limb and righted herself. Breathing heavily, all the fears of what could have happened ran through her mind in an instant.

With all her strength, she tightened the ropes, checked the knots, and tried to calm herself. The thought of what might have happened scared her to her bones. Carrie was wet, afraid, and alone. She wanted so much to be with her family, be that little girl and have her mother make dinners and wait for the streetlights to come on so she would run home for a family dinner. She hated Noah at this moment for leaving. Her sobs turned into full body jerks as she let loose a torrent of tears and emotions that had built up for months. She swung her arms widely about wanting to hit something, punch someone, force the negative emotions from her body. There wasn't anybody to hold her and tell her everything would be all right. Things hadn't been "all right" for almost three years.

Carrie sat there, tied to a tree above the forest floor, exhausted, panting. There were no more tears, no one was going to come and hold her and make everything all right. Her arms dangled loosely at her sides; her fingertips numb. There was nothing left inside. She reached for the knots that held her tightly and picked at the ropes. Ending things was probably the best thing. Since the event, she had been alone almost the entire time, fighting for survival, struggling to find food, shelter, friends. Carrie was spent—there wasn't anything left in the tank.

The first knot around her right leg was undone, the two ends of the rope fell on opposite sides of the large tree branch. Carrie fumbled with the second knot around her left leg, then the one around her waist. There was only one more rope securing her to the tree, the one around her chest. She would untie it, roll from the branch, and hope that from this height the fall would kill her. Then the thought came to her: what if she only broke her leg, maybe injured herself enough that she was left in constant pain. What if she lay there for days, hoping she would die—or if one of them came along and infected her, she would be one of them with a handicapped symbol on her back. She had never seen one of them with a handicap. Maybe they got eaten or left to die. Do they die on their own? Maybe they just lay there forever, unable to move. Instead, she thought she would shoot herself, take the handgun, point it at her temple and pull the trigger. But she might jerk the gun as she pulled the trigger, she thought, and just blow off part of her face. Maybe put the barrel in her mouth or under her chin.

She could do it in the tree; the scavengers would never reach her up this far and her body would decompose and eventually fall to the forest floor.

She formed a pistol with her right hand, with her index and middle fingers playing the part of the barrel. She placed it against her temple, her thumb won the part of the hammer, lowered slowly as

Carrie pursed her lips and let out a barely audible wisp of air, thinking that was the sound she would hear immediately before she died. She then placed the finger gun under her chin, discounted that, and stuck her fingers in her mouth. The thought of tasting metal before she died disgusted her. She moved her fingers back to her temple, pressed them hard into the skin, then imagined the courage it would take to pull the trigger. The bullet escaping from the chamber, breaking though her skull, ripping into her brain and destroying everything in its patch at it made its way to the other side. The bullet would blow a larger hole on the left side of her head, blood, brain matter, tissue and hair would follow. She wouldn't feel a thing.

Bugs and other insects would soon make their way into the cavity—eat, nest, lay eggs—and birds would feast on her eyeballs. Her body would bloat, break down and ooze fluid as her tissue decomposed. Scavengers would pace frantically around the base of the tree hoping for a morsel of flesh as it broke away from her body.

Carrie wondered if she used a length of rope, tied it tightly around the tree, then slid a noose around her neck and jumped, would the fall break her neck so she'd die instantly, or would she struggle as she slowly asphyxiated. Then she wondered, even if the fall did break her neck, would she still be aware for a few moments, if her brain still had enough oxygen reserves to understand what was going on. Would she swing and dangle, unable to move her limbs, fully conscious of the fact that in a few brief seconds she would be dead?

Carrie reached down, grabbed the two ends of the ropes, and tied them tightly around her waist, then secured each leg. Maybe it didn't take courage to kill herself, maybe it was the easy way out. It took courage to stay alive, hope, and work for something better.

Eyes closed, she wanted to cry, but there were no more tears to come; instead she listened to the sounds of the night—crickets chirping, cicadas, owls—hoping they would lull her to sleep. Carrie was days behind schedule and would need a miracle to make up the time and meet with her group.

She let her mind wonder, taking in the night sounds when one distinctive sound sent chills over her entire body—footsteps. They were unmistakable even in the dense bush. The sound they made was like no other animal or human—a lumbering, steady walk, mindless and without direction.

Carrie scanned the area knowing full well there wasn't enough light to see much beyond the end of the tree limbs. Soon all sound stopped as well, the same as when any predator comes within range. The footfalls remained steady, one after the other, no break. The cadence was perfect, getting closer, closer, then nothing. The sounds of the forest night went still. There was only silence. Carrie listened, waiting for whatever was there to move on. Nothing. She leaned over as far as her bindings would allow. Then she heard it breathing. For the past three years, Carrie could honestly say she had never heard any of them breath before. She didn't think they did breathe. Straining against the ropes, she got close, hoping to hear more, and then she heard it again. It was distinctive and regular; they do breathe.

Does that mean they also have a heartbeat and pulse? she wondered. Carrie was now more frightened than ever. *No one has ever heard one breathe before. Are they evolving into something more?* The very thought that they could become more, evolve into something worse, scared her. Perhaps she should rethink her suicide scenario.

It remained directly below her, unmoving. Could it sense her, smell her and know she was up the tree? They couldn't climb, run or rationalize. But if they were evolving, maybe they could form logical thoughts and become more deadly than they already were. There was only one option, kill it now.

Carrie reached for her pack, released it from the trunk and rummaged around until she found the pistol and a small LED flashlight. The light would blind it, giving her time to aim and pull the trigger.

Inside the pack, she cupped the end of the flashlight to shield the beam and flicked the switch quickly to make sure there was enough battery power to illuminate the area. Carrie pulled the gun from the pack, rested it on her lap, closed the pack flap and secured it to the rope around her legs so it wouldn't fall when she pulled the trigger.

She listened intently for the sound of breathing coming a dozen or more feet below her. There—she heard it again. She moved to her left and strained to lean closer to the sound. There it was again, steady, one breath every five seconds or so.

Like she had seen in countless police movies, she palmed the flashlight in her left hand, thumb on the switch, crossed her right hand over her left wrist and slowly cocked the hammer, then waited. She heard it again, steady; it was directly beneath her.

Carrie took in a deep breath of her own, held it, then thumbed the switch. The dim light illuminated an infected male. She steadied her hand to pull the trigger when it did something unexpected; it looked up at her, directly into the light. The thing looked like every other one she had seen or killed, but in the dim light she could see its eyes; they weren't blank like the others—they were sad—and it was staring into the light. They weren't supposed to be able to tolerate the light, yet it continued to look straight at her. For what seemed like an eternity, the two of them stared at each other. Carrie was certain it couldn't see her, but it continued to look into the light.

Then she realized it was the same one she'd seen before, the one wearing the suit. Was it following her?

She carefully lowered the hammer and moved the light around the base of the tree to see if there were any more of them gathered around. She positioned the light just to the right of the infected so the light didn't blind him. Carrie wanted it to see the anger on her face.

"Go. Leave me alone," Carrie screamed at the top of her lungs. She waited. No footsteps. The breathing from below remained constant. "Go. Leave me the fuck alone."

He looked at her, their eyes making contact, then he did something unexpected. He smiled at her. It was a forced smile, but a smile none the less. It softened his appearance, making him look almost human again. He didn't look as threatening when he smiled. She saw the dirt on his teeth, but she couldn't believe what she noticed. His eyes had something in them. It recognized another human.

Before she was fooled into believing this thing understood what it was doing, Carrie thought it might be a learned tactic to lull humans into thinking they understood what was happening right before they attacked. He continued to smile for a few moments, then looked away. Carrie turned off the light, expecting him to finally give up and leave.

There was a sound, a rustle in the leaves and pine needles on the forest floor, then nothing. Carrie shone her flashlight down to the base of the tree trunk. He was now sitting down, his back against the trunk, just staring ahead. Paying no attention to Carrie or the light coming from above, he placed his hand over the wallet in his jacket pocket to make sure it was still there.

This was the first time Carrie had seen one sit, or rest, or do whatever it was doing. Her flashlight was becoming dimmer, the old batteries finally failing, but she couldn't pull herself away from whatever he was doing. They usually had a single focus of just moving towards a destination. No one knew where the destination was, perhaps they didn't even know themselves.

There was a soft click, and she was in darkness again.

Day 918

Carrie woke long after the sun came up. Stretching, she recalled the guest she'd had the night before and looked below to see if he was still there. Nothing. A sense of relief came over her. Maybe she had dreamt the entire scenario, maybe it never happened. Maybe he understood her yelling at him and did leave.

Before loosening her binds, she drank half a bottle of water and found the last remaining bits of wild turkey. It was warm, old, but was still good protein for the hike ahead. She set her priorities for the day: reuniting with her friends, water, food—in that order.

Removing the ropes and bindings, she lowered her pack to the ground, then she waited for a few minutes to make sure the area was clear. Carrie surveyed the scene, then carefully climbed down. She coiled the ropes, tossed them in her pack, then hoisted it over one shoulder, all the while keeping her eyes and ears open.

She looked up into the sun; it was still early, maybe six-thirty or seven in old world time. Carrie knew if she kept a constant pace she could be at the rendezvous in an hour. She would be late, but they would have left a coded message indicating where they were going.

Once on the trail she broke out into a slow jog, the rifle bouncing in rhythm with her stride. Carrie's mind wondered as she ran; images, thoughts passed quickly, things that didn't matter any more. She forced them out. Carrie knew now that if she romanticized the past, it clouded her mind. Still, she was alone and scared, and it helped.

The time passed quickly. Her feet hurt, she paused only to sip from her water bottle, and would have killed for an Advil and a new pair of shoes. In between breaths, she tilted her head back and sipped more water. She wanted more, but until she could find another source, what she carried was all she had. Carrie smelled it first, then noticed the wisps of smoke above the treeline. It didn't appear to be that far away. She knew that smell. Fear spilled over; adrenaline coursed through her.

She capped the water bottle and ran, faster than she thought she could. The pack bounced on her back. She grabbed the straps and pulled them tight. Her feet were slipping in the loose dirt, but she kept her pace. Carrie could see the clearing ahead; the smell became more intense and now she was certain what she was about to see. She stopped short, her feet sliding in the dirt; then she let her pack drop to the ground. Pulling the handgun out, she stuffed it into her waist band, holding the rifle at the ready, knowing full well if it was an attack it would have been at night. If it was another group of humans, they wouldn't have fought unless something seriously provoked them.

Carrie burst through the clearing and found them. It was her group, dead, all of them. She stood in silence, panting, arms at her side. Some of the provisions were on fire and several bodies were still smoldering. It was commonly known that if someone received a non-lethal wound from an infected, they would set themselves on fire or someone else would kill them before the change took hold.

During a night attack, one counter move was to light a campfire and blind the infected. Carrie thought that during the attack someone must have tried to set the infected on fire and the flames spread quickly as the fight went on.

There were several infected bodies lying alongside her entire group. She thumbed the hammer on the rifle and slowly made her way to each body. There was no way of knowing what exactly had happened, but she wasn't taking chances. She found a large stick and poked any of the bodies that weren't charred beyond recognition.

Most of the dead were human. Carrie walked slowly among the

infected dead and human dead, listening for any sounds, looking for movement. Stepping over the bodies, she saw her friend. Years ago, she would have burst into tears, curled up in a little ball and sobbed. Today that person no longer existed.

She continued to poke the dead, the end of the stick pushed hard and deep into a section of soft tissue. Carrie didn't hold back. A few times the stick punctured the skin and sunk deep into the corpse. She had to be certain they were dead.

One of the infected corpses was still holding tight onto one of her friends. The side of its head had been blown away by a gunshot, but Carrie noticed it had a large chunk of flesh in its mouth from the leg of one of the group members. She knelt and turned the human body over. It was one of the younger girls she knew well. Carrie recoiled. The girl was maybe sixteen, her youthful skin had already started to turn gray, becoming leathery. Her pupils had blown and were solid black. There was no way of knowing how long it would be before her friend would completely turn. Everyone was different. Carrie couldn't take the chance.

Carrie stood back and looked in the young girls' eyes. She was gone, staring up blankly, unsure what was about to happen. Briefly, Carrie thought about the male infected smiling back up at her the night before. Its eyes had something behind them, these did not. She pointed the rifle at the young girl's head and pulled the trigger, once, twice. The back of her skull exploded, spilling its contents on the ground, turning the soil black. Her young pretty face was now broken and deformed. She was dead. Again. There wasn't any grief or sorrow for the young girl, she was already dead before Carrie pulled the trigger.

Carrie stood over the body, almost envious. She hoped that there would be someone who would shoot her if the time ever came. The smell of gun powder filled her nostrils, the sounds still echoed through the trees. She dropped to the ground next to the girl, crossed her legs then stared aimlessly at her dead friends. If she'd had any emotions left inside her she would have cried, but she couldn't. Carrie hated herself for not feeling something—anything—pity, sorrow, jealousy?

Carrie stood, then finished checking on the rest of the bodies. The entire group was dead. She was certain of that. From what she could determine, the attack had happened the day before. If she had been on time, she would be laying among the dead—or turned.

There was no reason to take time to bury the bodies; most were already completely burnt or still burning. More out of anger than worries of cross contamination, Carrie used her poking stick, wrapped in a torn piece of clothing, set it ablaze then set the rest of the bodies on fire. Again, no emotion, this was now a fact of life. Setting the last body alight, she stood back and watched them all burn. There was an intense heat and smell. Carrie began to chuckle—then burst into a full laugh. She wished she had marshmallows. Carrie laughed loudly to herself as she thought about roasting marshmallows over the dead, burning bodies of her friends.

Walking around the corpses, Carrie found a sealed container of dried meat strips. She wasn't sure what type of jerky it was, but it would help keep her alive. She ripped a bite and chewed on the leathery texture of the jerky. It was tasteless and hurt her jaw to chew, but it was good. She stuffed a few pieces in her pocket then sealed the container and tossed it towards her pack.

Carrie quickly collected guns, knives and ammunition that had been spread around the scene then laid out across the ground. Among the chaos of bodies and equipment, she found more sealed containers of food and water and placed them away from the pyre.

But any container that was open she considered spoiled and she tossed its contents on one of the many burning bodies.

Sitting with her legs crossed among the guns, Carrie looked across the mounds of smouldering and burning bodies. She pulled a piece of jerky from her pocket and bit hard on the meat strip. She wanted to feel something, anything, so she didn't lose her humanity. But those thoughts only got in the way of survival. She cast them aside and began to wonder what to do next. Then she placed the handguns in one pile, the rifles in another and counted all the rounds for each.

The handguns suited her small hand better. There were different sizes, but Carrie weighed the killing power of each before deciding to keep what she already had. She knew it and handled the gun well. Among the ammunition, there were over a hundred rounds more for her weapon. It would add weight to her pack, but it was an easy decision to make.

She collected the sealed containers of water and food. Opening one of the water bottles, she tilted her head back and drank the entire contents. In all, she found more than two dozen sealed water bottles. The infected hadn't figured out how to uncap or screw and unscrew the bottles so she felt safe drinking them. Carrie drank two litres of water and only stopped when she felt she was about to vomit. It felt good to be full. There was enough food to last her for weeks if she'd been able to carry it all. Instead, she stuffed as much protein as she could into her pack. She found a granola bar in one of the food containers and flipped it over. It had expired almost fourteen months prior. Carrie tore into it and sniffed deeply. The smell of its sugary sweetness filled her senses with memories of better days. With her eyes closed, she carefully took a small bite and hoped it wasn't bad. It was stale, dry, but the chemicals and sugars had done a wonderful job preserving it. It was delicious. She rolled the oats and sugar and nuts in her mouth until she had to swallow the food. Carrie repeated this several times until the entire bar was gone. She ripped open the foil wrapper and licked any of the sweet icing that had stuck to it. For those few moments, it was heaven.

Carrie turned her attention back to the cache of unused guns and ammunition. She wrapped them in whatever old garments she could find and buried them in a shallow hole off the main path. She placed several stones over the hole in a star shape. The infected would never understand, but any human would recognize the shape as being man made.

Looking up into the sky, the sun indicated it was mid afternoon. Carrie had a few hours at most to find a place to bed down for the night. With the weight added to her pack, her pace would be considerably slower.

The plan had already been set, and she knew where she was supposed to be. Yet Carrie wondered if she should follow the plan and continue south below the snow line.

Years ago, it was thought that if everyone moved to Northern Canada, the infected wouldn't be able to survive the cold or find food and would simply die out. Their numbers would be reduced and if any of them made their way north in the summer, they would be easy to defeat, given their limited numbers. The plan made sense, considering no one truly knew what they were dealing with. Most of the survivors had difficulty adapting with the cold and hunting in the winter. Many of the humans, who were not prepared or accustomed to living in the cold, died as quickly as the infected in the frigid weather.

Over the past few years, it became apparent the infected didn't feel emotions; it wasn't the cold that killed them, it was the inability to hunt in the snow. They couldn't be reasoned with or feel pain and had only a single objective: food. They had to eat, or they would die. Or whatever it was they did. They still consumed energy and had to replace it. They were violent, single-minded and had no other motivation than to survive. They didn't resemble their previous selves in any way.

No one had ever seen them reproduce in the conventional sense. Their numbers only increased as they infected more humans.

Carrie knew it would be best to continue south and hopefully meet up with another group for safety. Living alone now wasn't really a viable option with no one to help with food, shelter or hunting. She knew her limitations and became frightened at the option of being alone over the winter.

She sat on the ground, watching the flames slowly die out on each of the bodies. The smell of burning flesh once nauseated her; now, it was a common odour that Carrie had become accustomed to. She tapped her pack and rolled her fingers along the zipper, her dirty fingernail clicking along the zipper teeth. She strummed the zipper like a guitar and began to hum a tune. Her eyes closed, head tilted back, the sun felt good on her face. The tune wasn't from any band she could recall, it was just a little melody to help the time pass.

A few hundred yards north of where Carrie sat watching bodies burn, a fox began to wake. After the attack from the infected mouse, the fox had itself become contaminated through direct contact. Weak and unable to move as the virus burnt through its system, causing a cascade effect of changes within its DNA, it had buried itself in the underbrush and only woke early because, even unconscious, it smelled burning flesh and it was hungry. It opened its eyes, squinted against the afternoon sunlight, lifted its head, and sniffed the air. It was an unmistakable smell, food.

It pulled itself out of the underbrush and made its way to the edge of the woods. Once it got too close to the sunlight it stopped, unable to see or tolerate the pain the sunlight caused. It lay down and would wait until nightfall.

Carrie swung her pack over her shoulders, feeling the added weight of the extra provisions. It was always worth carrying the extra food, water, and ammunition. She would return to this site one day, if she survived, to retrieve the guns and bullets. There were dozens of stashes of provisions buried all over the Canadian and American countryside. In the years since the incident, it had become practice among some of the survivors of one group to help another. If two similar groups happened to meet, they would form one larger group to better the odds of survival. There were always the rogue groups who would kill other humans to take what they wanted.

A few hours later, the sun was just clear of the treeline. Once the sun set over the treetops, any of the infected would begin to wake up and start to hunt. Carrie realized she was running short on daylight and would have to spend another night up high in the trees. Scanning those along the path, she spotted a group of tall oaks without any branches or limbs until at least six feet up the trunk.

Before making the ascent, Carrie unclasped the chest buckle, letting her pack fall to the ground. She undid her belt, pulled down her pants, squatted and peed before bedding down. There was no reason for modesty or worrying about who might be around. Carrie wished she had toilet paper to clean up but that was a luxury she hadn't seen in over a year.

Carrie retrieved the rope, tied it to one end of the pack, and tossed the other up high into the tree. After years of tree climbing, she had become quite skilled at getting the weighted end of the rope exactly where it needed to be. It spun around a large limb, locking itself in place. She then pulled a shorter rope from the bag, swung one end around the trunk, caught it, tightened both ends around her wrists, and used it as leverage to pull herself up the tree. Once she'd chosen her branch for the night, she pulled her pack up and secured it. Carrie perched herself on the limb, wrapped her bedding ropes arounds herself and settled in for the night.

As he walked along the path, in the distance he saw a glow around the bend. As he got closer, the light from the fires became brighter—but not as strong as the fire ball in the sky. He squinted his eyes, then looked away.

The evening had not only awakened him, but it had also brought out the animals looking for food. Walking by the burning mounds, he saw a pack of coyotes had already gathered around the corpses and were biting and tearing chunks of flesh from the corpses that weren't burning any longer. They tore at the flesh, ripping morsels from the bodies. The animals only feasted on the bodies that had been recently killed. The infected bodies were left untouched, the virus emitting a scent which offended the animals. Several coyotes stopped feeding for a moment, noticing the man approach, and growled menacingly. They lowered themselves, guarding whatever corpse they had chosen and continued to snarl. The adversaries stared at each other. He felt no fear but still gave them a wide birth, walking around the pack along the edge of the clearing. Once the coyotes recognized he wasn't a threat, then cautiously went back to feeding, always keeping an eye on him.

He made his way along the treeline passing several of the burning bodies and inhaled an offensive odour. He didn't like it. Something else that was new that he didn't understand. Stopping, he inhaled deeply as smoke flooded his nostrils. The smell of burning bodies made his stomach turn. A wave of nausea overcame him, another new sensation. He rubbed his stomach, but it did nothing to stem the wave of nausea.

Scanning the area, he navigated a path away from the burning bodies until he was standing on the outskirts of the clearing. The light from the dying fires was faint and didn't bother his eyes as much. The smell continued to upset his stomach and it rumbled, causing mild discomfort. Was it the smell—or hunger?

Walking away with his back to the clearing, he heard a low menacing growl behind him. Turning slowly towards the noise, he came face to face with two coyotes, their hackles raised, ears lowered, and lips curled back revealing dangerously lethal teeth. He had never encountered a situation like this and stood motionless and silent. The aggressive animals kept low, snarling, never taking their eyes off him.

Staring down the two coyotes, he couldn't fully understand what was happening. As before, instinct took over. He began stepping back slowly, one foot then the other, methodically, until he had put some distance between himself and the coyotes. He kept his gaze low, not wanting to provoke the animals. With ten or more feet between them, the growling subsided, and they relaxed, but kept their aggressive stance. He continued his backwards walk until he lost sight of them in the darkness, then turned and disappeared into the night.

Carrie rolled to her right. Her leg and arms fell from the tree limb, but her binds held tight preventing her from falling to the ground. "Shit," she whispered, a soft whimper, and exhaled. She pulled herself back on the limb. She often slipped but had never fallen. There was a fine balance between feeling secure and being comfortable. Carrie preferred to be comfortable but didn't want to fall to the ground. She tightened the bonds and tested them before feeling that sense of security again.

The cool, damp night air made the hair on her arms stand erect.

She reached inside her pack, took a sip of water, and pulled out her jacket. With the ropes wrapped around her torso, she had to put the jacket on with the back panel against her chest. The extra layer added much needed warmth. Carrie tried to fall back asleep, but instead she looked through the remaining leaves on the tree to the stars in the cloudless sky. Each night it seemed there were fewer leaves on the trees and more on the ground.

"Star light, star bright, first star I see tonight. I wish I may, I wish I might, wish that ..." Carrie wasn't even certain if she had the saying correct, then couldn't think of what to ask for. "I wish that I could have," she paused, "wish that the world ..." She chuckled at herself. She honestly couldn't think of only one wish, she wanted several. "Only one," she said to herself. "I want to be somewhere far away from here."

Carrie knew her wish would never come true, but it was worth the effort. She stared at the brightest star and recited her wish over and over again. She yawned once, closed her eyes, and within a few minutes, fell asleep.

He kept a steady pace along the path, pausing to pick wild mushrooms at the roadside and golden crab apples from the trees. He stood beneath one of the trees, picking it free of all fruit. Moving on, he found another and feasted on more crab apples. He reached up higher, picking the larger fruit that the ground animals couldn't reach. Along the top of the treeline, the moon peaked across the edge of the branches. As he ate, he looked up, staring at the moon, not really knowing why it was there or what it was. He spit out the apple core, wiped his chin with the back of his sleeve, and reached up and found another. They were tart and juicy and the more he ate the less noise his stomach made.

He filled his pockets with as many apples as they would hold and continued along the path. Feeling the nights getting cooler, he sensed that he had to make his way south. He couldn't remember why or how or what was causing the days to become shorter or cooler, or what he had done in the past. He was a newborn with memories only a few days old. He feasted on the fruit he carried in his pockets as he walked along the narrow path.

Fifty feet behind him, eyes tracked his every move from the edge of the path. It followed him, stopping when he stopped, moving when he moved. It would slowly close the gap until it was close enough to strike.

Carrie fell asleep once again, although dreams were not coming easily, nor was it restful. Her mind kept flashing back to the clearing where she'd been earlier in the day. As much as she'd like to have thought she was hardened to those sights, and the loss of friends meant nothing to her, she was only lying to herself. She saw the broken bodies, some ripped open and bitten, all of them dead.

Carrie was standing over one of the bodies, the youngest of the girls. She had a visible open wound across her chest and was lying prone across two males, one of them an infected who had lost half his skull to a shotgun blast. As Carrie turned to walk away, a gentle moan broke the silence. She turned to see the young girl begin to move. The girl slowly rolled over, falling off the other bodies onto the ground. Her skin had already begun to turn grey. Her chest wound was now exposed, her blood had coagulated, and the skin ripped by an infected bite had begun to heal over. It would only be a matter of hours before she was one of them.

Carrie looked around, found an aluminum baseball bat someone had been using as a weapon, and pick it up. The silver colour was tarnished and stained dark with the blood of countless strikes to the heads of infected attackers.

With the bat in hand, she took a few practice swings to loosen up her shoulder muscles, asking the pitcher to place the ball where she could knock it out of the park. Stepping in close, Carrie placed the tip of the bat along the left temple of the young girl, slowly pulled back, then brought the bat down softly, touching her temple again, making sure her aim was true. Then she positioned the bat up high, planted her feet, and swung with the force it would take to crush her skull. As the bat came down, the young girl opened her eyes; they were blank, empty, seeing something, unaware of what would happen a split second later. The bat made contact, the sound of bone being smashed by a hollow aluminum bat filled the air along with the sound of soft tissue tearing away from the skull and the brain being torn apart. Carrie woke up with a start. She jerked, twisted, and broke free of her bonds, falling to the ground below. She landed flat on her back; the air ripped from her lungs. For a moment, Carrie couldn't inhale or exhale. She forced herself to breathe, but her lungs had to equalize the pressure before they would accept fresh air.

Finally, with a deep inhalation, she took in a breath and let it out with a sigh. Carrie sat up, wrapped her arms around her knees and took a few slow, long, deep breaths until she could breathe normally. A quick pat down along her arms and legs assured her nothing was broken, but she knew she would be bruised by morning. Looking up from where she had fallen, she realized that she was fortunate not to have injured herself.

She got on her hands and knees, then stood and turned. Carrie stopped short when she came within inches of him. They were face to face; she was so close she could smell his breath. Startled, she yelled and fell backwards again, landing on her ass. Even in the dim light of the forest, she could make out the figure before her. She reached for the gun she sometimes kept in her waistband but found nothing.

Everything she owned was still up in the tree. Digging her heels in, she clawed at the dirt moving along like a crab, never taking her eyes off him. Carrie stopped only when the back of her head hit a tree, now almost ten feet from him. She slid her back up the tree until she was standing and the two of them were facing each other a few feet apart. He hadn't moved, which wasn't like them. They usually attacked quickly, fought to the death, and if you didn't die from your wounds or weren't eaten, you became an infected.

Carrie wrapped herself around the tree, putting a barrier between them. Still, he didn't move.

Peaking around the tree, she looked at him standing immobile in the darkness. It was difficult to see him in the dim light. She darted to the other side of the tree, and with one eye, snuck a glance. He followed her movements, moving slightly to see her around the other side of the tree, but he didn't make a move towards her.

The stare-down seemed to last an eternity; this was the longest she had ever seen one of them motionless or not attacking. Carrie didn't know what to do. Her eyes locked onto him as she blindly fumbled along the ground, her hands searching for a weapon: a big stick, a rock, anything. Nothing. There wasn't anything within reach. Her mind raced with options: run, but humans couldn't outrun an infected; fight, with no weapon she would certainly fail. Her only choice was to find another tree and climb as fast and as high as she could and wait for daylight.

It would be difficult with the limited visibility, but she had no choice. Looking up, the tree she was hiding behind didn't have any branches she could reach. A quick scan of the surrounding area provided her with an escape. A little more than a dozen feet to her left, a maple tree had a few low branches she could quickly scale and climb high to wait out the night. It was close enough that if he decided to attack, she would most likely be able to get to the tree, but could she climb fast enough before he reached her. Did she break into a run or slowly move towards the tree to shorten the distance and see if he made a move?

Carrie decided to slowly walk towards the maple. She revealed herself from behind the tree, her eyes locked onto his. As she moved slowly, he cocked his head, causing her to jump in fright. He mimicked her gesture. Carrie continued her deliberate walk. This time he copied her, step for step, the distance between them remaining constant. She stopped, he stopped. She moved a hand; he moved a hand. Her apprehension faded slightly. Turning to the left, she saw she was now within reach of the first branch. Carrie looked back at him. He was standing motionless, still staring at her.

Each of Carrie's steps were calculated and slow until she was at the base of the tree. She kept her eyes on him as she reached up, trying to find the low hanging branch.

From the underbrush she heard a growl, then something raced towards her. In the darkness she couldn't make out what was running at her, but whatever it was, it was closing in fast. Carrie panicked. It was a fox, its fur tangled and mangy, looking sickly. Was it rabid or infected? It didn't matter, she turned and jumped high, grabbing the low hanging branch and pulling herself up. As she kicked at the tree trunk, she heard the animal growl, then yelp with a sickening bone crushing snap, then nothing.

Hanging from the branch, Carrie turned to see the man holding the dead animal in his hand, he was close enough to touch her. The smell of death, rotting flesh and decay surrounded him. If her stomach had had something in it, she would have thrown it up.

Carrie let her grip loosen as she dropped to the ground, her feet landing flat. They were within a foot of each other, staring, unmoving. He stood rigid, arms at his sides, emotionless. He attempted a forced smile that he mimicked from the photograph.

Surprised at what she saw, Carrie was confused by what had just happened.

He let the dead fox drop, its head landing on Carrie's foot. She shook it off in disgust. The dead fox flopped over in a heap.

Carrie had never been this close to a live infected before. He looked almost human. He had been human at one point, so it made sense he would look human. Even in the pale light, she could see that his pupils were blown, huge. There was very little white left around the black of his eyes. She never really connected the reason why the infected were only awake at night. They couldn't tolerate bright light because of their dialated pupils. With a wide grin he simply stared at her, and she stared back at him.

Carrie examined him carefully, as best as she could, despite her fears. He wore a tan suit that she imagined at one point must have been a nice suit—but wearing the same clothing every day for years would make even the most expensive suit look like tattered rags. His tie was loose around his neck and hung at an odd angle towards his right shoulder. The ends of the tie were shredded and all of it was matted with blood and dirt. She thought he probably hadn't a clue what the tie was meant for. If he did attack, she would grab the tie and use it against him; she'd grab it, pull it around back, and drop him to the ground. His suit sleeves were both torn at the cuff; what was left of his shirt underneath was dirty and thread worn. His hands were rough, like those of a labourer, and his fingernails were long, cracked, jagged and dirty.

"Now what?" she asked him. "Do we stand here until daylight and just stare at each other?"

He tilted his head to one side. His smile disappeared as he

opened his mouth, but nothing came out. His teeth were black, his lips cracked and dry. *Do they communicate telepathically?* she thought to herself. To her best knowledge, no one had ever captured a live, infected before. No one wanted to try, let alone study one.

His head tilt reminded Carrie of a puppy trying to understand his master's commands, hearing them for the first time.

"Do you speak?" she asked softly, not wanting to panic him. Carrie laughed to herself; she was the one scared shitless. Again, no expression, just an exaggerated head tilt.

"Can I leave?" Her voice was muted, barely audible.

No reply.

Standing face to face with an infected, even though he didn't present an immediate threat, Carrie still needed to formulate an escape plan. She took one giant step to her left. He copied her move. She took another, he did the same. Inside she chuckled, the tit for tat moves reminded her of "Simon Says." She took one more step to the left. He followed suit. Again, they were facing each other in such close proximity that Carrie could smell his foul breath.

For several minutes, the two stared at each other, frozen. Carrie knew she had to decide soon. The infected usually travelled in multiples, or if they were alone, they were looking for a pack to join. Her equipment was still up in the tree. It would be hours before daylight. Should she risk making a run for it without her gear, or climb back up the tree? She knew she had no choice other than to retrieve her gear.

Looking around, Carrie plotted each step she would take until she was less than ten feet from her tree. She would take each step, stop, wait, then take another until she was close enough to her tree to bolt and climb as fast as she could.

She took a step; he did the same. They looked at each other.

Carrie took a step, so did he. This was repeated several more times until she was close to the tree base. She paused, then ran. Carrie jumped, grabbed the low hanging limb and kicked and pulled herself up the tree. Wrapping herself around the limb, she positioned herself, reached up and kept climbing until she felt safe. When Carrie was on the same limb as her gear, she stopped and looked down. He was at the base of the tree, looking up, his mouth wide open in a silent scream.

Feeding the rope though itself, she undid the knots, lengthened the cord, and secured herself to the tree, this time, making certain she wouldn't fall again. When Carrie looked down, he was seated at the base of the tree, looking out into the darkness. A strange sense of pity came over her. He hadn't even tried to attack her. Now, he sat with his back against the tree, unmoving.

Carrie felt a sense of relief. The panic faded and disappeared as she wondered what had just happened.

He sat at the base of the tree, turned and looked up to see the girl sleeping. He wondered if she was the same as the ones he'd seen in the cabin—and in the photograph in his pocket. His mind kept flashing images of the girl from the photograph. He kept seeing her doing things in different places. He wanted to take his wallet out again, but instead he placed his hand over his jacket and held it there. It was secure and it would stay there.

Looking around from where he sat, he could see the dead fox lying on the ground. He went over to it, picked it up and tossed it into far into the woods. For some reason, it bothered him in some way he couldn't explain, and he didn't want to see the dead animal any longer than he had to.

Standing in the darkness, he wandered around the woods looking for more food and water. He foraged for anything he could eat. Despite being hungry, he couldn't bring himself to feast on the fox. He fumbled around for mushrooms, bugs and flying insects, anything to satisfy his hunger. When he had eaten enough, he made his way through the woods. He could no longer see where the girl was up in the tree. Circling the area, he came upon the remains of the fox, then walked about until he found the tree and saw her sleeping high on a limb. It made him feel something. He smiled softly looking up at her, somehow content.

He sat down, back against the tree, and fell asleep.

Day 919

Morning came quickly.

The first thing Carrie did was look down to find the infected man laying across the ground at the tree base with his head covered in dead leaves and loose earth. He looked dead, she thought. But they were already dead, weren't they? At least, that's what everyone suspected.

Could she risk jumping down and possibly waking him? No one she knew had ever woken an infected. In the past, if she came upon a sleeping infected, she would shoot it in the head. Easy choice. Perhaps that's what she should do here. Carrie retrieved her handgun, checked it, reset the safety and placed it back in her bag.

Carefully, Carrie lowered her gear to the ground then slid down the tree. Hanging from the bottom branch she let herself go, landing softly on both feet. Only the sound of the earth crushing beneath her feet echoed in the forest. He didn't move. Slowly she pulled the gun from her bag, cocked the hammer and placed the barrel against the back of his head. Her finger began to squeeze the trigger. There was no movement from the infected, yet something inside her caused her to hesitate.

She thumbed the hammer back down and holstered the gun. Picking up her gear, Carrie headed down the path. Moments later, the rustling of leaves made her freeze. She dropped her bag, grabbed the gun and turned to find he was standing only a few paces behind her. His head was lowered, his chin resting on his chest against the morning light, his eyes barely open. If they could squint, he was squinting.

"Go. Leave me alone," Carrie yelled. It was daylight. The infected were not supposed to be out in the sun. At least she had never seen one out during the day. He remained motionless. He raised his head slowly and they stood staring at each other, Carrie still pointing the gun at him. "Go away." She took two running steps towards him then stopped suddenly, sliding in the dirt. She expected to scare him, but he didn't move.

She lowered the gun and stuffed it into her waistband. Carrie picked up a small stone and threw it at him. It missed him and hit the ground far past him. He didn't move. She found another stone, took aim and hit him in the leg. He didn't move. "Do they feel pain?" she wondered. There wasn't any expression or movement from him. Picking up her gear, she turned and started down the path again. She could hear footsteps behind her. She stopped and the steps behind her ceased as well. Soon, they were playing the same game as last night. Carrie smiled to herself. She took another step, he followed suit.

"You gonna eat me?" Carrie yelled half jokingly. No response. "No?" There was no response. "Stop acting like my ex-boyfriend. He didn't answer me either," Carrie laughed out loud. "You two have the same personality." He stood silent.

"Oh, come on. That was funny. I expect at least a chuckle out of you." She paused, still feeling leery. "Well, come on," she ordered him as if talking to a stray dog, "But, I'm telling you now, make one wrong move and I'll blow your brains out." Carrie continued down the path, and not once did the gap between the two of them close. He kept his distance; she kept her hand on the handle of the handgun.

An hour or so into her walk, Carrie heard running water over the birds chirping. She stopped and listened, trying to find where it was coming from. Glancing back, she saw that he had stopped as well. She smiled. The sun was over the canopy and shone directly on him. He covered his eyes with his arm, staring directly down.

The sound of the stream was faint, but it was close. She turned, listening carefully to gauge the direction. When she spun around, Carrie saw her new friend doing the same. He was standing in place, slowly spinning around, his head still down, eyes away from the sun. He had been mimicking her every move. She laughed loudly. "Hey."

The spinning stopped; his eyes barely open as he gazed towards Carrie. She stood in amazement as her new-found friend remained immobile before her. She dropped her pack to the ground, dug through the contents, and pulled out an old ball cap and tossed it to him. The cap floated in the air, hit him in the chest, then landed at his feet. He didn't move.

"You wear it on your head," she yelled. He didn't move. "Like this," demonstrating how to put on an invisible cap.

"Pick it up."

Nothing.

Carrie found a long branch, inched closer to him, then used it to retrieve the ball cap. She took a few steps back then pulled the cap over her own head. "Like this." She took the cap off, placed it on the end of the stick, and held it before him. It took awhile, but he eventually reached for the cap and did as he saw Carrie do. As he applied the cap, she noticed the entire back of both his hands—wrists, hands and fingers—were pink, the same pink as her own hands. The rest of his skin, face and neck, were still grey. She hadn't noticed the pink on his hands when she first saw him at night. His pink hands stood out in stark contrast to his grey face.

Once the cap was on, he dropped his arms to his sides and stood before her. He slowly raised his head, his face in shadow from the sunlight. He looked proud of his accomplishment. If it weren't for the grey face, stench and clothing, he could pass as human.

Carrie turned her attention away from him and made her way

toward the sound of the stream. Less than one hundred feet from the path she found it—shallow, with clear, cold water running in the tall weeds. She forgot about him, dropped her gear and stuck her face in the stream, wallowing mouthful after mouthful of water. Feeling full, she pulled her pack closer, rinsed all her bottles, and using a piece of cloth wiped the insides clean, then refilled them with fresh water. Not far downstream from her, her new friend knelt in the grass, cupped his hand and spooned water to drink.

Staring at him, she thought he would have lapped water from the stream like a wild dog. Instead, he looked refined as he casually dipped his hand into the stream. It was then she noticed the water had cleaned the dirt from his hand. In the light of the late morning sun, his hands were now pink without a trace of the grey, rough-textured skin the infected always had.

Carrie stood, started to move closer, then stopped herself. He didn't notice she was approaching and continued to drink water. When he finished, he sat in the grass and kept his head low, protecting his eyes from the sun. She called out to him several times. He continued to sit alone, paying no attention to his new friend. She studied him, wondering what happened to cause this change in behaviour. And appearance.

Leaving him alone on the edge of the stream, Carrie went on the hunt for food. As she walked away, she turned back several times to check on him. He didn't move.

Despite wearing the cap, the light still irritated his eyes and made his head hurt. He couldn't recall ever having pain like this. If he'd understood fear, he would have been afraid of the pain in his head. It felt like waves of tension moving inside his skull. He had no way to comprehend the sensation or translate what he was feeling into anything he could interpret.

With his eyes closed, he began to rock softly back and forth where he sat. The morning sun's warmth wrapped around him, making him feel sleepy. He couldn't recall ever feeling that warm. Laying down in the grass, it didn't take long before he fell asleep.

Within an hour, Carrie returned with her pockets and hands filled with white acorns. As she made her way back to the site, she found her companion sleeping, curled up in the fetal position. He had pulled grass and dirt over his head to shield him from the sunlight. The ballcap had fallen from his head into the grass.

She didn't even try to keep quiet as she dropped the acorns to the forest floor in a mound. Taking off her boots, socks and pants, Carrie stepped into the cold stream and carefully began lifting rocks and small logs under the water's surface. As the crayfish scurried away, she scooped them up and filled her socks with the tiny crustaceans. Using skills honed over the past three years, within a few minutes both socks were filled with more than a dozen of the little creatures.

She filled a small pot she pulled from her pack with stream water and built a fire. As the crayfish were boiling, she peeled the acorns and ate the soft, white centres. Some were bitter, other were just bland, but they provided the protein, fat and calories she needed. She missed the days when she could buy a jar of roasted nuts, sit in front of the TV and eat them handful after handful—with all their salty goodness—and sip a cold beer.

After eating her share of the food, she rinsed her socks in the stream, placed them on sticks, and hung them close to the fire to dry out. Carrie loved the feeling of going barefoot by the ocean and walking along the beach.

She placed a small mound of acorns hearts and a few cooked and peeled crayfish on a rock by the sleeping man. It wasn't until well after noon that he roused and forced himself to sit up. While he slept, she'd had time to rinse and dry her other clothing and refill her water bottles again. She thought about taking a short nap, but she didn't trust him and didn't want to be unprepared to defend herself. Yet.

"Morning. Did you sleep well?" Carrie didn't expect an answer. "I'm really not sure what you eat, but I saved some food." She pointed to the nuts and crayfish, and cupped her hand, pretending to eat invisible food held in her palm, bringing it up to her mouth.

With his new pink-skinned hands, he found the ball cap that had fallen from his head and placed it awkwardly, low over his brow, then reached for an acorn and ate it. One after another, he ate until the nuts were gone, then started on the crayfish meat. Carrie looked at the infected man, still apprehensive and scared of the man that had most probably saved her life. She couldn't kill him after what he had done, nor could she just abandon him. She watched as he continued to eat with those pink hands.

Carrie had seen her share of people get infected and go through the change. It was a slow and painful process. Once the infection made its way into the host, it slowly altered the person from the inside out. Often it took days, sometimes as long as a few weeks. It was always assumed that their metabolism changed and the infected would live longer than a human. No one knew exactly how long they could live but they never seem to age. It had only been three years, but no one had ever seen an infected dead of natural causes. The only way to kill them was to kill the brain or cut their heads off. Otherwise, they would continue to live with non-lethal injuries.

Carrie knew if he made any type of threatening move, she would shoot him without hesitation, no second thought. But seeing this man now, silently sitting on the stream's edge, she wondered if it was in him to attack her.

Sipping from her water bottle, Carrie watched him sit quietly after he finished eating. With his arms laying loosely on his lap, he sat in the grass and gazed forward. Was there anything human left inside him? What was he thinking, or was his mind empty? She began to wonder a lot about him. He looked no different than the homeless men she would often see in the cities before the event; quiet, down on their luck and pensive. Was it possible she was feeling sorry for this man?

Carrie sat, dangled her feet in the water, and watched him. She wanted to know him, know what had happened to him, who he was, and what was happening now. "Hey," she called out. He didn't move. She called out again, louder this time. Slowly he turned towards her, his eyes shielded from the sun by the cap. She could still see his eyes, and if there was a way for an infected to show sadness, he did. He stared at her for a few moments, then turned back. No threatening movements, no sign of hostility. He was calm.

Inching closer, Carrie knew deep down it was a bad idea, but something made her. She wiggled her way in the grass, splashing the water with her toes, deliberately making noise so he wouldn't be frightened. It took a few minutes, but eventually, she was only a few feet away. She refilled the water bottle from the stream. "Hey." She took a sip from the bottle, coaxing him to drink, then placed the bottle on the grass.

Slowly he picked it up and held it to his lips and drank, water spilling down his chin. He drank until the bottle was dry then placed it back on the grass. Carrie carefully took hold of the bottle, avoiding where he had touched it, and refilled the bottle in the stream. She set it back on the ground beside him, and again he picked it up and drank until the bottle was empty. This time he refilled it himself and placed it on the grass between the two of them, offering to share with

Carrie. She smiled at him and gently slid the bottle closer to him.

Emotionless, he took the bottle and held it, looking forward across the stream.

Carrie slid back away from him, stood, and walked towards the fire sporting a broad smile. "One small step for man," she whispered.

By mid-afternoon, Carrie wanted to get back on the road heading south. She collected a few more pounds of white acorns, stowing them in her pack. Her water bottles were filled with fresh cool water and she made sure his bottle was filled as well.

She'd started down the path before she realized that he was still sitting on the stream's edge. "Come on." She thought about slapping her thighs like you do when calling a puppy but decided against it. He stood and began walking towards her, leaving his water bottle on the ground.

Carrie walked closely past him, without paying attention, retrieved the water bottle and held it out to him. "This is yours. Keep it with you." They looked at each other, close enough to touch. He reached for the bottle, their hands almost touching. For the first time, she was able to compare skin tones side by side and noticed his hands were almost normal. She brushed past him, taking the lead, feeling the anxiety of what she had just done, knowing how stupid and reckless it was.

As they walked the path, he had moved in front of her, leaving Carrie to try to keep pace. Despite his ragged clothing and worn shoes, he made good time. He was walking quite a bit faster than she was used to walking. Sweat dripped freely from her brow. She could feel the moisture in her arm pits and down her back. It seemed the rumours were true, the infected had endurance and strength that surpassed humans; why and how, no one knew. Maybe they just didn't feel pain or know what it was like to be exhausted. Either way,

Carrie needed a rest. "Hey," he kept walking. "Hey, stop." Again, nothing. She screamed, "Stop."

He did as he was told, turned and waited for Carrie to catch up. She walked up beside him, doubled over, hands on her knees, trying to catch her breath, "I'm exhausted. Are you not even tired?" No response. Again, she caught herself standing close beside him. She shuffled to the left as gracefully as she could, hoping he wouldn't notice or even care. He repeated what she had just done, his worn-out leather dress shoes, kicking up dirt. He was now close beside her again. Still bent over, she saw their feet side by side. She took one giant step to the left. He did the same. Once more time, she thought. He followed suit. Carrie began to laugh softly, then it turned into a bull belly roar. Out loud, she asked him, "Just for shits and giggles, one more time?" She took another step; he did the same, then she began a soft jig, moving back and forth to imaginary music, her arms swaying side to side, her hips keeping rhythm with her movements. He began to shuffle his feet while the rest of his body, still rigid, moved robotically, but he made an attempt to mimic Carrie. "I have my own God damn infected," she exclaimed, laughing aloud.

Carrie stopped, facing him. She had finally caught her breath, "Do you speak at all?" There was a new level of trust. "Anything?" He returned her questions with a blank stare from beneath his cap. "OK, let's try something simple." She placed her hand to her chest, "I'm Carrie." She patted her chest, "Carrie."

Nothing.

Again, patting her chest, "Carrie."

He still had a blank look on his face. Without thinking, she patted his chest, then patted her own chest again. "Carrie," then placed her hand on his chest again.

Reaching inside his coat pocket, he pulled out his wallet and held it before her. Carrie was shocked. For a moment she was frozen, then she slowly took it from him. As she flipped it open, the first thing she saw was the photograph of the man and his daughter. Something came over her and she became to cry, then fell to her knees and openly sobbed.

Carrie finally regained her composure. He was standing over her, emotionless. She wiped the snot from her upper lip, the tears from her eyes. She stood to face him, looked at the photograph and the driver's licence in the window pocket beside it, folded the wallet and handed it back to John Dwight Munroe.

He reached for his only possession, holding the wallet as if it were priceless, then tucked it away in his jacket pocket. Carrie placed her hand on John's chest where he stored his wallet. Not only was she no longer afraid of John, but she also felt sorry for him.

He was human at one point, not much older than herself; a good-looking man with a young daughter.

Carrie had forgotten that the infected were once human. They were easy to kill because of what they had become, because everyone was afraid of becoming one themselves. A few days earlier, she would have killed John without remorse, without thinking twice about doing it, without knowing he was once a father. How many mothers, fathers, sons or daughters had she killed over the past few years?

Her hand moved from his chest to his shoulder, then slid down his arm. Carrie took hold of his hand and squeezed. A sign of affection she knew he wouldn't understand. As she was pulling her hand away, John did something that shocked her, he softly squeezed her hand back. She looked down, his pink fingers with their long, dirty cracked nails were wrapped around her hand. A feeling of warmth came over her. Carrie looked up at John, hoping he would suddenly be human or be able to respond like a man.

Instead, he looked at her, staring with blank black eyes. Yet she noticed there was a small amount of white in one eye around the large, blown pupil. It was small. Maybe it had been there before and she just hadn't seen it. If it was new, perhaps it was caused by the same thing that was turning his hands pink, and the reason John wasn't aggressive like the other infected.

"It's getting late, we have to make camp before nightfall." Carrie pulled her hand away and started to walk. John stood his ground, not following this time. She turned around. "Come on, it's gonna get dark soon. I need to find someplace safe for the night." She chuckled. "You know …" A coy smile. "From guys like you used to be." Carrie curled her index finger. "Come on."

Expressionless, John began to follow her. His pace was constant, keeping his distance a few feet behind her. Down the path, Carrie turned to watch John following her. The sun was low in the sky, already below the treeline. It wouldn't be long before dark and the other infected would begin to come out if there were any around. When they slept during the day, groups of infected would scatter, yet somehow, they knew how to reconnect when they awoke.

There was still enough light to hunt for a meal before bedding down. Carrie stood on the edge of the forest line, scanning the trees to find a nest. She found a maple tree, her favourite type, tossed her rope over the low branch and pulled her pack and gear up high. As she worked, John stood back, studying her every move. She watched him as she readied her perch. "You gonna stand there or do you want to help?"

John took a step towards her, then stopped in his tracks. Carrie looked at him, stunned, amazed that he might have understood what she was saying. "Can you help me?" They stood looking at each other. She desperately wanted to have John understand what she was saying. He didn't move from his spot. "Good try anyway, bud." She continued to hoist the gear up, secured the line to the tree trunk and told him she was going out to find dinner. Motionless, John stood his ground and watched as Carrie walked away.

It wasn't long before she returned with two rabbits. They were small and normally she would have eaten both herself, but this time she wanted to share. She dropped the dead rabbits on the ground when she noticed John wasn't where had she left him. It was getting late and calling him by name didn't get his attention. Instead, she ran back and forth across the path from treeline to treeline looking for him.

After several minutes of fruitless search, she stood in the centre of the opening staring further up the path. Carrie wanted to yell his name, but even calling out for someone who wasn't infected would only attract unwanted attention. Frustrated she placed her hands on her hips, guessing John's instincts had taken over and he had continued to move south. She was saddened her friend had decided to abandon her; but in retrospect, he was still infected and could pass along the disease if she wasn't careful. It was probably best, she thought. Still, she stood looking out into the forest for him.

It was going to be dusk soon. If she wanted to have cooked rabbit instead of raw, she would have to start a fire before the glow could signal her position.

Carrie skinned the dead animals, skewered them, and hung them over the fire pit. As she sipped from the water bottle, she kicked off her boots and socks and rinsed them with some of her drinking water, then placed the wet hosiery on one of the hot rocks surrounding the fire. Turning the spit, she felt sorry for the pair of rabbits she'd killed, but she needed to eat. Laying down on the grass, Carrie stretched out and closed her eyes wanting to drift off to sleep.

She whistled random songs and dug her toes into the grass, forgetting about John and life all together. For a few moments things were as they were supposed to be. The meat began to crackle and pop as the rabbits cooked over the fire. Over the sound of her whistling and the fire snapping Carrie heard footfalls behind her, getting closer. With reflexes honed by three years of survival she pulled the gun from her bag, rolled on the grass, pointed and took aim.

Unaware of what was happening, John kept walking towards her with a blank look and a steady gate.

"God damn it, John." Carrie stood and lowered her gun, "You realize you almost got yourself shot."

John kept walking towards her, unwavering, until they were face to face. He stood before her, opened his hands and dozens of acorns fell to the ground at her feet. Carrie looked down; the light brown nuts were scattered around in the grass. She thought about picking them up, then stopped. Unsure if they were contaminated or not, she left them.

Carrie realized she'd already had skin-to-skin contact with John and didn't want to risk eating nuts that he might have somehow contaminated. She scooped up the nuts and held them out; John opened his hand and graciously accepted them.

By now, the rabbits were almost fully cooked. They were edible for John at this point, but Carrie would have to wait until hers was cooked more before eating it. The meat would be dry and bland without any spices, but full of protein.

Carrie pulled one of the skewers from over the fire and handed it to John. She was certain he had eaten raw meat in the past, and most certainly something worse than her cooking. He looked at it, sat down, and began to break the acorn shells and eat the nuts. One by one he shelled and ate them, ignoring the rabbit meat.

Carrie was shocked by what she saw. In the past three years since the global extinction event, Carrie had never seen the infected eat anything other than flesh. Watching John choose nuts over meat confused her. The man in the tattered suit sat in the grass peeling nuts with his long, jagged fingernails. As he brought the nuts to his mouth, the pink skin of his hands stood in contrast to the grey skin still on his face, his eyes shadowed by the brim of the hat. He uncapped his water bottle, drank until it was empty, then tossed it to the grass.

For the first time, she took a long look at the soles of John's dress shoes. The leather was worn and separating from the uppers. It wouldn't be long before he would be walking barefoot.

Carrie replaced the first rabbit over the fire and waited a few minutes before pulling the second skewer that was still cooking over the pit. She held the rabbit like a popsicle, biting into the meat, ripping chunks of flesh from the bones. The rabbit was small and she was secretly happy John had rejected her offer. She took bite after bite from the carcass, eating almost every morsel of meat on the bones. John paid no attention to Carrie as he continued to eat his acorns. They sat in silence, only feet apart. Carrie was still amazed that she had befriended an infected. She sat looking around their surroundings, watching for any signs of strangers walking past. She still wasn't used to having John as a travelling companion. He sat silent, unmoving, staring straight ahead.

"John," she called out to him as she pulled the second skewer from the fire and bit into the crispy flesh.

No response.

"John." Carrie tapped the side of his pant leg.

Machine like, he turned towards her, expressionless.

She pointed to the sky, "It's gonna be dark soon. I need to find shelter. You wanna help me?" Carrie finished the last bit from the second rabbit, stood and began to kick dirt over the fire. As she continued to douse the flames, John stood and copied her kicking movements. He didn't throw much dirt on the fire, but it was fun to watch him make the attempt. Carrie chuckled and kicked harder. John followed suit. Carrie broke out into a full belly laugh and started to kick dirt with both feet as John tried his best to copy her. The fire was long put out, but the two continued to play in the dirt. John kept up as best as he could. When they stopped, Carrie was out of breath, bent over, hands on her knees. John simply stood and watched as she fought to catch her breath.

Finally, Carrie gathered her gear and slapped John on the back. "Come on. Let's go find a place to crash for the night." She made her way to the trees, turned and saw him follow.

As she made her way among the trees, John stopped and watched.

Carrie found her perch, retrieved a blanket, then secured her gear with rope and hauled everything up the tree. Before climbing, she went back to John and tugged at his sleeve. He followed her to the base of the tree. "Sit," Carrie ordered, the same way you tell your dog to sit for a treat. John didn't move. Carrie put her back up against the tree, lowering herself to the ground, showing John what she expected of him. "Sit."

Carrie stood and again asked John to sit. This time he did as instructed. She wrapped the blanket around his shoulders. "Sleep tight my friend. I'll see you in the morning."

Before climbing the tree for the night, Carrie walked a dozen feet into the woods, pulled down her pants and squatted to pee. When she was finished, as she turned to make her way back to her tree, she bumped into John, who had been watching her. She let out a yelp that spooked him as well. He made a slight facial expression of surprise. It was the first time Carrie had seen John express any type of emotion other than the blank dead stare he always wore.

"Christ John! What the hell are you doing?" He remained silent. "You don't do that, okay? It's not nice." Once again, Carrie was short of breath and a little embarrassed. "Did you see anything?" She chuckled. "I'm not sure you'd would know what you were looking at anyway." She walked back over to the base of the tree, picked up the blanket, flicked it in the air to get the dirt off, not that John would have noticed, ordered him to sit, and wrapped him in it. "Night. And no more peeking."

Moments later, Carrie was secured to the branch twenty feet above John. Looking down, she could see him sitting, his ball cap moving side to side. He seemed unsure what to do. Until recently, he would have been awake at night, sleeping in the day. She hoped he would get some rest, then thought, *maybe they don't sleep*. She began to think how it all started, remembering where she was, how she felt the first time she saw an infected; and worst of all, the first time she had to kill one to survive.

These were memories and thoughts Carrie wished she'd never had to experience or imagine.

She pulled the collar of her jacket up high, shrugged her shoulders and hugged herself for warmth. The nights were getting cooler quickly and it wouldn't be long before the snow came. The last few winters had been difficult, and she had barely survived—only with the help of her friends. They were all dead now, and Carrie was alone. Alone except for the infected man sitting beneath her tree.

Carrie looked down. John still had the blanket wrapped around his shoulders, his head still moving side to side. She smiled, feeling comfort in having her own sentry standing guard.

With heavy eyes, and a chill in her bones, Carrie felt herself dozing off.

John sat at the base of the tree, legs straight out in front, tugging at the blanket around his shoulders. The garment was new. He'd never had to worry about extra clothing, he never felt cold or warmth; he was just what he was. As he looked out into the quickly darkening forest, John had difficulty seeing as he used to. This was also something new for him. Seeing in the dark had never been a problem, but over the course of the past few days, as he was able to tolerate more daylight, his vision at night was being compromised.

As he sat there, he had an unusual feeling—perhaps contentment, or rather, satisfaction that he had eaten. Oddly, he'd enjoyed his choice of acorns and insects. John touched his stomach; he felt the area where he had first felt pain. He recalled having the wound, but not how he got it. He ran his hand over his shirt where the wound should have been, but now felt nothing more than a tender area. It had begun to heal, and the pain was gone.

A noise from the darkness broke his thought. John turned towards the sound. Nothing. It was gone. Then he heard another; a twig snapped, then leaves rustling underfoot. The noises became more frequent, louder. John stood, and the blanket over his shoulders fell to the ground.

Three infected, two females and a male, emerged from the darkness, walking towards the area where Carrie slept. Their walk was slow and robot like, just a quick, steady pace without interruption. The lead female had her nose in the air, sniffing. She was a large woman, a formidable opponent. She turned and headed directly for the tree where Carrie was perched. Stopping at the base, she paid no attention to the blanket that lay in the dirt. Instead, she looked up and inhaled deeply. Another infected woman, slight in stature, moved to the back of the tree, and the male took guard beside the large woman. Their eyes, pupils blown, could take in more light in the darkness than any human, and they saw a girl in the tree, secured to the limb, sleeping. It could have been two hours or two minutes, the three infected remained perfectly still, looking up.

For the past few days, John had unknowingly been watching Carrie walk. She picked up her feet instead of dragging them, walking silently along the path. John copied the way she walked, approaching the three infected from behind. With the skill of a professional baseball player, he raised the heavy broken tree branch he'd found not far from where he'd been sitting and swung it hard against the back of the male. There was the sound of spinal vertebrae shattering as the branch made contact. The infected didn't speak or make noise. He opened his mouth, possibly in pain, as he fell to the ground, paralyzed from the fracture site down.

John pulled the branch back as the smaller female turned to face him. He swung upwards catching her under the chin. Teeth broke loose as her head snapped back and she fell to the ground.

The large female turned and lunged at John. He side-stepped her, kicking the water bottle Carrie had given him into the underbrush. He surprised himself by how quickly he was able to move, avoiding her attack. She missed him, tripped over the male with the broken back, and fell forward to the ground. John turned, raised the branch high over his head, and brought it down with as much force as he could gather. The back of her skull split open with a sickening crack and blood splattered in all directions.

The male, still having use of his arms, grabbed John's ankle and pulled. John turned and kicked the man in the face with his free foot, but the infected held firm. He attempted to grab John's other ankle, but John kept that leg back and out of reach. He could see the man's mouth open, wanting to scream or yell, but nothing came. John kicked him in the head a second time. The man refused to the let go of John's leg. John pulled hard against the grip on his leg, but determined, the infected tightened his hold. John raised the branch and brought it down hard. He felt the hold on his ankle let loose. He raised the branch a second time, then a third, and fourth, until the infected's skull was shattered and his brain leaked onto the forest floor. John looked down, emotionless, still unsure what he was doing.

The female with the broken jaw tried to regain her senses and fight back, but the head injury was too severe. She stumbled, getting to her feet, then fell back again. Her jaw was fractured in several places and hung at an awkward angle. She got to one knee; blood flowed freely from her mouth. She tried to stand, stumbled, falling back to the forest floor. John casually walked over and grabbed her wrist as she tried to fight and dragged her off deeper into the woods. He returned a few moments later, alone.

DAY 920

Carrie squinted as the sun broke over the trees and shone directly upon her. Her legs had cramped up overnight; she rubbed her thighs and calves until the feeling returned in her toes. Once she was fully awake she looked down to where she had left John the night before. She felt a sense of relief seeing him sitting at the base of the tree, the blanket hung over his shoulders, his head moving as he looked about.

"John," she called out to him. He stood, looked up and stepped away from the base of the tree.

Carrie loosened her bindings, lowered her gear to the ground and climbed down. Her legs were still tingling so she bent over, massaging her calves and thighs. She noticed a large dark spot in the earth and wondered what it could be, then dismissed it.

"So, how was your night?" Carrie coiled up the rope and stuffed it in her pack. "I slept great. Well, as good as can be expected when you're tied to a tree." John stood before her. The soiled patches on his suit disguised the droplets of blood from the previous night's assault.

"Hey bud, where's your ball cap and your water bottle?" Carrie spun around in place, looking for the cap; instead she noticed the ground had been disturbed. "Rough night?" No answer.

"I'm sorry you lost your cap. I'll try to find you a new one, OK?" She cast John a sad look then tasted her morning breath. She looked for her water bottle in her backpack, pushing items aside, still unable to locate it. Then she recalled taking a sip of water in the middle of the night and sticking the bottle between two small branches. Carrie looked up and saw her favourite bottle secured up high in the tree.

"Excuse me. I'll be right back."

Carrie jumped, grabbed hold of the first branch, then pulled herself up and started the climb. When she reached her sleeping perch, she took hold of the bottle and stopped. As the sun came higher over the trees, Carrie noticed something odd. Something large and black was up high among the trees. She waited a few minutes for the sun to rise a little higher.

Excited, Carrie jumped from limb to limb, making her way down. She jumped down, gathered up her gear, then tugged at John's sleeve, "Come on. Let's go."

She made her way through the thick underbrush, away from the winding path, pushing branches aside, forgetting that John was behind her. It was only a short distance away, but it took longer pushing through the dense forest. Then Carrie stopped, dropped her gear, and stared at the log cabin partially obscured by trees. If she hadn't seen the large, black plastic rain barrel on the roof she could have easily missed it, the path winding away from the cabin. The sides and front of the structure were almost completely engulfed in overgrown trees. They snaked their way up the walls, covering the only front-facing window. The metal roof was buried under years of dead leaves and new growth vines. It was nature's way of reclaiming the cabin.

"Anybody home," Carrie yelled out. John finally caught up and stood beside her. She cast him a glance, "What do you think?"

"Hey." She yelled even louder.

She knew if there was somebody home they might be sleeping, and if she walked up without notice, the owner could open fire and shoot them both. Having an infected standing with her didn't help.

"Hey, anybody home." Carrie yelled as loud as she could. They both stood outside the cottage, waiting for a reply. Several minutes passed without an answer. She found a large stone, took aim and threw it at the front door. The stone hit hard, echoing a loud thud in the forest. Again, they waited, but finally Carrie turned to John and shrugged her shoulders. "I was aiming for the window," she said, and winked.

Secretly, she wished John could understand what she was talking about.

Carrie took his sleeve and pulled him into the woods and placed his back up against a tree, holding him tightly. "Can you do me a favour and stay here please? If there's anyone in there, well, that's human, you will scare the shit outta them and get me shot. And you too."

John remained expressionless, looking at Carrie. She forcibly exhaled in frustration, knowing speaking to him was like talking to a puppy. They looked at you, watched you speak, but understood nothing.

She took a few steps and turned, expecting to see John following her. To her surprise, he hadn't moved from the tree. Carrie extended her arm, hand straight up. "Stay," she said, and chuckled to herself. It was a command meant for a dog, but it worked with John.

Making her way to the cabin, she made no attempt to remain quiet as she approached the front door. "Anybody home," she yelled out several times. Scanning the area surrounding the cabin, Carrie looked carefully at the trees—at the base of the trunk and up high—for anyone who might be hiding, waiting to open fire. Standing near the front door, she paused and listened. Other than the sounds of the forest there was nothing, just eerie silence.

Taking in a deep breath, Carrie approached to the door then turned towards John, checking on him. He remained still, exactly where he had been when she commanded him to stay. She rapped on the door, "Hello" she said in a soft voice. She strained to hear any noise coming from the inside. Silence. This time she knocked harder, still no response. *Damn* she thought to herself. *This time I'll knock hard enough to raise the dead. Bad choice of words.*

She shrugged, and wailed on the door, "Hey come on. Anybody there?"

Carrie took a few steps back, waiting for someone to finally come and open the door. After several minutes she decided the cabin was either deserted or the occupants were away. She grabbed the doorknob and twisted. Locked. She went to a window she spotted to the right of the door, tore through the brush that grew up and around the sill, then cleaned the accumulated dirt. She cupped her hands around her eyes and peered through the thick glass into the dark cabin. From what she could see between the partially closed curtains, the interior was clean, nothing out of place to indicate a struggle. The glass felt funny, and the view was blurry. When Carrie pulled back, she tapped the glass and it echoed back with a dull thud. The glass wasn't glass but thick plexiglass.

Walking away from the front of the cabin, Carrie turned to John. "No one's home," she told him. "Come on. Wanna help?" and waved him over. He seemed to understand and began making his way closer to the cabin. Around the east wall, another window was overgrown with brush. She pulled at the vines and branches, snapping and tearing them away from the plexiglass window.

Inside, Carrie saw more of the same; the cabin appeared clean, as if someone spruced up before leaving for the season and never returned. In this case, it could have been the literal truth. The two of them walked to the back and found another door. It, too, was partially covered with vegetation. Carrie cleared the area of moss, vines, and branches while John stood and watched. Beside the door was a small box which held some pre-cut wood for a fireplace or pit.

The wood was weathered and old. Carrie pulled at it and the bark peeled away easy. *Old*, she thought.

She grabbed the doorknob; it refused to turn. Carrie wasn't surprised. She looked around, wondering where the key could be. No one would hide it under a rock, been done too often. There were two trees with a clothesline hung between them and one had a clothes pin bag. Making a bee line for the bag, she flipped it over watching the contents spill to the ground. The wooden clothes pins had begun to fade and crack from being left out in the elements for years, and among them was a tarnished door key. Carrie picked it up, blew off the dirt, then rubbed the key against her pants.

She looked up at John. "Let's hope this works," she said, and ran to the back door, inserted the key. The knob turned easily. Carrie pulled the key from the lock, kissed it and pocketed it. She pushed the wooden door in slowly, the hinges creaking from lack of use; then it stopped. She gave a gentle shove to see if it would open any further, but it remained where it had stopped. Carrie peaked in and saw that the door had come to rest against a small closet.

"Helloooo," she howled, before stepping in.

A dank, musty smell greeted Carrie and she sneezed several times. The breeze from the open door forced the latent dust into the air and filled the inside of the cabin with floating particles that assaulted her nose. She wiped it with the back of her hand, sneezed once again, then apologized to John. Secretly, she would have loved to hear "Bless you," from him. Carrie turned to see that John was still just outside the door, motionless. She reached back, took hold of his sleeve, and pulled him in. "Come on."

Carrie began to scan the interior of the small cabin while John stood beside her, unimpressed, unemotional and expressionless.

She was enthralled to be standing in a relatively tidy cabin.

Despite the dust, the space appeared to have been cleaned before the owners left and never returned. Perhaps they became infected themselves or were some of the lucky ones and died instead of turning. Carrie slowly walked around the inside of the small space, running her finger along the edge of the dining room table. The dust was thick, several year's worth Carrie surmised. She went to each window and pulled the curtains aside to let in some light, then unlocked the front door and opened it wide for fresh air. The breeze blew through to the back door and brought up more dust. The air was now thick with particles, but the stale air was quickly replaced.

The structure was much smaller than the one she'd found her aunt and children murdered in. Carrie wondered how long it had been since she had set fire to that cabin. She didn't count the days anymore. It felt like weeks but had been less than one.

This residence was only a single room, with a sleeping loft above the main area. The kitchen had a small counter, with a wood stove at one end, tucked into the corner; and an old-fashioned hand pump stood at the opposite end emptying into the huge sink. She thought it was a great idea to have the water source in the house instead of out in the yard. Carrie took hold of the handle and began to pump up and down. Stiff at first, it loosened up a little then spurted and coughed before water dripped out then began to flow. It smelled of rust as it left the spout, swirled around the drain, and disappeared with a hollow sound beneath the counter. She continued to pump for several minutes, giving her arm a good workout, until the water ran clear. Carrie placed her hand under the chilly water, as it flowed between her fingers. She continued to pump the handle a few more times, cupped her hand and carefully took a sip.

Carrie turned to John. "Fresh water." He looked back, expressionless. "Smile John, this is a good thing," she said, and slapped the side of his arm. He touched the area where she'd slapped him and rubbed it. She smiled. "Don't be such a pussy big guy. I barely hit you," she said, and stroked his arm.

Above and below the sink were hand-crafted rustic kitchen cabinets. Opening the first door, she gasped at what she saw. She quickly opened the next door, then the next. Each cabinet was lined with canned food, jars of preserves, dried pasta in glass containers, canned meat and bottled drinking water. The bottom of the cabinet was littered with mouse dropping, but the owners had been aware of the rodents' destructive capabilities and taken steps to preserve the food. It was all in metal or glass containers to keep the little buggers out. Carrie grabbed a jar of tomato sauce, turned it over and over, looking for an expiry date, then realized she wasn't even certain of the date anymore. It had been years since she'd had spaghetti with sauce. She began to salivate, grabbed the jar of pasta and placed it beside the sauce on the counter. Once she finished searching the cabin, lunch would come next.

Carrie made her way past the kitchen to the only door inside the tiny cabin. She opened it to reveal the luxury behind. Letting out a soft squeal, Carrie went directly to the small claw foot tub, squatted and gently ran her hand across the edge, feeling the cool porcelain on her palm. Along the back wall was a selection of bath salts, lotions, soaps and a razor. The single tap was connected to a copper pipe and disappeared through the wall. She stepped out and noticed the copper pipe tightly coiled around the wood stove vent pipe then ran up the wall, through the roof. She darted outside to see where the pipe went and found it connected to the fifty-five-gallon, black plastic drum secured to the roof. A lid covered the top. It was a homemade water heater where rainwater would filter through the series of screens on top, fill the barrel, and the sun would warm the barrel during the day. When you turned on the tap, gravity-fed water would run down the copper pipe wound around the wood stove vent, be heated even more, then empty into the tub. She assumed the water never really got hot but would be warm enough for a relaxing bath.

"I think I just wet myself," she said, laughing out loud. Carrie turned, slightly embarrassed by her own comments, to see John again, wearing a blank look. He didn't understand.

Back inside, she braced herself against the bathroom wall, her gaze never leaving the tub. Carrie contemplated the next few hours: lunch, bath, then shave her legs to make herself feel like a woman again. The cabin was rustic, barely a shed, but after years in the wild, it was a five-star hotel with all the amenities.

She returned to the main room and looked upstairs at the loft. A flimsy ladder led up to a sleeping area seven to eight feet above the kitchen. She took hold of the side, place her foot on the first rung, and bounced several times to test the strength. It was affixed to the bunk frame that held the bed in place. "Here goes," she said softly, shrugging her shoulders; then taking each rung with care, slowly moved up towards the bed. In the past, she had found animals and rodents making new homes in abandoned areas of houses and cabins, often in old mattresses. Reaching the top, she peeked across the neatly made bed. The covers were still smooth and unwrinkled. She doubted anything had slept there or made a home inside the mattress. Bracing herself on the ladder, Carrie swung her fist, landing hard several times on the covers. Years of dust sprang up, filling the loft, and she felt a huge sneeze coming on. She turned her head and let it loose.

Down below, John jumped back, startled by the noise. Looking down from her perch, Carrie noticed his reaction and laughed. "Well mister. Turns out you are human." He looked up towards Carrie.

She wanted nothing more than for her new friend to talk to her. She light-heartedly yelled at him, "Work with me John."

"Humpf."

Carrie almost fell from the ladder, "Did you just say something?" She scrambled down and stood before the man and took hold of both his sleeves. "John, say something."

He let out a barely audible moan.

Carrie hopped up and down, stomping her feet and tugging on his sleeves. She thought about how she'd managed to make him respond, then realized something. She stood before him and looked him the eyes, "John."

"Humpf."

"Oh my God. You know your fuckin' name." Tempting fate, she said his name again. He responded in the same manner.

"You know your name." Carrie let loose her grip, testing him, she turned her back and said his name, "John."

Behind her, she heard him answer, "Humpf."

"This calls for a celebration. How does spaghetti sound?" she asked. He didn't reply. "John."

"Humpf."

Carrie jumped up and down, taking hold of his sleeve once again, excited that he had made another step toward humanity. "I think this calls for lunch. I'm starving and we have lots of food for a change."

She let loose her grip on John's sleeves then went to the wood pile out back. A stack of cut logs had been left under an overhang. She grabbed a few, along with some loose kindling on the ground, and returned to the kitchen. John was exactly how she had left him. Carrie shook her head and smiled. He was progressing slowly, but she wondered if the infection would completely disappear. Walking past him, she placed the dried twigs and logs in the small wood stove and lit the fire with a match. As she blew softly at the base of the fire, the flame grew, took hold of the twigs, and spread. Carrie closed the stove door, realizing how excited she was for two things she used to take for granted: a bath and a simple spaghetti dinner.

It would take some time before the fire got hot enough to boil water or heat bath water. Carrie went out to fetch more wood for the stove, stacking the logs in the corner. John remained in the same position.

"Come on. I have to climb up on the roof; you have to spot me." Carrie walked past John; he didn't move. She raised her voice, "John." He turned, following her outside.

Unable to find a ladder, she scanned around the roof, scampered up a tree and across a large limb, then paused, looking at the steep pitch before hopping to the roof. The metal sheets covered in years of dried leaves and pin needles made her footing tenuous. Carrie stood on the angled slope, took a single step and slid. She knelt, planted her foot for traction and held firm. "Shit," she thought. "That was close."

Slowly standing, she twisted her boot, moving the debris beneath it until the rubber soles found metal to grip against. Testing her position, she lifted the other foot and started the slow ascent to the barrel. Once she was close enough, she reached out, took hold of the edge of the plastic drum and pulled herself up. There was a metal screen that was almost completely covered with vegetation. Holding the rim tightly, Carrie swiped all the leaves and needles from the screen. Once cleaned, she ran her hand around the edge, found the two latches that held the screen in place, lifted it off and saw the barrel was almost full of clear water. The tight weave of the protective screen had kept most of the debris from falling inside. She replaced the lid, set the latches and made her was back to the tree branch.

Son of a bitch. I didn't think this through. Carrie knew there was no way she could jump the distance from the roof up to the branch. Without a solid footing, she would never clear the distance.

Leaning forward, she looked down to the ground below. It was less than a ten-foot fall. She could still break her ankle if she landed wrong. Lowering herself to the roof, she sat, lifted her feet and slid off the edge, falling to the earth. Her feet barely touched the ground, then she tucked and rolled before coming to a stop. When she opened her eyes, John was standing beside her with his hand held out to help her up. Not thinking, Carrie took hold, feeling the strength in his grip, and was pulled to a standing position. He let go and looked at her. She already knew she had natural immunity to the infection but was still apprehensive about touching him, "Thanks, John."

"Humpf."

She smiled again, slapped him on the shoulder. "Let's go see if we can make lunch."

Carrie found a pot, filled it with water and placed it over a circular plate on the wood stove. She kept adding wood to the fire, bringing the flames up until they were bright red and orange. While she waited for the water to boil, she went to the tub, opened the tap and let some of the stale water in the pipes drip out. The water had already begun to warm up. She turned off the tap before going back out to the kitchen.

In the cabinet, there were large mason jars of spaghetti, bowtie and egg noodle pasta. Over the course of the past few years, Carrie had eaten raw pasta she had found in her travels, but this was going to be a treat. She selected the egg noodles, and when the water was at full boil, placed two large handfuls in the pot.

She emptied half the jar of pasta sauce into a smaller pot. Without a fridge, the sauce would turn in a few days. Pasta would be on the menu tomorrow, she told John. He replied with his now infamous, "Humpf".

She set the tiny wooden table that obviously did duty as dining table, coffee table and other functions, for two. Carrie had wiped the table down and cleaned some cutlery and dinnerware, ready for fine dinning.

John remained where he was, statue-like, watching Carrie move between the sink, stove and table, preparing for the meal.

The boiling water filled the cabin with a moist scent of pasta while the heating sauce added the aroma of tomato to the mix. The kitchen felt warm and comfortable. All worries about the infected and life for the past few years disappeared like the wisps of steam rising from the pot of boiling water.

The pasta was drained, placed on each plate, then a large scoop of sauce nested on the top of coiled egg noodles. Each plate was carefully set on the table beside the cutlery and a bottle of water. Carrie took hold of John and walked him to a chair, forcing him to sit, then moved around to the other chair. Realizing she'd forgotten to remove the cap from his water bottle, she reached across the table and uncapped it.

Carrie sat back, sighed heavily and felt a little nervous. It was a first date of sorts. John sat at the table, unmoving, staring at her. She lifted her bottle of water. "Here's to our first real dinner. Cheers." She extended the bottle, waited for John to reciprocate. He left her hanging. Carrie smiled—"Klink"—pretending that wine glasses had just met across the table. She took a sip, placed the bottle down and picked up her fork. "I hope everything is to your liking," she said, and twirled a mouthful.

Casting a quizzical glance at John, she noticed the skin around his eyes and cheeks was almost entirely pink, and his pupils had receded even further, allowing more of the white to show. The smirk she made was purely self-indulgent. It was like a work in progress, she surmised. Her efforts were paying off.

The sauce lingered in her mouth. If there was a way to imagine taste buds coming alive after years of overcooked game meat, no spices and bland food, Carrie was experiencing just that. She couldn't recall if this brand of pasta was one of the best, but it sure tasted that way. The hint of garlic, spices and tomatoes, mixed with pasta, was heavenly. Carrie didn't chew the food, but let it rest in her mouth, the flavours flowing across her tongue and around her mouth in waves of enjoyment.

Eyes closed, she let out a gentle moan and finally began to chew, then swallowed. "Oh my God. That was so amazing." When Carrie opened her eyes, John was staring at her; he still hadn't eaten.

"Like this," she said, demonstrating with her own food. She placed her fork into the pasta and began to twirl, the pasta wrapping itself around the utensil and mixing with sauce.

Instead of a fork, John used his fingers, picking up a single egg noodle and lifting it from the plate. It continued to uncoil itself from the rest of his pasta, dripping sauce as it left the plate. He raised his hand high until the strand was completely detached from all the other noodles. He dangled it until the loose end landed in his mouth and he began to chew. The length of pasta slowly shortened as he ate. Once he finished, he picked up another strand and repeated.

"Good enough. That way works, too."

Carrie finished her plate, went back for seconds, then sat before John. He continued to eat one piece at a time. His hand and face were covered in red sauce. She looked at him, paused, felt a sickening feeling rubble in her stomach and felt immediately ill. The image was causing flashbacks of images she thought she had forgotten. The sauce reminded her of times when she'd come face to face with infected who had attacked friends; instead of pasta sauce, their faces covered in blood. The survivors knew the infected didn't single them out, they were simply a food source. They attacked animals with the same viciousness as they assaulted survivors. Now, Carrie was sitting across from John as she would have on a coffee date.

She grabbed the moistened cloth from the sink she used for cleaning and washed John's face and hand. He remained motionless, like a young child allowing itself to be washed. Dropping the cloth on the corner of the table, Carrie went back to her seat and looked at John. The images had been rinsed clean from her memories like the sauce from his face.

"Sorry. I couldn't look at you that way. It brought back too many bad times. I'm sorry if I hurt or scared you."

Her mood had changed; Carrie no longer wanted the second helping, but couldn't let the food go to waste. She swirled the fork in the thick egg noodle pasta, spinning over again and again. John continued to eat each piece slowly with his fingers.

Carrie's plate sat in front of her; some pasta and sauce remained, but she couldn't eat another bite. John's plate had finger swipe marks running through the pasta sauce. She stood, picking up both plates. John remained sitting at the table while she cleaned the kitchen and put everything away, placing the dishes in the sink, ready for the hot water. "Typical man," she said to herself with a chuckle.

Rummaging under the sink, she found several bottles of dish soap and other cleaners. Carrie picked up the dish soap and recalled the days when she and her mother used to wash dishes together and talk about school. Her father offered several times to buy a dishwasher, but her mother wanted nothing to do with it; this was their time, and a dishwasher would take that away. Carrie recalled how they would chat about school, get advice on boys and trade opinions on clothing. It felt like a perfect time to cry, but that was a waste of energy.

She placed a pot of water on the stove, stoked the fire and readied the dishes in the sink. John, forever the man, remained sitting at the table, looking forward, unmoving. When the water was warm, she added a small dollop of dish soap to the bottom of the sink, poured in the warm water and swirled her hands to make suds. The temperature of the water felt good on her skin; the soap has a smooth texture. It was that bubble bath she wanted, but for her hands. There weren't many dishes. Soon they were cleaned and stacked neatly on the counter beside the sink. Carrie would let them air dry.

The entire time she was doing the dishes, she kept thinking about that bath. Checking on the fire, she made certain it was glowing. She could feel the temperature in the small cabin increasing. Tiny beads of sweat had already formed on her forehead. John sat motionless, no signs the heat was bothering him. It was the cold they hated, not the heat. Before going to the bathroom, Carrie locked the exterior doors, and checked the entire cabin and wood stove. Only then did she feel secure enough to indulge in personal time.

As the fire grew hotter, Carrie cleaned parts of her new home, sweeping up mouse droppings, swiping away cobwebs and dust. Once she felt the accommodations were as least adequate, she went to the bathroom and turned the tap over the tub. The water initially came out cold, then warm. She slowed the flow, letting the water warm up as it ran through the copper coils and passed around the vent. She added a small amount of soap to the water, and again whipped the soap into a frenzy with her hands until large bubbles covered the surface.

She went to check on John, who was still sitting at the table. Carrie stood at his side as he turned to look at her, "I'll be busy for a bit. Don't move. Don't go outside. Don't touch anything." She laughed, leaning in; she almost kissed him on the forehead, but pulled back as she realized what she was doing.

The bathroom door only had a flimsy antique gate lock and hasp. The previous owners never considered security, she assumed. She set the lock, stripped, tossed her old dirty clothes in a heap beside the tub, and lowered herself into the warm water. She couldn't recall the last time she was in hot water, or for that matter, had a proper bath or shower that wasn't in a stream or a lake. She used the bubbles to wash herself, letting the silky soap strip away dirt and filth from her body. She dunked her head beneath the water, then washed her hair the best she could. She played with the suds, making shapes and mountains, feeling more relaxed than she had in months. Carrie laid her head back on the tub and closed her eyes. Maybe it was a few minutes or an hour, Carrie didn't know. When she opened her eyes, the door was slightly ajar, and she could see John standing outside, one eye visible through the open door.

"Jesus, John," she yelled, "Close the door and go sit down." He remained standing at the door, not moving, not blinking, one eye staring at her. Carrie felt violated, but understood; John didn't know what he was looking at or what he was doing. The bathroom was small; she reached for a towel, wrapped herself tightly, took hold of the door and slammed it hard. Feeling immediate regret, she opened it again; John was still standing there. "I'm sorry. You spooked the hell outta me John." He replied with a "Humpf."

Carrie chuckled, closed the door and made sure she set the lock properly. She quickly dried herself, patted her hair and smelled the stale aroma of the towel, then wrapped it around her body. "Laundry.

Housework. I could get used to this," she mumbled to herself as she walked out of the bathroom.

John stood as he always did, unmoving, expressionless, just outside. Carrie took him by the arm and guided him to the table, forcing him to sit. She tried to explain privacy, but all she got back was his typical blank look. Trying to explain privacy to John was like disciplining a puppy.

Leaving John at the table, Carrie found some clean jeans and a sweatshirt and some boy's underwear and socks. She felt like a million bucks wearing clean clothes that she considered almost new. There was enough clothing to get her through the next year. She was used to wearing the same things for months on end and pulling clothes from dead, uninfected bodies. It was something else she didn't think twice about. It's not like the dead needed clothing anymore.

Walking around the tiny cabin, Carrie pulled open drawers and looking into every box and container to inventory the entire contents of her new home. There were several puzzles, board games, a cribbage board and a deck of well-used playing cards. Pulling open another drawer, Carrie stopped as soon as she saw what was inside. With a trembling hand, she pulled a cell phone out and held it before her. It was too much to ask that it would still turn on. She closed her eyes and held the power button down for several seconds before releasing it. She opened her eyes to a blank scene.

Carrie flipped the phone over. The back didn't come off, it had a non-removable battery. Looking inside the drawer, she didn't see a charger, so she blindly dug her hand deep inside, then felt a cable and something flat. Grabbing hold, she pulled out a solar charger and power cable. Carrie began to jump up and down letting out several shrieks. Normally unaffected by noise, upon hearing Carrie,

John let out a dry growl of his own. Excited, Carrie grabbed John by the arm and squeezed. He simply looked up at her.

It wasn't much past noon, there was still plenty of daylight left. Carrie took the cell phone and solar charger outside and searched for the brightest and most secure place to lay the phone down. Back inside, John was where she'd left him. She was giddy, holding out hope the solar charger still worked and that the phone wasn't damaged.

* * * *

Two men who at any other time in history would never have been friends, through necessity, became the best of friends. Dunkin', the name given to him by his family because of his love for their coffee, was the taller of the two. He was once a lawyer in a Boston firm that handled divorce and family matters and he'd had to kill his wife and two daughters when they became infected. His natural immunity to the disease kept him alive. Dunkin' was glad his immunity wasn't passed down to his daughters. Having seen what happened to young, pretty girls, he convinced himself every day they were better off dead.

Every night, Dunkin' dreamt of when he discovered his wife had started to turn. He went to the bathroom and switched on the light. She complained it was too bright and demanded he turn it off. In the morning, when he woke up, she was laying in bed beside him, her head covered by blankets. When she refused to come out from under the covers, he pulled them back to discover her skin had already started to turn grey and her pupils were blown wide. Without hesitation, he knew what he had to do. Her body was still under the covers, so he climbed on top, pinning her to the bed. Placing his hands around her neck, he began to squeeze tighter and tighter and he cried until she was dead. He had expected she would fight, show emotion, but there was nothing; her large eyes were emotionless, failing to understand what was happening. But Dunkin' knew she was already gone before he placed his hands around her neck. He fell and lay beside her, wrapping his arm around her as he pulled her in tightly and cried.

Leaving the master bedroom, he went to the girls' room to tell them their mother had passed away during the night only to find them in a dark room, heads covered and quiet. It had been even more difficult having to kill both of them, but he never thought of that. Instead, he focused his anger on survival, and mistakenly hoped one day to find the person who had started the epidemic—to murder him or her the way he had his family. Within less than an hour of waking up that morning, the man affectionately known as Dunkin' by his wife and children, had killed his family and left the home he'd shared with them.

Dunkin' was ashamed of what he had done but knew they were better off. Countless times, he'd felt the barrel of his mother's five-round revolver in his mouth. He considered himself a coward for never having had the courage to pull the trigger. He kept the small snub-nosed revolver in a holster on his belt. It was a horrible weapon for anything other than close or confined fights. It had been a present from her father, engraved with his mother's birth date. The last box of ammunition for the revolver rattled around in his backpack. Before the epidemic, Dunkin' had always dressed in a suit, shaved daily and worked out at his home gym in the basement. Since that day he seldom spoke, his thick black hair was grey and thinning, and he sported a long beard.

The second man, Taylor, was a drug dealer from Baltimore.

Both his arms were covered in sleeve tattoos that, at one time, meant something in the gang he belonged to. Today they were useless markings that he kept covered up. He stood only a few inches shorter than Dunkin' and kept his hair cut short with the razor-sharp Bowie knife he kept strapped to his leg. He used it to shave daily; he had hated facial hair his entire life.

Taylor had been arrested more times than he had birthdays. When the infection hit Baltimore, he was in jail waiting for his trial to begin for a killing he was most certainly guilty of, and was sure he would never see daylight again. Inmates and guards throughout the institution became infected, changed before him, trying for days to attack him. The same jail cell that kept him confined prevented the infected from killing him. He survived on a small stash of candy bars, junk food and tap water, and was at death's door when Dunkin' discovered him.

Dunkin' rescued Taylor when he went to the jail looking for ammunition. They figured he had killed more than a hundred infected in the prison before coming upon Taylor. Dunkin' discovered dozens of dead infected inmates in their locked cells. That was when they understood that even the infected could die if they didn't eat or drink. No one was certain how long it would take to starve an infected, no one wanted to test the theory.

When it came to making decisions, Taylor took the lead and Dunkin' seldom objected. Taylor was the muscle and the brains, but had lost the will to live. The only thing that kept him going was his hatred for the infected and his desire to kill more.

It was several months later, as they travelled south, that they heard everyone was heading north to Canada, as far north as they could to keep away from the infected. They had once been part of a larger group that split in New York City. They had heard the other half of their group was wiped out in an ambush by survivors who needed to eat. Cannibalism, rape, and most other crimes didn't shock anymore; they were mainstream in the larger cities. Dunkin', Taylor and a few others made it out alive; but some of their group had been killed, some committed suicide, and others decided to head off on their own. It was Taylor who had kept them alive. Now, it was just the two of them.

Dunkin' stopped on the path, pulled the paper map of the Northeastern United States from his cargo pocket and unfolded it. It was held together with clear packing tape to prevent any more tearing or water damage. "I'm pretty sure we are on this side of Missisquoi Bay," he said, tapping the map with his index finger.

Taylor had stopped questioning Dunkin' long ago. His "pretty sure" was more accurate than most people's certainties. He nodded in agreement.

"I think we can go for maybe another few miles, then hunt a bit and make camp." Taylor wiped his brow with the back of his arm. "You know we'll have to find a place to hunker down for the winter before the snow starts. And we need to find a place and get more gear before that. Last count I had twelve rounds left for the rifle, two full clips for the Sig and we're running low on water. How far west is Missisquoi Bay?"

Looking around, Dunkin' tapped the map again. "We're west of Interstate 89, maybe a good ten, fifteen miles south of Quebec. Along here, this is Welcome Center Road. We should find customs buildings, and if they haven't been ransacked already, we might get lucky and find some clothing and gear. If not, we'll have to decide whether to go west along the banks and find some cottages and see if we get what we need. If things hold, most of the 'fected are still moving south, but they like the woods. If we go too far towards the

Bay, we may run into some of them. If we wait until we get to Canada, I'm not sure what we'll find. I heard the Canadians still have border patrols and kill anyone they think is infected. I haven't been there since I was a kid. You ever been?" Dunkin' cast an eye towards Taylor, who chuckled.

"You know damn well I never been outta Baltimore."

"Okay. You call it. West towards the woods or east and hit the Interstate and check out the abandoned cars. The walk will be easier. We'll be out in the open but make better time."

There was no hesitation, "West. Find some cabins, get some gear. We need to hunt to eat today, and we can get some water from the lake. Can't do that along I-89."

Dunkin' folded the map along the repaired lines and tucked it in the cargo pocket. There was no argument; it wasn't his way anymore. He pulled the hunting rifle from his shoulder and held it out front as they made their way west into the woods.

* * * *

Guarding the phone and solar charger, Carrie waited patiently to see if the charging light would illuminate. It had been more than an hour since she placed both the phone and charger in the bright afternoon sun. The tiny LED light finally blinked white; it was pale, barely visible, but Carrie saw it. She jumped and spun around. When she stopped, she noticed John was standing at the door watching her.

"It's charging. It's charging. Do you know what that means?" John didn't answer even though she really wanted him too. "I don't know if the cell towers are working or if the GPS satellites are still up there either, but we can check. Isn't that great?" Carrie's voice was excited, almost shrieking. No response. "John," she yelled.

"Humpf."

Carrie smiled back. "Humpf to you my friend," and went back to staring at the phone. "Once it's charged, I can check to see if it's locked. I hope they didn't feel the need to put a fingerprint or PIN lock on the phone. If that's the case, I'll never get in. I'd have to wipe it and we all know, there won't be any updates." She chuckled at herself knowing John wouldn't understand. He stared blankly at her, "Humpf."

"If the GPS satellites are working, we won't be randomly walking north. We can actually decide on a route and make it a hell of a lot faster. That's if we don't decide to stay here for the winter." Carrie paused, "What do you think?" She hoped that there would be more than a "humpf" of a response. John stared, failing to understand anything that was going on.

It took more than an hour of solar charging before the battery icon even began to register on the screen. Carrie had been staring at the phone waiting for signs of life and began to jump around when she finally saw the green light indicator.

Holding her breath, she pressed the power button and waited for the phone to spring to life. The black screen turned gray; a small circle appeared, then the screen went black again. Fortunately, it meant the phone was starting to charge. Carrie had no clue how long it would take to charge a dead battery on solar power only. However long it took, it was worth it to find out if the phone was unlocked so maybe she could get some of the features to work.

Carrie looked at the sky and realized it wouldn't be long before the sun would set along the treeline and she would have to wait another day before she could fully charge the phone. She carefully unplugged the cable from the base and brought both inside. The entire time, John stood by the cabin and watched her move about, completely unaware of what she was doing. Carrie passed him without a second thought as she went to the cabin through the back door. She had become comfortable having him around.

When the phone was securely placed back in the drawer for safekeeping, Carrie returned to the yard to find John exactly where she'd left him.

* * * *

Dunkin' and Taylor pushed their way deeper into the woods. They had both become quite adept at walking quietly through the brush. Dunkin' kept his rifle held out before him; a round always in the chamber. He scanned the area around him, careful of his next step.

As they made their way closer to Missisquoi Bay, Taylor spotted movement not far ahead of them. With military precision, he lowered himself to the forest floor and ordered Dunkin' to do the same. He pointed off to his right, Dunkin' understood and raised his rifle. Through the scope, twenty yards from their position, Dunkin' made out a large boar that didn't care about remaining quiet. The boar was big enough that it had few, if any, natural enemies. Its snout and tusks rooted through the earth for worms, snails, bugs and tubers. Dunkin' guessed it must weigh almost two hundred pounds. He aimed for the spine, lowered the rifle for a moment, then raised again; panning to the left, he pulled the trigger. The boar took off running into the thick brush.

"Missed?" Taylor whispered.

"Nope. Went for the smaller one."

Taylor squinted, eventually seeing a much smaller boar lying dead. "We could never eat all that meat. Most of it would have spoiled." Dunkin' said, emotionless as he stood and shouldered the rifle. "It probably would've taken more than one shot to take that big guy down. Waste of a good bullet."

He casually made his way to the animal, and with a hefty kick confirmed it was dead. One single shot through the head, behind the left eye, had killed the smaller boar instantly. Dunkin' was content it never felt anything. On the inside, killing still bothered him. He handed his rifle to Taylor, picked up the boar and slung it over his shoulder, guessing the weight was less than fifty pounds. "We should get about twenty pounds of meat outta him."

Before the sun had set, the two men had started a fire, placed the young animal on a spit and tossed the carcass, skin and some of the unused organs into the bay. They would have plenty of cooked meat for a few days. They had two cans of beer left over in their pack and it seemed like as good a time as any to enjoy them with their meal. While the meat cooked, the cans cooled in the water.

Dunkin' and Taylor sat quietly, staring into the fire as the flames licked the bottom of the small boar on the spit. Every few minutes, Taylor would turn the meat over, trying to even out the cooking. Gone were the days when he could order a burger or steak rare. Everything had to be cooked beyond well done.

With his hunting knife, he cut a long strip from the leg and handed it to his friend, who pulled it from the end of the blade, blew on it and bit off a chunk. He chewed, nodding his appreciation to Taylor. He stood, went to the bay's edge and pulled the cans of beer from the water. He cracked one, presented it to Taylor, then popped his own can open and sipped from it before sitting down.

"Stale beer and overcooked, bland meat," Dunkin' cracked a half smile. It was the most emotion he had expressed in weeks. Taylor reached over, tapped beer cans, "Here's to stale beer and overcooked meat and staying alive."

As he chewed another piece of boar meat, he quietly added, "And the best fucking table in the whole damn place."

Both men had their fill of food and beer. They pissed on the fire, dousing the embers, then wrapped the rest of the boar in a game bag to keep insects away and suspended it high in a tree. They each found their perch for the night and secured themselves tightly to a tree.

It had become a nightly ritual, before it got too dark, for Dunkin' to pull a worn photo from his breast pocket. The edges were frayed and white; cracks blurred parts of the image; yellowed packing tape on the back held the print together. It was the only picture he had of his family. He cursed technology and the men that created it. He wrongly blamed technology for the infected and for digital technology. All the birthday, anniversary and date night pictures he had were locked in digital format in his phone, which bounced around in the bottom of his pack. If, he promised himself, if he ever found a power source, he would charge his phone and find a working Wal-Mart, if they still existed somewhere, to print off all those damn pictures so he had more than a faded, cracked photo that he knew would eventually break into a dozen pieces. He never wanted to forget the faces of his children or his wife.

Taylor squirmed against the bindings, trying to make himself comfortable. He brushed his long blond bangs back as he turned his cap around and pulled the brim of his red "Make America Great Again" ballcap low to keep his hair out of his face. He swallowed hard, fighting back the tears the way he did every night, wishing he could have seen his mother one last time. He hoped against all hope that she didn't have to see what had happened, but he knew she was strong, and would have fought as long as she could against attackers or the infected. He smiled inside, picturing his mother with a shotgun, blowing away those bastards as they came for her. She was as strong, maybe stronger, than he was. He knew any thoughts he had of going back to look for her were nothing but fancy.

"Night John-Boy," Taylor called out.

"Night Jim-Bob," Dunkin' responded, barely audible.

Each man, tied high up in a tree, wished themselves dead; but knew that the next day, they would fight to stay alive.

* * * *

Carrie shook the dust from the sheets in the bunk before making the bed again. She made small talk with John about sleeping in a bed. Occasionally, he would reply with his trademarked "Hmmpf" and watch her work.

Finding an oversized T-shirt rolled up on the bed, she went to the bathroom, closed the door and prepared for her first night in the cabin. It had been longer than she could recall that she didn't have to tie herself to a tree and put on layers of clothing to keep warm. She striped down, hanging her new clean clothes on hooks in the tiny space and slipping on the T-shirt. Carrie loved the feeling of the flowing loose material, feeling almost naked.

Looking in the faded mirror, she pulled back her hair, turned one way, then the other, wondering how she could cut it. It had been more than three years since she'd had a professional haircut. She pulled her hair down, then back, and longed for the days when she enjoyed dressing up. Opening the bathroom cabinet mirror, she paused when she found items that made her weak; scissors, and a toothbrush and toothpaste. She filled a glass with water and could care less who had used the toothbrush last. She knew an infected would never use a toothbrush and replace it. She chuckled at herself.

Carrie vigorously brushed her teeth; she could swear the tartar was being ripped from the enamel. Several times she added more toothpaste and continued to brush. It was only when she spit and noticed the frothy toothpaste was blood tinged, that she stopped. She rinsed several times, curled her lips, then looked in the mirror running her tongue along the front of her teeth, feeling clean for the first time in months.

Carrie then picked up the scissors, grabbed a handful of hair, and watched clumps fall to the sink. She dared not look in the mirror until she was done. Cut hair continued to fall and she smiled, feeling almost childlike as more chunks of hair fell from her head. She led out a loud gasp when she noticed a few gray hairs mixed in with her locks. Finished, she looked in the mirror turning from side to side. Her new cut was lopsided, her ears exposed, but she felt lighter and free.

She stepped out to find John exactly where she had left him. She grabbed the bottom of her T-shirt, spun around a few times then shook her head, "Well, what do you think?"

John was expressionless, offering no opinion. "Men," she sighed. "Infected or not, you're all the same." Carrie took him by the hand and led him to the bathroom, forced him into the tub and made him lay down. Grabbing a spare towel, she covered his head, "Go to sleep dear John. I know you're becoming human again, but I can't take the chance. I'm gonna lock the door so I can sleep. I'll see you in the morning."

In the cabin, Carrie rummaged around until she found a small toolbox with a length of rope. She used it to secure the bathroom handle, preventing John from leaving in the middle of the night. Unsure of the cabin's security, she locked the doors and jammed a chair under each of the door handles before climbing into bed.

Pulling back the blanket, a whiff of stale air rose. Carrie ignored it, longing for a night in bed. She crawled under the blankets, fluffed up the pillow sliding her handgun beneath it, then laid her head down and began to cry.

* * * *

Two men and four women wound their way through the forest, instinctively heading south. A large woman led the way, the other five followed in line, stepping in the previous ones' footsteps. She had trained them well. They followed her lead and accepted her position without question.

In her previous life, Debbie had been a truck driver, never taking abuse or shit from anyone. A lifelong chain smoker with an eating disorder, her days had been numbered by her doctors; lung cancer had metastasised to her liver and brain, and she was a hundred pounds overweight. At the time she became infected, she had been driving along the Maine coast, still smoking, and knew she had less than a month to live. The cancer had started to eat her from the inside out. To compensate, Debbie began to eat more and more and vomited almost as much. Becoming infected had been her salvation.

Unknown to Debbie, the infection had killed the cancer cells in her lungs and liver. Mankind had found the cure for cancer—living a life as a dead person. She was still overweight; that would never change. Debbie continued to eat whatever she could, even as an infected.

She stopped short and the other five followed suit, maintaining their distance between each other. They stood still, unmoving, waiting for Debbie's signal. Time had no relevance to the infected, they could remain motionless for hours, never tire or feel pain. Debbie took a few steps forward, not making a sound, and pounced. The squeals from the raccoon wailed through the night. She held the animal down with her weight as she bit into its neck. Injured, the raccoon whirled around and sunk its fangs into her face. The animal pulled back and tore most of her nose off, Debbie felt nothing. Lifting her legs off the ground, her mass began to crush the animal. It attempted another attack and bit her hand, ripping the little finger from her right hand. Debbie felt no pain. In a matter of moments, she had crushed the animal with her weight.

Debbie stood, holding the dead animal by the back leg, ripped it from the rest of the body and began to eat it. Flaps of skin from her nose entered her mouth as she took a bite from the raccoon's leg, and she ate part of her own nose along with the fur and flesh of the animal. She tossed the carcass at the five, who fought for whatever morsel they could tear from the dead animal.

Waiting for the others to finish, Debbie wiped her mouth with the back of her hand. She didn't even notice her nose was missing.

Once the raccoon was nothing more than bones, Debbie began making her way along the riverbank. She stopped, walked into the water and submerged her head to drink. While the other five drank from the river, Debbie stood and scanned the area. Even without her missing nose, she could still smell. The scent of recently cooked meat hung in the air.

The others rose to see Debbie walking side to side in the water, trying to follow the scent of meat in the air. With her head high, she walked blindly through the current. The others followed without question or reservation. The current hit them hard, making it difficult to find a secure footing. Debbie fell beneath the water several times and got back up. Each time, she found her footing and made her way closer to the other bank. The others also lost their footing but managed to get back in line.

One of the smaller men in her group, standing in the middle of the current, fell beneath the waves. He wasn't aware he should panic or try to find the bottom of the stream or right himself, but the water pushed him further downstream to the deeper parts of the river. He had no sense of urgency as his head came above the water then rolled back under.

Debbie continued to follow the scent. None of the other four offered to assist the smaller infected or even looked his way as he tumbled in the water. He couldn't call out to them; they had lost the ability to speak.

It would be several days before the body of the small, infected man was discovered by a group of humans. In the past three years, no one had realized that they could drown.

Debbie finally made it to the opposite bank, the other four not far behind. The smell of meat was strong here. They searched for almost half an hour before finding the tree. She looked up and saw a bag dangling high up from a branch. The other four soon crowded around her, all five of them knowing what they wanted, smelling the cooked wild boar meat Taylor and Dunkin' had secured in a meat bag. The five moved around under the bag, necks straining to see the bag and mesmerized by the aroma.

One of the four infected inadvertently placed her foot in the fire pit as she looked up. Her foot shuffled a few times, kicking up embers from deep under the coals that started to warm the tattered pant leg of the unknowing infected. The bottom cuff of her pant leg dragging along the coals began to glow red, then a flame ignited and eventually took hold of her pants. She turned to look at what was happening and couldn't comprehend the seriousness of the situation. Eventually, the flames started to move up her pant leg. Only the dampness of her clothing stalled the flames before she was completely engulfed. She twirled, tripped over the rocks around the fire pit, and landed flat on her back. The glowing embers burst around her, eventually igniting her clothing. She began to flail around, still unable to scream.

The others just moved aside as they continued to look up at the meat bag, wondering if it would simply lower itself so they could feast upon the contents.

The bright flames of the female rolling around on her back woke Dunkin'. He was barely sleeping, he never slept well. He looked down to see one of the infected, completely engulfed, flailing but silent. Standing too close to the burning female, a male infected allowed the material of his pant leg to heat up and ignite into flames. The fire began to creep up his body until he too became a raging inferno. Debbie and the others ignored him, simply moving away to avoid catching fire themselves. They all looked up at the meat bag, wondering how they could retrieve it.

"Taylor," he whispered. "Taylor."

There was a moan from the other tree as Taylor woke from a deep sleep. Straining against the bindings, he turned, and before he could respond, the flames caught his attention. Looking down, he saw two bodies fully engulfed. A normal person would be screaming, rolling about. Instead, one of the infected was more concerned with trying to right itself after being on its back. The other was simply laying there, most likely now dead, as the flames continued to cook the body.

The light from the flames illuminated the remainder of the group who ignored her plight, focused on the bag of meat suspended above their heads.

Taylor never did look over at Dunkin; instead, he took out his side arm, cocked the hammer back, aimed, and one by one all the infected fell, including Debbie. One bullet for each, no wasted shells. The one on fire was still flailing well after the others were killed. He pointed a thumb at the carnage below, "Is that what you woke me up for?"

"Yeah. Damn fine shooting. All head shots."

"They didn't get to the meat, did they?"

Dunkin' shook his head side to side. "Think we should douse the fire before it attracts more of them."

"No way I'm climbing down there, and I doubt either of us have a bladder big enough to put out the one still rolling around on the ground. How long do you think that thing will continue burning? It's fucking disturbing to watch."

"If it bothers you, shoot it."

"I'm not wasting another bullet. Let the fucker burn. I'm going back to sleep."

Taylor pulled his tattered MAGA red cap low again, tugged at his jacket against the chill and pretended to fall asleep, as if the killings and the burning body didn't affect him. He glanced at Dunkin', who couldn't pull his eyes from the sight below. Taylor closed his eyes and hugged himself tighter. He heard a single shot.

From beneath his cap, Taylor smiled. "I'm not cleaning that mess in the morning," he said, hoping he would be able to get a few more hours of sleep before sunrise.

* * * *

Carrie jumped up in bed at the sound of the first shot in the distance, pulling the gun from beneath her pillow. She sat still in the darkness and heard more gunshots, then a few moments later, one more. They were faint, far off in the distance. Carrie waited until she heard only silence. With all mechanical equipment broken or unusable, loud noises were easy to identify.

Sliding out of bed, Carrie went to the bathroom door pressing her ear against it, there was nothing but silence. Best to let John sleep.

Carrie climbed back into bed, once more securing the handgun under her pillow. Her first night in a real bed in years was not proving as comforting as she had hoped. Her hand slid under the pillow, grasping the butt of the pistol; her finger rested beside the trigger guard. As her hand squeezed and relaxed around the gun, she heard the sound of rain beginning to strike the tin roof. The sound was familiar, a memory from her past. Carrie shrugged her shoulders and pulled up the blanket as the rain began to pour down and the drumming became a constant rhythm above her. Closing her eyes, she longed for her own bed and stuffed frog. She thought briefly about Mulder in his pond before sleep overtook her.

* * * *

Dunkin' and Taylor woke to the feeling of rain whipping against them as they lay strapped to the limbs. Getting rained upon wasn't something new, but adding the night chill made sleep almost impossible. They both pulled nylon covers from their packs and covered themselves, then pulled their hoods tight around their faces with the drawstrings.

Dunkin' tilted his head back, sticking out his tongue to catch fresh rain. Cool rainwater was always welcome. Every few moments he could swallow whatever amount he'd caught, which wasn't much, just enough to wet his mouth. He glanced over to Taylor who was curled up tight on the tree limb. Despite the man's shortcomings, Dunkin' had grown to appreciate having someone like Taylor with him. His attitude and skills were exactly what were needed to survive. Curling up tight against the rain, Dunkin' fell asleep.

DAY 921

Taylor woke as the sun broke through the trees. He noticed there were fewer leaves every day, and those remaining were developing brighter colours. The fall foliage didn't provide much cover against the previous night's rain. He stretched, felt a full bladder, then cupped his hands and blew into them. They were cold; he was cold, the night air becoming a little brisker. The outer layer nylon jacket and pants still had tiny beads of morning dew on them from the evening rain. It wouldn't be long before he and Dunkin' would have to find a place for the winter. He strained his neck, the vertebrae cracking one by one. It felt good to relieve the tension.

Looking across to the other tree, he saw that Dunkin's branch was vacant. Below, the bodies were no longer scattered around the fire pit. He knew his friend's conscience had got the better of him.

* * * *

An hour before the sun rose, Dunkin' couldn't sleep; he had barely slept all night. He loosened the bindings, lowered himself to the ground and packed his gear.

Standing a few feet from the bodies, he scanned the carnage that had lasted barely a minute the night before. He was surprised other infected hadn't found the bodies and eaten them overnight. That meant the area was clear for a mile or so. Their scent hadn't been detected by animals either.

As Dunkin' walked around the bodies, the hand of one of the dead infected still twitched, its fingers moving as if typing on a keyboard. Maybe it was a muscle memory from its previous life, typing out a memo, or a book never to be published—something, he hoped, that was good and honest, not something evil and perverse that it had done after becoming infected. Despite all that had happened, Dunkin' still wanted to believe that the infected remembered what they'd been before, and some repressed memory of their previous life would push it's way to the front and remind the host of the life that had been taken away.

"I'm a fool. A fuckin' idiot," he said under his breath.

Finding a large stick, he poked at the bodies until he arrived at the one with the twitching fingers. He poked it hard in the belly. It didn't react. Dunkin' walked closer, leaning over; the side of its head was missing. Taylor's bullet had entered the back and exited where the right eye should have been. Not wanting to get too close, he swung the stick softly, striking the infected across what was left of its head. It didn't move, but the fingers kept typing the memo.

Rope was a precious commodity, but Dunkin' could spare a small amount. Cutting a six-foot piece, he created a noose, fished it over the foot of the finger typer and dragged the body away to a clearing. He did this for all the bodies, even the burnt one. Out of sight, out of mind. Remembering his mother always told him, "Everyone deserves respect."

* * * *

"Everyone deserves respect. Remember that. Your daddy, your brother and even your sister. Me too. And you know who deserves respect the most?" Dunkin's mother stood over him as a little boy. His nose dripping with blood, tears still streaming across his cheeks.

Dunkin' shook his head, "Nope."

"The bad men. Not all people are mean or bad. Some are born

that way. The Lord just didn't have time for them. Some are bad because they don't know any better and some are mean because life dealt them a bad hand. But they still deserve respect. Do people not deserve respect because they have less than what the Lord gave to everybody else?" Dunkin' shook his head again.

"Everybody does, so don't be giving mouth to people just because you're bigger and stronger. There's always someone bigger and stronger than you. You just haven't met them yet. You understand?"

Dunkin' quietly agreed.

"Oh, one last thing. You know how you always manage to find lost and injured animals and you bring them home and we try to make them better? You sleep with them, feed them and treat them right. That's respect for those little animals. Sometimes they die and sometimes they live. The Lord makes the final decision, not you. But all of the Lord's creations deserve respect. You done right by those little animals. You keep that up. They can't protect themselves when they are young, so they need someone like you to help them when they're hurt and alone. Someday you will need help and, the Lord willing, you will find someone like yourself to be there for you. You're a good boy. Just don't pick fights anymore. You kiss your momma and go back out and say you're sorry to that boy that got the better of you."

Dunkin' wanted to protest that he didn't start the fight, but he knew better than to argue with his momma.

* * * *

Looking down at the pile of infected corpses, Dunkin' wondered if they were the Lord's creation and if they deserved respect. If they did, this was the best he could do under the circumstances.

He gathered dry twigs and leaves, placing the loose brush around the pile of infected corpses, then covered as much of the bodies as he could and lit the edge. The fire spread, quickly consuming them. Through the flames, Dunkin' saw the fingers were still typing the end to the unpublished story. He waited, standing motionless, until the fingers stopped moving.

* * * *

Carrie's eyes opened to a strange and unknown environment. There was a slight moment of panic before she recalled where she was. She stretched her arms above her head and pushed her palms against the wall above the pillow; her leg muscles tightened, toes flexed, and nothing cracked or ached. She curled up under the blanket thinking how nice it would be to wake every morning in a warm bed, without the fear of being attacked while she slept.

There was no way to tell what time it was. Between the overgrowth and the plexiglass, the window didn't allow much light into the cabin. Carrie looked across the room, and for the first time in a long time she had no idea how long she had slept or approximately what time it was. Jumping down from the bed, she landed on a wood floor, not dirt. Her back felt great, her legs didn't have any cramps. Carrie doubted she moved much through the night after waking to the sounds of gunfire.

Carrie slowly entered the darkened main area of the cabin, moving the obstacles blocking the bathroom door. She pulled on the handle, attempting to limit the creaking of the hinges. John had barely moved from the night before. Like a sleeping baby, he rolled his head, eyes hardly open, and moaned. This was the first time she had heard any noise from John other than Humpf.

John pushed himself up, stepped over the side of the tub to join Carrie. They stood inches apart and she felt no fear. Even in the darkness of the cabin she noticed something; she took John by the sleeve and led him outside, where she immediately saw that his face was now completely devoid of any grey. His skin was now an even shade of pink. Pinching his suit cuffs, she turned his hands over, looking at the pinkness of the skin on his palms and the backs of his hands. His fingers were an even shade of pink, the off-colour sections of grey had given way to flesh tone.

Holding onto both sleeves, Carrie tugged and pulled at John's jacket, elated that the virus might finally be in remission. She smiled at him and he stared back, still unable to comprehend what was happening. Until now, no one had dared to hope that the virus might only be temporary, but John was showing signs that he was becoming human again.

Without any forms of communications, global or even local, the receding signs and symptoms of the infected may have already happened in other parts of the world, but there was no way to pass the news from one country to another. Maybe John was the first. Carrie hoped that there were more infected who had already changed back in other parts of America and the world.

The sun had just topped the trees, which were losing more leaves every day. If time still mattered, she suspected it was before eight. Despite feeling the cool fall dirt on her bare feet, Carrie dragged John into the clearing, where the rising sun provided the best light. John did something she had never seen an infected do. The bright sunlight didn't affect him at all. He didn't squint, shield his eyes or divert from the morning light.

Excited, Carrie turned him directly facing the sun, out of the shade. Startled, she almost fell backwards, "Holy, fucking shit." The colour of his facial skin was normal, not a patch of grey remained. His pupils were normal sized, his facial appearance was totally normal.

Carrie removed the wallet from his suit jacket and handed it back to him. He accepted it, holding onto it tightly. She tugged at his tattered suit jacket and pulled it from his frame, loosened his tie, slipped it over his head then undid his dress shirt and pulled that off too. It was only then she realized that John had body odour. It was known the infected didn't have body odour, no smell whatever. The odour they emitted was from the rotting tissue and blood of their past meals that splattered on their clothing. This odour must be something new. She looked at this chest, running her hands over the skin, expecting to feel something, anything out of the ordinary. Instead, all she felt was skin as pink and as normal as hers. John watched as Carrie's hand ran over his chest, down his abdomen and stopped at the scar where the bullet had wounded him.

"What's this? You got shot, not that long ago. Look at this, no exit wound." Her fingers ran around the edge of the entrance wound. "When did you do this?" she asked him as she walked around and checked John's back. Not a single patch of grey anywhere. There was no indication of the infection remaining, just dirt on his skin, the bullet wound, and the goosebumps on his arms and chest.

Carrie took John's hand and guided him back to the cabin. Locking the door behind her, she led him to the tub and forced him to sit on the edge. She started a fire in the kitchen, and while waiting for the temperature to get hot enough to heat the water, Carrie went back to the bathroom and stood before him. "I'm not sure if I should do this, but I want you respectable and out of those clothes. Can I have the wallet?" She carefully took the wallet and placed it on the edge of the sink. "You can have that back after." John watched as his only possession was secured on the sink. His eyes never leaving the wallet.

Like a mother carefully removing the clothing from her young child, Carrie stripped John naked and guided him to sit in the tub. She doubted he was able to comprehend embarrassment or understand the concept. He didn't react to being naked in front of her.

She set the rubber stopper in place, reached for the tap and slowly started to let the water pour into the tub. When the cold water made contact with John's feet, he let out a child-like whimper. Carrie chuckled at another new sound coming from him. She ran her hand under the water and felt the cold water give way to tepid then warm as the water heated in the pipes wrapped around the fireplace exhaust vent pipe.

Carrie found a rag and a bar of soap, wet them both and slowly began to wash John's arms, rinse them and moved to his legs. John watched and followed Carrie's every move. The clean water went from clear to brown the more she scrubbed at the years of dirt from John's body. Not a single patch of grey remained.

John's hair was matted with years of mud and debris from sleeping with his head below ground and washing his hair proved to be more difficult than she thought, but the results were worth the effort. He looked, Carrie thought, human again. She chatted as she bathed him, small talk, and instead of a blank stare, he watched her without glancing away. Progress, she thought.

After years of fighting and killing infected, the general consensus was that the virus caused the body to go into some sort of hibernation. Their hair and beard stopped growing; it was assumed they never voided and never had a bowel movement, but they had a voracious appetite and needed to eat constantly. So little was known about the infected because none had ever been captured, and even if one had been, who would study them?

Carrie pulled the stopper, watched the dirty water swirl down the drain, and helped John stand to dry him off. He stood naked before her, unmoving, letting her do what needed to be done. Leaving him alone, Carrie went into the main room and dug through the closet until she found some clothing, she thought might fit him.

When she returned to the bathroom doorway, she stopped short, letting the clothes fall to the floor. John's wallet was on the floor, he was carefully holding the photograph, his eyes never straying form the image and for the first time, Carrie could see emotion in his eyes. For several minutes they stood before each other, silent, Carrie waiting for something more from him. Eventually, he retrieved his wallet, cautiously secured the photograph back inside, then placed the wallet back on the edge of the sink.

After a few moments of awkward silence, Carrie picked the clothes up from the floor and helped John dress. She brushed his wet hair back, then to the side, then back again. She preferred it that way. He stood there in oversized faded jeans and a large, bulky sweatshirt. She liked that John didn't have a beard yet, all the men had beards now since they couldn't shave. Her hands slid across his cheeks, feeling the smoothness of his skin against her fingers. Soon, she hoped, his facial hair would start to grow in, another sign of being human. The colour of her fingers and John's skin was almost the same shade of pink. In that moment, she was so happy she made a decision.

Taking his hand, she led John out of the bathroom. He walked casually behind her to the kitchen without his usual rigid gate, and she sat him at the table. Carrie prepared more pasta using the remaining sauce before it spoiled. It wasn't the eggs and bacon she longed for, but not having overdone game meat without spices was still a treat. John watched her attentively as she made breakfast. His eyes followed her around the room as she readied the meal.

Carrie placed the bowl before John, then took her seat. There was a moment of silence before he picked up his fork and shoveled a mouthful. Carrie didn't eat; she was too amazed at what she was witnessing. An infected had almost fully transitioned back to being human. His skin, now almost completely back to normal skin tones, his gait, no longer mechanical, was now smooth and fluid. She marveled at the sight before her.

Every so often, John would look up at Carrie with a pensive look, one of discovery. The transformation was almost complete. It appeared that he was learning how to be a man, behave like a person, and this might signal the end of the infection.

John looked up at Carrie from his meal, wondering why she was staring at him. He'd awakened that morning more aware of his surroundings, but the last few days his mind had still been a fog. All he could recall were fragments of events. Sitting across from him, he watched as Carrie simply smiled at him.

Carrie rested her chin in the palm of her hand, proud that she'd taken a moment to be compassionate. She felt like a mother watching her child grow and learn to be independent and was proud of every new thing he did.

It was the start to a good day.

Later that morning, the phone charger sat on a large stone in direct sunlight as it charged. Carrie felt anticipation growing and she wanted so much to press the power button. As she cut branches to further camouflage the cabin, she prayed silently to whatever God would listen that the phone didn't have a password. Each time she passed the phone, she looked at the tiny LED in the top right corner;

first it was a pale yellow, then the yellow became brighter, then the battery percentage appeared at ten percent. Carrie let out a soft squeal which drew John's attention. He looked up and rushed to her side.

Carrie stood dumbfounded at John's movement and mannerism, almost human. This time he had a look of concern on his face that shocked her. She smiled back, took his hand and squeezed. Nothing would have pleased her more than if he had squeezed back. Instead, his hand simply wrapped around hers.

"In time. Right?" she told John, then let his hand fall free.

He stood silently looking at Carrie, then he turned away. She could swear he was grinning. He went to the edge of the clearing and planted himself with his back to her, looking beyond the treeline. She watched him for a few moments, wondering if his mind was also reverting, if he was beginning to remember the days before he became infected, remember the family in the photographs, who he was.

John stood silently, staring into the forest. He shivered at the cool air biting through him, feeling an odd sensation, but the sounds coming from the woods were pleasant and made him feel at ease. This was new for him; he was at ease, comfortable. And the person he was with was becoming more familiar. John recognized her each time he saw her, and he could recall recent memories and events with this girl. They would all come together in a string that flowed from one day to the next, but didn't go back very far. No matter how hard he tried, his first memory was still in that cabin, feeling pain in his abdomen.

John reached down and rubbed the wound. It no longer hurt; the pain had left. His entire existence started at that very moment he awoke feeling the wound in his abdomen.

He turned to look at Carrie. She was busy cutting fresh branches, confused by her constant repetitive actions of stacking twigs and branches against the cabin. He watched her lay them along the sides as high as she could reach then go back to the woods and cut more. Each time she passed the big stone she looked, paused and looked at it, then went back to her chore to keep them safe.

When Carrie's back was turned, John casually walked into the woods.

Despite the cool temperatures, Carrie's brow was wet with perspiration. She paused at the phone, wiped her forehead with the back of her arm, and noticed the battery was now at twenty percent. Dropping the branches she was carrying, she sat beside the stone and held the phone, a trembling finger hovering over the power button. With her eyes closed, she pressed firmly, felt the vibration under her finger, then released the button. The triangle, circle and square began their programmed dance, swirling around, blending together and pulling apart again. The anticipation was too much, Carrie wanted the bootup to end and to know whether the device was unlocked. She closed her eyes, waited, then opened them slowly, nervous at what she might find.

The brightly lit screen made her jump. The phone didn't ask for a PIN or a fingerprint to gain entry. The background had a picture of a couple on their wedding day, standing on the beach, facing each other, a calm blue ocean in the background. "Destination wedding," she whispered. There were a few icons at the base of the screen: a phone, a mail app, texting app and camera. Swiping left, the next few pages were filled with icons from top to bottom. Carrie found the photo app and tapped it lightly. The photos began to populate one by one and filled the screen. The first were of the couple, whom Carrie assumed owned the cabin. Selfies and pics of them inside the cabin and on the grounds around the property. As she scrolled down, she saw pictures of what looked like their wedding, the airport, the honeymoon at a beach resort, and when they arrived home. As she continued to scroll down, the couple were living their lives, meeting friends, going out for dinners and drinks. A normal life before the event.

Carrie closed the photo app and flipped between the pages and stopped short at the music app. Her stomach turned. With a gentle tap, the list of songs began to show on screen. Before it finished retrieving the entire file, she hit Shuffle and placed the phone back down on the stone. The music started.

With her eyes closed, Carrie allowed the melody to envelop and overtake her senses. It had been almost three years since she'd heard a song of any type. The song, she didn't recognize it, nor did it matter, played softly through the phone's speaker, the sound thin and one-dimensional. It was the most beautiful song she had heard. The music had the power to make the reality of the day disappear like wisps of smoke into the air from a campfire. Lowering herself to the ground, still with her eyes closed, Carrie let the next song play, then the next and the next. Relaxed, she felt herself drifting off with songs playing one after another, softly filling the air around her. When she awoke, perhaps fifteen minutes later, the music still played. Looking up, she saw a few leaves from the trees overhead begin to float to the ground, cutting in and out of the rays of sunlight as it shone through the barren trees. If not for the circumstances of the past few years, it would have been a perfect day.

Carrie had work to do; laying about in the dirt wouldn't accomplish anything. She rolled to her side and abruptly stopped—surprised to see John laying on the ground next to her, his eyes closed as well, relaxed, perhaps mimicking her. As she gazed upon him, wondering if he understood the words or the melody of the songs, she realized it didn't make a difference. He was acting human, and that, that was all that mattered. Standing as quietly as she could, Carrie turned to pick up the pile of branches she'd been using to hide the cabin. To her astonishment, the pile was now three times as high.

If she'd thought it prudent, she would have kissed his forehead. Instead, she grabbed an armful of branches and made her way to the cabin, the soft sound of music, barely audible, played not far away.

* * * *

Dunkin' and Taylor gathered up the last of their things after breakfast of boar and wild berries. As Dunkin' ate, he wished for a cup of coffee, holding the warm cup in his hands, the smell of a fresh pot in the morning, but it had been months since he'd had his last cup of java. He had found some Keurig pods and emptied the grounds into an old tin can, boiled the water, let the it brew for a few minutes, then sipped the strong black coffee. After he finished, Dunkin' wrapped the wet grounds in a sock and it remained in his pack for a several days, providing an aroma he sorely missed. Instead, today was just cold stream water.

The entire boar carcass had been stripped and cooked, the hot meat wrapped in rags, and half put in each of their packs. The plan was to make ground for the border if possible. The days were getting shorter, the nights cooler. When winter arrived, they would be safe, safe from the infected who were unable to tolerate the temperature extremes and hunting in the snow.

Not much was said in the mornings, most things that needed to be said already had been, stories told twice, sometimes more. As they spoke, Dunkin' thought again about a hot coffee with his breakfast; Taylor wanted a beer. He adjusted his red Make American Great Again ball cap, pulling it down low, feeling the frayed material from the brim between his fingers. The next time he saw another cap from the Trump era, he would take it. The caps were extremely rare and difficult to come by.

Kicking dirt on the campfire extinguished the flames quickly, but for assurance both men peed on the fire to douse the embers before gathering up their gear and heading north. Their pace was slow, the ground had softened with freshly fallen leaves and rainfall from the previous cool night. They walked the northbound lane of I-89, making their way along the side of the highway.

Grass on the road's edge was overgrown and trees provided coverage that could easily hide an ambush from other survivors, but they discussed it and agreed that was unlikely. The road appeared barren, with brown weeds growing wildly between the cracks. A few abandoned cars remained, the doors, hoods and trunks propped open. They peered in as they passed. Weather had taken its toll on the interiors and most of the engine components were missing. Taylor twisted the gas cap off the first vehicle and inhaled. There wasn't any odour; all the fuel had been drained. The trunk was filled with water from the previous night's rain. With a scooped hand, he took a sip. It was fresh and clean; he took a second and third drink. Dunkin' held his rifle at the ready; it was always his nature to be suspicious.

Not far up ahead, Ethan Allan Highway crossed I-89. Taylor ran up the bank and onto the highway, scanning the area east and west, then north on the path they were heading. "Looks clears." Overhead, powerlines followed the highway and cut north and south to homes just off the roadway. "I think there might be some houses close by. What do you say we take a look see, never know what we might find?"

It was still early; they could afford to spend some time rummaging through houses looking for much needed supplies. He tightened his grip on the rifle and made his way up the hill. "Which way?"

Taylor pointed. "East."

Dunkin' pulled the tattered map from his bag, then pointed, "The road goes east then north and curls back up to I-89 right here." He tapped the paper "It looks like there might be quite a few homes. If they aren't ransacked, we can grab some new, warmer clothes, socks, maybe even some canned food and find some rounds. With what we've got, we won't last more than a few months even if we play our cards right."

Looking down, Taylor kicked the dirt, "I needed new boots about six months ago. This might be what we need for gear and food. What say we head over and see what we can find?" He paused for a moment, "You know what?"

Dunkin' didn't look over.

"I need to put some weight on."

"No shit," Dunkin' laughed, "You know what I want? I want a big fuckin' extra-large Dunkin' coffee with a donut—no, make that two. I don't mean those shitty plain donuts; you know those shitty ones that are just dough and nothing else? I mean those big mother donuts topped with lots of sweet icing, maybe some jelly inside or caramel or something sticky. Maybe have a third coffee; maybe have so many of those icing topped donuts with that creamy filling that I puke."

Taylor began to walk past Dunkin', without saying word, but let out a small chuckle. "You have the weirdest fantasies. Please tell me the girl that serves you is hot."

"I don't care about the girl. All I want is a hot, fresh coffee with a donut. Maybe a whole dozen; I doubt I could eat an entire dozen, but I'd certainly try. Could you image eating an entire dozen; talk about a sugar rush. Give you a wicked headache. What I wouldn't do for an open Dunkin' Donuts. I'd stand in line, happily, place my order and leave a tip. Then I'd go to the park, feed the pigeons, and eat all the donuts."

Taylor had fallen behind and was watching Dunkin' as he rambled on. "You are obsessed with coffee and donuts. I can't believe we have finally run out of shit to talk about. That's gotta be the fifth time this week you've told me that. Tell me about the server. Is she hot? You know, like some hot blonde, no redhead, maybe a little curvy. I'm tired on seeing skinny people. That's what I want to hear about, not donuts. Do you get a woody when you think about coffee and donuts? What about your mom's meatloaf, maybe some apple pie? I tried sugar pie once when I was kid when we visited Quebec. Sweet and creamy. Wow. Now that was good."

Dunkin' laughed then stopped in his tracks, "Fuck. Really? We need to find some more things to talk about." He laughed out loud. "But man, I'd still kill a hundred infected for a coffee and a donut. I'd like to try that sugar pie. Mom made a lousy meatloaf."

Without looking back, Taylor began making his way east along the highway. Dunkin' folded the map, stuffed it in his pack and followed behind. Nothing more was said about coffee and donuts as they approached the first house on the south side.

Both men had guns at the ready scanning the area for movement. The house was a single-level dwelling, small by any standards; all the windows had been broken for some time, the roof had a large hole directly above the door. The house had been compromised several times over the years. Dunkin' had his rifle trained where the picture window should have been as Taylor made his way to the rear.

Taylor ran up to the house, his back hitting the clapboard siding with a loud thud just to the right of the front door. Dunkin' scanned the area back and forth, the barrel of the rifle leading the way, his finger tightly wrapped around the trigger. Other than the sound of wind blowing through the trees pulling the leaves free from their hold on the branches, it was dead quiet. The dried leaves rustled and rolled along the side of the house as the wind gusts blew. With his hand on the door handle, he gave a gentle twist; the handle rotated without resistance. Taylor cast Dunkin' a quick look, then barged in.

Outside, Dunkin' could hear his partner's footfalls in the house as he kept watch. From experience, they both knew that homeowners would often wait outside until the attacking party was in the house, where the invaders were at a disadvantage. Traps would be set, making it difficult to navigate the unknown halls of the house, with the fear of death or serious injury always a possibility. Slowly Dunkin' moved in closer, his back to the building, looking high in the trees and low along the weeds and overgrowth. In the past, he had seen trap doors spring up after a group walked over them. Snipers would pop up and shoot the invaders in the back. From experience, they'd learned to walk separately along the paths so that if a sniper did spring up from beneath a trap door, the person walking behind could shoot them before they got a round off.

Inside the house, Taylor made his way around the debris, dunking under cobwebs and watching for potential traps. He had seen most of the common ones, so he had an eye for anything that might be off. From the front door he turned right, down the hall to the kitchen, each step calculated and methodical, heel to toe. It was more difficult to spot traps when the house was in a dilapidated condition. When Taylor came to the first room on the right, he turned—no one behind him—forward again. He looked quickly in the room and then back. Nothing. He then ducked down and peered in, making certain the room was clear, then stood and entered the bathroom. It was small; nowhere to hide, no closet, the tub's shower curtains had long been torn down.

Entering the hall as carefully as he had the bathroom, Taylor looked up. Cobwebs dangled loosely from what was left of the ceiling. It had already been ripped down by someone looking for hidden guns or a food stash in the attic. He swiped at the cobwebs that tickled his face then continued to the door on his left. The only bedroom had also been ransacked; the mattress was up against the wall, loose clothing on the floor covered in debris and old leaves from the open window. His focus was on the mattress; someone could be hiding behind it. With military precision, he stepped over the clothes, quietly reaching forward, and pulled down the mattress. Mice darted off in all directions as it hit the floor, causing loose debris to take flight.

Breathing a sigh of relief, he turned to the dresser that had also been toppled over; each one of its drawers had already been pulled out and clothes piled in the centre of the room.

"Fucking waste," he whispered, seeing all the clothes on the bedroom floor. Rain had soaked the clothing over years and the rodents had chewed and nested inside the garments. It was impossible to find new clothes; most people would still sort through the clothing he dismissed on the floor, find a few pieces worth salvaging, wash them and save them for later. Taylor kicked at the pile, flipping them over, hoping a single piece would be worth saving. Nothing presented itself.

Taylor was beginning to relax; the house was small and didn't hold any secrets. He called out to Dunkin', signalling the "all clear." Dunkin' double-checked the exterior then made his way inside. He lowered his rifle and walked in, checking over his shoulder again to see if any hidden enemy had decided to attack while his back was turned.

Dunkin' joined Taylor, who was now in the kitchen rummaging through the cabinets for anything of value. The house had been ransacked time and time again; anything worth taking had been taken. There weren't any canned good, jars or useful boxes of food anywhere. The only remaining boxes of food had been chewed open and eaten by the resident rodents.

Taylor leaned against the kitchen counter, dejected but not upset; failure was commonplace now. They considered themselves lucky if they were able to find some odd scrap worth keeping. "Nothing here, ready to move onto the next?"

Dunkin' nodded in agreement.

The men exited the house and continued east a few hundred yards. A driveway on the north side of the road led to a house, partially covered by growth. A large tree had toppled over in a windstorm, crashing through the roof. From the look of the roof, the damage had happened several years ago. Standing back, Dunkin' and Taylor looked at the house with its white vinyl siding. Without saying a word, each man knew it was a house that had most likely hosted a large family: mother, father, maybe three or four kids, a dog in the back yard—a black lab or German Shepard—and maybe a cat—and most certainly they were all dead.

Both men recalled the first white vinyl-sided house they had come upon, similar to the one before them, not long after they met and began their journey together years ago. They couldn't recall which city, not that it mattered anymore; cities didn't exist, nor states or countries. But the white house had been beautiful, pristine; the lawn once manicured now overgrown, yet you could still see the remnants of its previous life. They were the first to entre the house shortly after the event. Nothing had been disturbed. It was as if the family had decided to leave on vacation and simply closed up the house. The curtains were drawn; everything was in its place, the house immaculate. Their guns were always cocked at the ready, both men vigilant for what might be lurking in the shadows. As they made their way through the house, nothing set off alarms of anything being amiss, only a slight buzzing sound. Taylor went upstairs, Dunkin' to the basement.

As Taylor rounded the corner on the second floor, flies buzzed and bounced off his head, filling the entire hallway; he knew the meaning. He followed the stench of death and decay that pierced his senses. As he passed each room, he glanced in to see that the beds were unmade, furniture tossed about, a fight had taken place in each room. Taylor figured the family had been attacked as they slept. Either a band of roaming humans or the infected had entered the home in the night through an unlocked door. He didn't want to see what was creating the fly frenzy, but he was driven.

The largest of the clusters were just outside the room at the far end of the hallway. He raised his rifle high and kept inching forward. The stench grew stronger closer to the room, a fresh assault stung his nostrils, and made his stomach turn. As he neared the doorway, the flies created an audible buzz that grew louder as the odour increased. Keeping close to the inside wall, he pulled the barrel of the rifle up close, finger on the trigger, then pounced to the opposite and looked in. The site almost made him vomit.

Dunkin' walked silently down the hall towards his partner. Taylor didn't move as he continued to stare at the carnage in the room at the end of the hall. Dunkin' stopped beside him, whispered, "Go downstairs and grab whatever food and weapons you can find. I'll be down shortly." Without a word, Taylor slid to the end of the hall and down the stairs.

Dunkin' saw the pile of decomposing corpses against the far wall, maybe four or five, one laying on top of the other. Their skin was dark and waxy, faces no longer recognizable; fluid had secreted from their bodies creating a large pool of thick dark goo on the floor. It appeared that each body had been partially eaten, hopefully after death. It was definitely the work of the infected. From the look and smell of the flesh, the bodies had been there for some time, stacked like boxes in a warehouse. He had never seen the infected do this before and was unsure why they had done it. Perhaps the infected who attacked the family ate as much as possible, and because of some dormant memory of their past human lives, the need to stack the bodies was still ingrained in them. Whatever the reason, Dunkin' stood there wondering if his family was still lying in their beds where he had killed them, their bodies decomposed and a breeding ground for flies to lay eggs. He took in a deep sigh; he didn't notice the smell; his mind was back in the day when he killed his family. He felt a knot form inside his throat and had to swallow hard to make sure he didn't start crying. He turned from the scene and made his way to the next door.

Dunkin' went into the main bedroom, yanked open the closet and found new shirts, pants still on hangers, and shoes and boots lined neatly on the floor. Selecting his new wardrobe, he carefully laid each garment on the bed, then went to one of the dressers and found clean underwear and socks. He sat on the edge of the king-size bed, flies buzzing around his head as he undressed and changed clothes. What he was currently wearing hadn't been washed in over a month and was showing signs of wear.

He stood before the full-length mirror in a new, clean pair of socks, new underwear, a pair of clean jeans, an Under Armour T, with a plaid shirt and a leather belt. They were all a little big for him, but he liked his clothing loose. He grabbed a few extra pairs of socks and extra underwear, another pair of jeans, a T and a heavy shirt, and a full change of clothes for Taylor. In the ensuite bath, he found Advil, Tylenol, toothpaste and the toothbrushes in the holder looked better than the ones they currently were using. There were also two bars of soap still in the wrapper. "Sweet," he whispered. He saw the razor and foam, and for a moment considered shaving, but it was a fleeting thought. The toiletries were stuffed in his backpack along with whatever other treasures were in the room.

As he made his way downstairs, he saw Taylor was sitting on the sofa, a pile of food covering the coffee table. "A present," Dunkin' said, tossing the extra clothes he had taken from the fathers' closet next to his friend. "What did you find?"

Taylor undressed as he spoke. "Lots of canned goods, might be a little heavy to carry, and a canned ham. Check this out, the expiry date isn't for another two months," he chuckled. "I found some boxed almond milk, still has some shelf life." Taylor was now trying on his new duds. "I found Tide Pods; I know you don't think we need to worry about cleaning our clothes, but I'm taking them anyway. There is nothing like fresh laundered clothing. Hey, while I was going through the kitchen, I can't believe what I found," he said as he tossed a bag to Dunkin'.

Dunkin' knew what it was before he caught it. He turned the foil bag to see the label: Dunkin' Original Blend Medium Roast. He cast his friend a look, nodded softly. "Thanks man. I mean it." He opened the corner of the bag, spreading the foil seal, and inhaled deeply. The coffee, still fresh, played classical music with his senses. It was the most tantalizing aroma he had ever experienced. Eyes closed, the scent brought him back to Sunday mornings, bacon, eggs, the thick weekend paper, and the family around the table. Kids yelling, each wanting something different—he would be watching, taking in the nuances of the moment as he sipped his coffee. These memories of Dunkin's family were brought back with the simple smell of ground coffee.

Taylor was not yet fully dressed in his new clothes, but he admired the dead man's fashion sense. "Nice shit. Fucking funny. I could never afford these labels before the event, now look at me; I'm wearin' an Under Armor T and sweatshirt. Pants are big, makes me look like a homey, but hell man, this stuff is almost brand new and feels good," he said, running his hands over his new shirt. "I feel like a rich man."

Dunkin' smiled at his friend. "You look good," he said, as he went through all the food on the coffee table. "This stuff will weight about twenty-five to thirty pounds if we try to take it all. What do we really need?" For the next half hour, the two men divided their spoils, loaded their packs with food, and filled their stomachs with what they couldn't carry. They both found newer boots in the front hall closet, and they left a note on the front door warning the next group that visited the house about the room upstairs, and pleading that they not trash or burn the house down, but leave whatever supplies they could for the next group of survivors. They left their old gear folded on the kitchen table in case someone needed it.

The two men stood before the white vinyl-sided house with the tree through the roof. "You figure there's anything in the house like what we found before," Taylor asked.

"This house looks like it's been picked over by buzzards and vultures and trashed a hundred times. Fucking idiots. Do you think we are all reverting back to being animals, not caring about anyone else but ourselves?" It was rhetorical; Dunkin' didn't expect an answer. He had asked Taylor the same question hundreds of times.

"Should we even bother going in?"

Dunkin' turned and started walking east again. "I think we are probably about two years behind on all the homes on this stretch of road. All the houses have been picked over and stripped of anything worthwhile. But it isn't causing much of a delay. Let's keep on going; who knows, we might get lucky and find a few things. Stay optimistic."

As they walked east along US-7, the wind picked up, blowing multicoloured leaves across weed infested and cracked asphalt, pulling the remaining foliage from barren trees. The silence was aggravating for both men. For years, there hadn't been anything to create sounds other than nature. Both men had grown up in the city where silence was not the norm. They detested the lack of noise.

If not for the gravel road, they would have missed a large multi-unit storage facility almost completely obscured by tall grass and weeds. A quick walk down the path revealed all the metal doors had been ripped from the frames, the contents looted, the vehicles which had been parked outside were also destroyed. They left without taking the time to see if anything was still left inside any of the units.

House after house along the road had been vandalized and ransacked for every last possible piece of clothing and equipment. It was becoming apparent that this was a bad decision, but they had committed to the task and would see it through. Thirty minutes into their walk, Taylor stopped at a dirt road which connected north from US-7. There were houses on both sides, each all but destroyed, their windows and doors broken. The roof on one of them had been opened by a fire and exposed to the elements. Still, he continued to stare down the path.

Dunkin' stopped a few feet ahead, turned, "What's up?"

"Notice anything?" Taylor never took his eyes off the path.

"Come on. We don't have time for this."

Taylor never moved.

"Fine, two houses, one big, one small, both look like something out of a horror film. Let's go. We can meet up with the main highway by noon if we keep the pace going."

"If there's only two houses, why are there four mailbox posts." Taylor pointed to the broken posts barely visible in the grass, then to the four mailboxes that had been toppled at some point. "I'm wondering if anyone has checked out the other two homes?"

Dunkin' didn't say a word, but started making his way down the path that used to be either a dirt road or driveway. Further up, the lane disappeared under overgrown trees and grass. Despite the early hour, the area beyond the trees was dark and an ideal spot for an ambush. Both men held their guns high, their senses on alert as they made their way down the lane.

* * * *

Carrie piled the branches and twigs along the south side of the cabin as far up as she could reach. Her hands were bleeding from tiny scratches and puncture wounds from the freshly broken limbs. She wove the branches as best she could so the pile wouldn't collapse under its own weight. As she did that, she wondered how birds could create such intricate nests while her pile of twigs looked just like a pile of twigs stacked high. Regardless, the task was made easier by the music playing in the background. The volume was set low to avoid making it a calling card for anybody close by.

She had already decided this was going to be her home for the winter. There was more than enough food, she was used to hunting daily for anything she needed. At the rate John was progressing, Carrie hoped he would continue to improve and become more helpful around the cabin. Winter had always been an infected-free season, a time when they hibernated and those immune to the virus were able to feel normal for a short time.

As she wove the branches into one another, John approached, dropped the armful of branches, then turned and shuffled his feet in the dirt as he went back into the woods. He remained silent, emotionless, and in the morning sun Carrie noticed his skin seemed even more pink than it had earlier. A sense of pride warmed her as she watched John working, comfortable in her decision not to leave him behind or kill him when she had the opportunity.

Despite the chill, Carrie had beads of sweat dripping from her brow. As she glanced up at the sun and the treeline, she wondered if she could build some blinds as a defense against an attack by infected or other marauders as they passed by. If she could find the cabin by chance, surely others could too. The cabin was far from any foot paths, which must have been why it had gone unnoticed for years. With the cool temperatures and wind, leaves were beginning to fall more quickly, and it wouldn't be long before her new home would be more easily visible. She scanned the area, realizing she should camouflage the black water drum on the roof. There were several evergreens surrounding the area that could be used as a blind for defense. Lots of work, she thought to herself. Carrie stopped and watched John gather twigs and branches, and knew that the workload would be shared, even if John was only able to do a small share.

* * * *

The overgrowth of trees, shrubs and weeds leading up to the two houses kept the area secluded and in perpetual darkness. Dunkin' slowed his pace as he pulled the rifle up high and placed his finger on the trigger. The hairs on the back of his neck stood up. "I don't like this," he whispered.

"Yep." Taylor's eyes never stopped scanning the area. "Can't for the life me figure out why I've got a bad case of the heebie-jeebies. Something is not quite right."

"Wanna turn back?"

"We need supplies badly. I bet they have guns and ammo. Lots of it. I'm willing to risk it if you are."

Dunkin' didn't answer. He kept his pace steady, staring at the treeline. "You think it's dark enough to fool the infected into thinking it's night? Look around, it's like sunset right now."

As the clearing opened, two homes separated by a common driveway came into view. Despite being midday, the overgrowth of trees kept the area in relative obscurity. The two homes hiding from the world; a world which no longer existed. One of the homes had a large Ford pickup parked in the front, covered with leaves and dirt. All the glass was still intact, tires inflated; if not for the covering debris, it wouldn't look out of place pre-pandemic. Dunkin' motioned with a head tilt towards the truck.

Taylor glanced quickly at the truck then back towards the houses. "It's still in one piece. I have a hard time believing no one found this place in all this time. You figure people still live here?"

"That's a possibility, but look around; nothing to indicate anyone's been here for some time. Either we got lucky as shit or something is really fucking wrong here—and I don't believe in luck. I think this is a set up. Someone's still living here, and we are sitting ducks."

Taylor broke off and made his way to the pickup. Each step was calculated and precise, his eyes scanning the area constantly. "See anything?"

"Nothin'. Quiet as a church mouse. Be careful."

Before opening the driver-side door, Taylor looked inside the truck bed then inside the back seat and the front. He released his hold on the handle and directed his attention back to the truck bed. Other than leaves piled up along one side, it was empty, as was the inside. If someone was hiding under the leaves, they would have to be ridiculously small. Taylor used the barrel of the rifle to push the leaves aside to make certain no one was hiding there, ready to attack.

He pulled back relaxing his grip on the rifle and tugged at the door handle, expecting it to be locked. The door snapped open and gave way with a loud creak. The tiny roof light illuminated dimly; there was some power left in the vehicle's battery. A thick, musty odour filled his senses. The truck hadn't been used in years and smelled of mouse urine and feces. Other than some rodent damage, the cab looked clean. Sticking his head inside, Taylor found the keys in the ignition. "I think we're clear. The keys are still in the truck. If someone had found this place, they would have taken this thing years ago. You want me to try and turn it over?"

"No. No way. If there is someone here, you'll give us away. I'm feeling a bit better, but no sense in ringing the dinner bell and letting everyone know we're here."

Taylor gently pushed the door closed and rejoined Dunkin'. Together they make their way to the closest house on the left. It had a raised front porch, and in Dunkin's imagination he could see the family sitting outside after dinner, the kids playing in the yard, mom and dad chatting about the day—something he would have liked. He shook the thought from his mind and carefully took the few steps up to the top of the veranda. Taylor had his back to him to prevent an attack from behind. He stepped backwards up the steps. "Clear."

Dunkin' peered into the window to the right of the main door.

The house was empty. Shadows pulled lines long across the walls and floors; corners remained hidden, colours muted in the darkness. A jacket or sweater had been casually tossed over the back of the sofa; a throw pillow was on the floor beside the coffee table which had an empty wine glass resting on a coaster. It was difficult, but he could make out a fine layer of dust on the table directly under the window. Everything was in its placed; nothing indicated any recent activity. Something he had seen far too often—a home that looked as if the family had just gone out to grab a cheeseburger or ice cream and never came home. He looked across the yard to the other house and wondered if that was the grandparents' house. It made sense that two homes so close would have related families.

"Look in; tell me what *you* see."

Taylor slung his rifle over his shoulder, cupped his hands around his eyes, pressing them tightly against the glass. "Nice home, everything in it's place, lots of dust. I doubt anyone's been here in a long time. I'm beginning to think we're getting fucking paranoid." He leaned back from the glass and pulled the gun from his shoulder.

Dunkin' smirked and placed his hand on his friend's shoulder. "Being fucking paranoid has kept us alive. No?"

"You're right. Shall we?" Taylor made an exaggerated motion like a butler inviting a guest into his employer's home, indicating they should entre the premises by trying the front door. He twisted the knob slowly, expecting the door to be locked; instead, it popped open and swung freely. "Country living. No one locks their doors," he chuckled. "After you."

Dunkin' was careful. He looked around for booby traps or anything that might be out of place. To his right was the living room where the wine glass sat on the coffee table. To his left, the dining room had a large family-sized table with an open laptop and a tablet casually placed on it. There were open school books and a child's knapsack still slung over the chair back. Dunkin' went into the living room. The wine has long since dried up, leaving a dark red ring around the bottom of the glass. He ran a finger along the coffee table making a wavy line in the thick dust.

"Been some time since there's been someone here. Take a look." He motioned for Taylor.

The two men stood in the living room. Despite the dust and cobwebs dangling from the ceiling, it still had the feeling of a carefully decorated home. It had quite some time since anyone sat on the sofa or had turned on the big screen television that hung on the wall. Taylor picked up the dust-coated remote from the coffee table, pointed it at the TV and pressed the red power button. The television remained black. Taylor shrugged his shoulders. "Wishful thinking, I guess," he said, and tossed the remote to the sofa cushion sending a small puff of dust into the air.

The country decor was different from Dunkin's home back in Boston, but the furnishing still made him feel comfortable and welcome. A warm feeling overcame him, reminding him of a time when his family lived a simpler life in a place not too dissimilar to the room he was standing in. Taking in a deep breath and one last look around, he suggested they split up and look for anything of use.

As he made his way down the hall, Taylor turned left into the kitchen and stopped when he saw the cabinets still closed. He could feel his pulse race and he stepped forward; his hands paused on the tiny door pulls. "Please. Please. Please." He didn't believe in God, but he was asking any deity that might be listening to answer him. Slowly he pulled the doors open and revealed a cache of canned and boxed food. "Holy fucking shit." Taylor's voice echoed in the house.

Still in the living room, Dunkin' ran to the kitchen then stopped short. All the kitchen cabinets were open revealing the hidden treasures behind them. Taylor was almost crying. "Look. Look at this. There's enough food here to last us through winter. We could even put on a few pounds," he said jokingly. "If this place checks out, I think we should stay here." He was almost giddy.

Dunkin' walked slowly to the cabinets, wrapped his arm around his friend's shoulders and gave him a quick hug. Taking in a deep breath, he scanned the food store in the kitchen. "Nice. Good job buddy," he said, then tightened his hug again. "This is fucking amazing." He moved along the cabinets and saw something he had always enjoyed with his children. He pulled out a can of pears and rolled it in his hand. "Wow. I haven't had pears in so long. I used to put them in a bowl, cover them in vanilla ice cream, then pour the pear syrup over the top. The kids loved it."

"I doubt the ice cream is still any good," Taylor chuckled, "but after we finish checking out the house, you can sit in the living room on the chesterfield and enjoy a bowl of pears." He took the can from Dunkin's hand and stuffed it in his friend's backpack. "Don't loose this," he ordered jokingly as he walked away, leaving Dunkin' alone with his memories.

Taylor left the kitchen, turned left, and continued down the hall to the bathroom on the main floor. Other than dust, cobwebs and insects, a washer and dryer were stacked against the far wall and the toilet seat was up. "A guy used it last," he thought to himself. He lifted the lid off the tank, empty. The water had evaporated and held no secret stash other than a chlorine puck that had dried out and cracked. Over the sink, he opened the cabinet mirror to reveal medical prescriptions, Tylenol and Advil, tampons, a razor and shave cream. He tossed the two bottles of pain killers in his pack then closed the cabinet. He looked at himself in the mirror, rubbed his beard and contemplated shaving it off.

Dunkin' thought about his wife and children as he inventoried the stash of food—inspecting each cabinet, cans pushed aside to see what was hidden behind the ones in the front. He found jars of peanut butter, jams, peas, corn niblets, creamed corn, stews, potatoes. They'd both had roast wild boar not long ago, but Dunkin' wanted a meal free of meat. He imagined spooning out peanut butter from the jar or warming up the potatoes and pouring creamed corn over them. He began to salivate as he lined up the cans on the counter, pushing them through the dust and mice droppings. By the time he had the majority of cans and boxed food organized and out of the cabinets, he had counted over seventy-five containers, separated into vegetables, soups and stews, pasta, rice and condiments. Based on their current food consumption, Dunkin' surmised they had almost two months of stored food, longer if they rationed their meals, hunted and added wild game to the menu. He held onto the refrigerator door handle, wondering if he should risk opening it. The last time the smell of rotten food was so overpowering he almost vomited. Instead, he opened the small pantry to the right and wondered if they had a cold storage in the cellar with more canned and dry food. He hoped he would be able to put on a little weight. Dunkin's mind was already made up; they would stay for the winter before heading further north come spring.

Upstairs, Taylor found the master bedroom and rummaged his way through clean clothes still folded in dressers and hanging in closets. They smelled musty, but were still cleaner than anything he had on. He found pants, shirt, underwear and pulled a few pairs of socks from the dresser at one time. He assumed they all belonged to the father of the household. Everything was laid out on the bed, where he would be able to sleep tonight.

At the far end of the room, a door led to the ensuite bathroom that boasted enough toiletries to clean off weeks or even months of dirt and sweat. He pulled back the shower curtain; the tub was filthy, coated with dust, dead insects and cobwebs. Taylor turned the water taps, no burp, no drips. All rural residences worked on sump pumps, to keep their basements dry, and wells that needed electricity to draw water from deep underground, not unlike any other rural home they had investigated. Except this house hadn't been ransacked or destroyed by vandals. Any attempts to power the water pumps would have to wait. Once he finished his investigation, Taylor decided this would be the bedroom he used.

By the time Taylor made it back downstairs, Dunkin' had cleaned the living room, the sofa was dust free and the windows were open, exchanging the musty, stale air with a cool fall breeze. Dunkin had his boots off, his gear laid out on the floor. He had stacked pillows up against the side arm of the sofa and was spread out, fast asleep. On the table sat an open bottle of Jack Daniels, more than half empty, the twist top on the table. He wasn't sure how much Dunkin' had consumed before passing out; it didn't matter, getting drunk was something Taylor had wanted to do for a long time. He took the bottle by the neck, tilted it back and finished what was left. He sat down in a chair and kicked off his boots, closed his eyes, and fell asleep.

* * * *

Carrie completed stacking enough branches along the wall facing the woods where she'd first noticed the cabin, attempting to conceal it from anyone who wasn't paying attention as they passed. She stood back, admiring her handywork, wondering if it was worth the effort.

She looked at her hands; they were cut, bleeding and bruised, her fingers stiff as she opened and closed her fists. A sound directly behind her caused Carrie to jump. Startled, she leapt forward and turned to find John had quietly walked up behind her without making a noise. In the past, John had shuffled his feet as he walked.

"Jesus, bud," she said, clapping her hand to her chest. "You nearly gave me a heart attack." Carrie's chest heaved as she tried to catch her breath. John softly stepped forward, raised his hand and put it where hers had been. She could feel the pressure—and her heart beating against it. "That's my heart." She placed her hand upon his and pressed his hand more firmly on her chest. "Feel that?"

John looked down at his hand, puzzled. One hand remained on Carrie's chest; he placed his other hand on his own chest. Immediately, Carrie slid her hand under John's, directly on his chest; nothing. Despite the new colour of his skin, there was still no heartbeat; but his hand was cool, no longer cold. She felt sad for John. The Tin Man needed a heart, and the Wizard wasn't around. But as she was about to pull her hand away, she felt something that made her own heart jump. With John's hand still upon hers, she placed his free hand on top, then hers—four hands pressing against his chest. For almost a minute, the two waited in silence, standing close to each other, until she felt it again. This time she was certain. She pulled back, spun around, squealing with delight. John, motionless, watched as Carrie stomped her feet then placed her hands over his heart again and waited. Eventually, she felt another beat.

Carrie looked up at John, smiled and hugged him. He stood in silence as she squeezed him with all her strength. Softly, he moved his hand up and placed it in the small of her back. She felt his hand and squeezed him harder, knowing it meant that he was potentially the first to revert back to being human. It could mean the infection was running its course and those infected with the virus could be healing themselves. Maybe John was the first—and here was hope—something Carrie had given up on long ago.

Carrie pulled back and John's hand slipped free. She kept her head down, covertly wiping a tear from her eye. "Well, enough of that," she said. "We have work to do. We need to trap dinner, maybe have a barbeque."

Carrie headed out into the woods for more brush. John remained where he was, placing his hand back on his chest, waiting for whatever made Carrie so excited. He felt his heartbeat, then another and another. For all he knew, it had always been there. Nothing to get excited about. John turned in the direction she had gone, watched, and waited. A moment of clarity entered his mind and he wondered why he'd suddenly begun to question all the things that were happening around him. His memory still wasn't clear, but he wanted to know why Carrie had become excited; why they were camouflaging the cabin; why he suddenly awoke days ago with no memory of who he was or why he was. John placed his hand over his chest, waiting for the thump that was so exciting to his friend. He felt it—once, twice— steady; something was bouncing in his chest. It meant nothing to him.

Walking through the woods, Carrie wiped her eyes. She was happy, happier than she had been in a long time. Her mind raced with thoughts of what all this meant; was John the first to turn human after being infected; was he one of many; could his blood help make a vaccine to help the infected or prevent any further infections? She wasn't even certain if laboratories that were attempting to find a cure even existed anymore. Carrie only knew it was good news.

With her arms full, she was making her way back to the cabin when she stopped to pick up a few extra branches and noticed the ground. Carrie was standing in the middle of a large square, maybe forty feet by forty feet, free of trees or brush. But it had odd plants in what looked like row upon row of planted crops. Dropping her pile, Carrie reached for one of the plants and pulled. In her hand she held a long, bright green stalk, and at the end was a bright orange carrot covered in dirt. She turned, looking down the aisle of stalks. There were several rows of the same plant sticking out of the ground. Beside the carrot stalks were tall stalks with broader leaves, many of them yellowed and turning, but she was certain she knew what they were. She dug her hands into the dirt and unearthed several potatoes. There were hundreds of carrot and potato plants, enough to feed them for the winter.

It was late afternoon by the time Carrie made it back to the cabin, where she dropped half a dozen potatoes and even more carrots into the sink. After washing them under the water, she decided she couldn't wait to cook them, so instead she sunk her teeth into a raw carrot. It was sweet and delicious, something she hadn't had in years. As she was squatting down looking in the lower cabinets, John stood silently in the open doorway, apparently waiting for an invite to entre the cabin.

"Get in here and close the door. It's getting cool out and I can start dinner soon. How do you feel about mashed potatoes and carrots? I know I saw powdered milk somewhere in this mess of preserves." She turned to watch John close the door and latch it, surprised he remembered how to do that. "We can have a nice vegetarian dinner, no meat. It won't be the way my mom used to make mashed potatoes, but we can whip something up that would make her proud with what we've got to work with. We haven't had milk, I mean fresh cows' milk, in years, so no butter; but I can mix the powdered milk and boiled potatoes and I know for certain I saw brown sugar in a mason jar somewhere. We used to make these sweet honey-garlic roasted carrots with sesame seeds. Oh John, they were so good and sticky."

With her hands full of mason jars, Carrie stood, placing the ingredients on the counter, "This will be a cluster of a dinner, but we have to try new things. Right?" Carrie realized she had been talking nonstop while John stared at her.

She took him by the hand to the washroom, ran the water and began to wash his hands, "Honestly, I don't know what I'm going to do with you," she chuckled. John pulled his hands away from Carrie's, then began to mimic the action, rolling one soapy hand over the other. "Look at you. I'm so proud of you." Carrie put her hand on his shoulder as she watched him. With clean and dried hands, she led John to the table as she prepared the next gourmet dinner.

As Carrie peeled and cut the carrots and potatoes, feeling secure and confident that the coming winter season would be relatively stress free compared to the past few months. She was feeling very domesticated as John stood, moved close to her, watching her prepare the meal, still not helping.

Day 922

Dunkin' woke as a wave of panic overtook him. He bolted upright, swinging his legs over the edge of the couch, his bare feet landing on the carpet. The feeling of skin on carpet scared him, causing him to jerk his feet back. When he finally relaxed enough to put his feet on the floor, he looked out into the darkness. It took some time before the haze cleared and he realized where he was. Dunkin' had been asleep for hours after drinking half a bottle of Jack Daniels. He rested his head in his hands as his stomach rumbled and tried to decide if it would expel its contents or not. Regardless, he didn't feel well. He fumbled through his pack and found the shaker flashlight he kept in the side pocket. Vigorously shaking the light to charge the battery cells caused his head to pound even more. He moved the weak beam of light across the room, barely illuminated his surroundings, but enough to make Dunkin' recall where he was.

He grabbed his boots, made his way to the front door, locked it, then moved down the hall to the stairs. Not having been upstairs, he shook the flashlight once again as the light began to dim. Walking slowly, Dunkin' scanned and checked each room. When he found what he was looking for he undressed, killed the light, then lying down on top of the bed covers, reached out and rested his hand on Taylor's. With a gentle squeeze, Taylor took hold of his friend's hand.

* * * *

Hours later Taylor sprang out of bed, awakened by strange sounds in the house. Years of being vigilant made him weary of the unknown. In the dark, he quickly dressed in the new clothes he had set out the night before. Pulling his hair back, he donned his MAGA cap to keep the hair out of his eyes then put his pack over his shoulder. Holding the rifle, he cocked the hammer.

"Wake up," he whispered. He heard nothing from Dunkin'.

"Hey!" A little louder. Still nothing. Taylor made his way over to the other side of the bed and punched his friend hard in the side.

"What the fuck?"

"Shhh. I hear something in the house."

Despite his head still spinning, Dunkin' sat up and listened. The room was dark; he could barely make out Taylor beside him. Then he heard it too. "There's someone downstairs." It was then, he realized, his pack and weapons were all downstairs in the living room. Dunkin' dressed quickly, placing his hand on Taylor's shoulder as they moved with military precision out of the bedroom, down the hall to the top of the stairs. They stopped, listening for any further sounds. Dunkin' leaned in close. "My gear is in the living room."

Somewhere in the house a floorboard creaked, not once but several times. The noise continued for some time before it stopped.

Step by step, the two men made their way down the stairs as Dunkin' shook the flashlight until he knew the cells held as much of a charge as they could. The beam would still be weak, but it would provide enough light to see in the pitch-black darkness of the night. Every few steps they paused to listen. The noise they'd heard had stopped. At the bottom of the stairs, Taylor, still in the lead, peaked around the corner with one eye. Seeing nothing, he slowly stepped along the hall towards the living room.

Dunkin' moved quickly, laced his boots and donned his jacket, slinging his pack over both shoulders. He thumbed the hammer back on the rifle, then both men remained still and waited. Several minutes passed, the noises they had heard earlier were gone. One room to the next, they scanned the house then out the windows. Whatever had been making the noises was gone, or had stopped moving. Out of the darkness, the crunch of leaves broke the silence, then again. Outside, the moonlight cut through the bare tree limbs and cast distorted shadows across the ground. Dunkin' noticed the movement first, slowly positioning himself to the side of the window and peering though the musty curtain. Taylor remained motionless, watching Dunkin' as he investigated, straining to see where the noise originated.

The infected walked slowly from the house out to the woods, single file, mindlessly following the leader. Each one was dressed in the clothes they'd worn when they became infected. Their blank eyes, pupils blown, were perfect for seeing at night but showed no emotion. Unwilling or unable to think for themselves, like cattle in a pasture, they followed whoever was first in line. The line was unending, it flowed from the house out beyond the treeline. Finally, the last infected lumbered her way into the woods, following the others before her. She was only a child, still wearing nothing but a dirty and tattered night gown with bare feet, her entire body stiff, only her legs moving, keeping up with the line.

Dunkin' pulled back from the window, his heart racing, and turned to Taylor. "Did you see how many were out there? We didn't even see the front of the line. I started counting and stopped at over thirty. I've never seen a group that size before. Jesus Christ, where the hell did they come from?"

Taylor tapped the heel of his boot on the floor, "Down in the cellar. Remember all that creaking we heard, I bet they were walking up the stairs to get outside. All of those fuckers were downstairs this whole time?"

Dunkin' closed his eyes, horrified at the thought that only one floor separated had them from a few dozen infected. "We should have done a perimeter inspection before coming inside. We got lazy. Unless they figured out how doorknobs work."

"They would have been through the entire house if they'd figured that out. We have to find the door to the basement and close off their access from outside. I didn't even see a door going downstairs, did you?" Taylor voice was quivering with fear.

Taking in a deep breath, Dunkin' thought about it. "I was so pre-occupied with all the gear and food in the house, I forgot to check all the doors and see where they go. You checked, right?"

Taylor nodded.

"I didn't see one going to the basement; it's probably hidden. A lot of older homes sometimes have doors to root cellars at the back of another closet. I bet we missed it. Let's get down there, close the door and secure it so they can't get back—"

"What if they try another door to get back in the house?" Taylor demanded. "We don't want them coming in through the windows or the fucking front door."

"Seriously? Have you ever seen one of them open a door or a window?"

"You wanna tempt fate?"

"OK. One problem at a time," Dunkin' responded. "We know they haven't figured out how to open doors. Let's find the door on this floor, make sure it's locked and nailed shut, then close the door outside. Keep them out. K?"

Taylor nodded in agreement. "If the basement door is in a closet, I bet it's the one across from the kitchen," he said, heading toward the door before he even finished speaking. Opening the closet, he pushed the contents aside and felt around for a handle. His hand found a latch against the back wall. Pulling down then to the side, the latch slid open, the door creaking on dry hinges. He took in a deep breath. "I'm going down."

He squeezed through to the back of the closet and through the door to the basement. Pausing at the top step, he shouldered his rifle and pulled out his handgun. He waited, listened for movement, and for his eyes to adjust to the darkness. At one end of the basement, a faint hint of moonlight broke through the open door that had been used by the infected. Taylor paused, pulled in another deep breath, then, heart pounding he took the first stair, then the next. Despite a pale beam of moonlight breaking through the open cellar door only then realizing he had left his shaker light with the rest of his gear. Scanning the shadows and corners for any movement or noise, he took another step.

Crammed inside the closet, Dunkin' stood guard for anything out of the ordinary. Other than the creaks of the stairs from Taylor's weight, not a sound came from the basement. Like his friend, Dunkin' opted for his handgun in such cramped quarters. The hammer cocked, the barrel followed his line of sight, ready for anything.

Listening for any noise—rodent, owl, infected—Taylor heard no movement. But as he took another step, something grabbed his ankle through the open riser under the stairs. Tumbling down the stairs, he landed hard on the earthen floor, knocking the wind out of him. He lost his grip on his handgun and it skittered somewhere in the darkness. Taylor opened his mouth to take in air. He rolled over quickly and the rifle fell from his shoulder. He grabbed it, pointed towards the stairs and pulled the trigger. Like a camera flash, the muzzle flash brightened the cellar, revealing several infected at the back. He pulled the trigger again and again. Each time he shot, one of the infected in the front of the group fell, making it difficult for them to advance.

Dunkin' had watched in horror as Taylor fell, rolled and armed himself, firing at something he couldn't see. Not wanted to get in the line of fire, he yelled, "I'm coming down." He took two steps, pointed his handgun behind the top step, and fired. The bullets didn't strike the back wall; instead, they hit more of the infected, causing them fall. Yet a few began to make their way around the bottom of the wooden steps, moving towards Taylor.

Taylor fired. "I can't make it up the stairs," he shouted. "I'm going outside, then running around to the front of the house. Unlock the fucking front door. And make sure you lock the basement door," Taylor screamed between shots, then ran out the door leading to the backyard.

Dunkin' pulled back, slammed the door at the top of the steps, making sure it was locked, closed the second door, then ran to the front door. He unlocked it and bolted outside and around to the side of the house as Taylor was rounding the corner. Taylor slipped in the long, damp grass, fell and rolled, accidentally firing a round. The flash startled Dunkin' but what he saw scared him even more. For only a moment, the rifle flash revealed the infected walking towards Taylor. The fire fight had brought back the others from the woods.

"Move your ass. They're right behind you," Dunkin' screamed. Taylor knew better than to look back. He attempted to right himself and slipped on the dewy grass and fell flat again. Above him, shots rang out. Like before, with each shot the flash showed the horror they were facing. One fell, then another—but the infected kept coming from the treeline—and Dunkin' kept firing. Taylor kicked his heels in the grass, finally getting some traction, stood and was about to make a run for it when something grabbed his backpack. He was yanked backwards. Another rifle flash from Dunkin', another infected fell, but this time it fell on top of Taylor. He pushed it off but felt hands from all direction grabbing at him, keeping him pinned to the ground.

Despite making himself a perfect target as the infected attacked Taylor, Dunkin' kept firing, killing more of the assailants. Several injured or dead landed on top of his friend, shielding him from direct contact, but preventing him from making an escape.

Taylor's first thought was to remain calm and let Dunkin' kill them one by one, then crawl out from underneath the pile. But as the pile grew, it made it hard to breath as the weight upon him increased. Then, he felt it. Something bit his leg, digging its teeth deep into his thigh. He screamed as he felt a large chunk of flesh rip away. He kicked and screamed again, flailing about and causing the bodies to roll off him.

Dunkin' heard Taylor's scream and kept firing. A never-ending stream of infected kept emerging from the woods, making their way to the melee, summoned by the screams. The sight was made even more horrific by the pale moonlight and shadows cast by them. He had never seen so many infected together at one time. Under the pile, Taylor had broken free, but he kept screaming. The scent of blood only made the infected more rabid and they continued to gnaw, bite and scratch at him. Dunkin' kept firing until he had run out of bullets, then he dropped the rifle, pulling out his handgun, aimed and fired. One head shot after another, the infected fell.

As Dunkin' looked at the pile, he paused. Taylor was screaming. He was in the middle of the scrum, his arms pulled as the infected bit and ripped flesh from his body. Dunkin' steadied himself and took aim. Taylor wasn't looking at him. He doubted he could do what needed to be done if he'd had to look into his friend's eyes, but he knew it was the right thing to do. Dunkin' pulled the trigger. The MAGA hat was blown off Taylor's head. The screaming stopped.

Dunkin's heart sank. He lowered the gun, thinking for a

moment he would let the infected attack him, then changed his mind. He raised the gun and fired but the mass of infected only grew. He turned to run back into the house, but his path to the front door was blocked. Several infected had come up the steps and were making their way to him. Looking around, he saw that his only immediate protection was the old pickup. Blindly firing behind him, Dunkin' ran for the driver's door. He was within reach when he felt a sudden backwards jerk. Fighting against the force, he turned and saw that one of the infected had a solid grasp on his pack. In one move, Dunkin' relaxed his shoulders, allowed the pack to fall away, and grabbed for the driver's door handle. Jumping into the truck, he slammed the door and instinctively pushed the lock button down, then did the same on the passenger door.

The infected swarmed the truck from all sides, blocking his view. Dunkin' had never been this close to the infected before. He could see their dead eyes and grey skin as they slapped the glass and attempted to bite at the vehicle. The pickup began to rock from one side to the other and creak under the weight of the attackers as they climbed onto the hood and into the bed.

Dunkin' realized the interior light had come on when he opened the door. He wondered if the truck would survive the onslaught until the sun came up. Then he considered; after all this time, could there be enough juice in the battery to turn the engine over? He righted himself in the driver's seat as the constant pounding on the glass increased in intensity. The key was in the ignition. He held his breath and turned it. A slow whirl signalled the engine attempting to turn over, then again and again. The whirl became faster and faster—then caught. "Yes," he screamed. He floored the accelerator giving the engine some needed gas and heard the eight cylinders roar.

With power, he could turn on the head lights. He fumbled for the high beams and lit the entire scene. The infected in front of the pickup turned away, blinded by the light. The others kept on their relentless pounding on the glass and biting at the metal truck body. He put the vehicle in reverse, stepping on the accelerator then braking, jerking the vehicle backward. Some of the infected fell to the ground from the truck bed and others fell away from the windshield, revealing the horror. Directly in front of him, several infected feasted on Taylor's remains. Despite the bright light and noise, they continued to eat and rip flesh from the body.

He shoved the gear shift from R to D and accelerated, steering towards Taylor. Unable to hold on, the infected either fell underneath the truck or away from it. Dunkin' kept a steady pace and hit the group feeding on Taylor's body. The heavy metal bumper crumpled as it smashed into several bodies and the tires crushed more of the attackers as the truck ran over them. Dunkin' slammed on the brakes, the rusty rotors squealing from years of rust as the tires slid in the tall, wet grass. He turned, looking out the back window. More of the infected had already moved in on the body to feast. With the vehicle in reverse, he floored the gas, crushing more of the assailants in his path, then ran over those eating Taylor, cranking the steering wheel hard as the front of the vehicle spun around. He took one last look at his dead friend, jerked the shifter into drive, and made his way down the lane away from the house to the highway. As the headlights brightened the roadside, they revealed scores of infected along the shoulder. The line continued for several hundred feet. For a moment, anger overtook him and he aimed for a group of infected as the walked single file along the road. But he pulled away at the last moment, not wanting to damage the truck any further.

If it hadn't been for the terror he'd just experienced, Dunkin' would have enjoyed driving again. As the anger subsided, he took stock of what he had; he had lost his pack with all his gear and had just a handgun with only a few rounds left. A quick scan of the interior showed he had almost a full tank of gas, the battery was charging. One of the headlights had been damaged and was pointing low, but otherwise the truck seemed fine. His kept his speed to a constant twenty miles per hour. There was no reason to drive any faster; he had nowhere to go, and his fuel would last longer.

Dunkin' reached for the radio, turning up the volume as static filled the cab. The CD icon was lit so he pressed the Select button until the music started. He didn't recognize the tune, but it was noise, something he needed to help him forget. He pulled the latch for the glove compartment, letting the door drop as several CD cases spilled to the floor. The dim light of the glove box bounced off something metallic. Reaching in, he felt a small pistol, pulled it out and flipped it over in his hand. At first Dunkin' thought it was a child's toy, but the weight and feel confirmed it was real; small, but still potentially deadly. He placed the gun on the seat beside him.

It had been several minutes since he had seen any infected on the road. Dunkin' was getting tired, the adrenaline had worn off and he was exhausted. With heavy eyes he found a side road, turned off the highway, killed the engine, turned off the headlights and let the vehicle coast to a stop. He lowered one of the windows, listening for signs of movement from anything out of the ordinary as he examined the tiny handgun, a Ruger 22 calibre. After several minutes of crickets and wind blowing through leafless trees, he cranked the window up tightly and lay across the seat, holding the gun in his hand. It didn't take long for him to fall asleep.

* * * *

Inside the cabin, Carrie and John sat upright at the table. She was scared, her left leg bounced with fright. John stared at her, still unaware of what was happening outside their home. She had been awakened by the sounds of repeated gun shots in the distance. Leaping from her bed she'd grabbed her rifle, making sure she was prepared for whatever might happen. It could have been humans attacked by infected and were shooting their way free. Or humans versus humans—something she hoped wasn't happening.

Now, the rifle lay across her lap, her finger resting softly on the trigger, with extra rounds on the table ready if needed. Each time she heard another shot in the distance, Carrie closed her eyes trying to determine if the gunfire was getting closer or further away. The echoes of the firefight remained constant. It didn't sound as if the gunshots were getting closer, but there were definitely different types of guns, handguns and rifles she assumed.

Eventually the sounds of gunfire stopped for a moment, then started again, but that didn't make Carrie feel more at ease. There was still so much to worry about. Any armed conflict could spill over and catch her and John in the crossfire. The cabin, hidden in the bush, hadn't been found in years; but if she could stumble upon it, so could someone else. Despite her efforts at camouflage, it would only take a wrong turn for someone to find it, the way she and John had.

Not long after, the sounds of gunfire stopped completely, then silence. After waiting for what seemed like a few hours, Carrie breathed a sign of relief and relaxed her grip on the rifle. She waited a few more minutes, checked the door locks again, then took John by the hand, leading him back to bed in the tub. She tucked the blanket tightly around his neck, combed the hair out of his eyes with her fingers and wished him a good night, then climbed back into bed herself. She kept the rifle beside the bed, loaded and ready. Laying there, Carrie couldn't help but wonder what had caused the armed conflict she'd heard. She ran through possible scenarios, but none of them bore any resemblance to what had actually occurred. It wouldn't be long before she knew the truth.

Day 923

Dunkin' woke up as the sun broke through the passenger window blinding him with its morning rays. He stretched his legs, kicking the truck's door. It was then he recalled where he was and what had happened the night before. With a heavy heart, the memory of shooting his best friend came flooding back. Sitting upright, he scanned the cab and noticed the Ruger on the floor, picked it up and rolled it over in his hand. Thinking of the previous night's events, anger mounted. Dunkin' wanted revenge against those who had taken so much from him over the years.

Dunkin' stepped from the truck, the cool fall air cutting into him, and realized he didn't even have a jacket. He walked to a tree and peed as he scanned the area. Steam rose from the tree where he voided. He no longer had a map. Had he turned himself around as he sped away from the house, had he taken a turn he didn't realize? Dunkin' knew he was lost and had essentially no gear, only what was in the cab of the truck and the clothes on his back. He zipped up and walked to the roadside, his eyes following his tire tracks in the dirt and the flattened grass. Looking both ways, he knew where he had come from, and thinking about Taylor, he knew what he had to do.

Slamming the driver's door, he keyed the engine to life, cranked the wheel hard and headed back to the house. Rage grew as he got closer, certain of what he was about to see. The music played from the CD in the background, annoying him with its lyrics of love on the farm and a woman who had done the singer wrong. Turning off the radio, he didn't want to calm down, he wanted to get back at those who had attacked him. Dunkin' rolled down the driver's window allowing the brisk morning air to revive him, secretly hoping he would wake up and realize that what he was about to do was a very bad idea.

Not long after, he saw the driveway and pulled up the lane to the house he and Taylor had found the previous day. Slamming the brakes, the truck bit and dug into the dirt coming to a stop not far from his backpack. Looking through the windshield, Dunkin' froze at the sight before him. It was even worse than he'd thought it would be. Tucking the Ruger into his waistband, he stepped from the truck and paused at the carnage on the overgrown yard beside the house. He reached for his backpack and tossed it into the truck bed. Then Dunkin' walked through the tall grass past dozens of bodies that lay scattered, some broken from being run over by the truck, others shot—then there was Taylor's body. Not much remained of his friend; he had been almost entirely eaten by the infected. His blood-soaked MAGA hat lay in the grass, part of the hat ripped apart by the bullet that ended Taylor's life. Dunkin' had wanted to keep the hat as a memento, but it was too badly damaged. He picked up Taylor's rifle and slung it over his shoulder. It too was covered in dried blood.

Turning away, Dunkin' noticed that most of the dead infected had been partially eaten by other infected. As he made his way among the bodies, he heard movement in the grass. Pulling the tiny gun from his waistband, he carefully walked toward the noise, stopping several feet from one of the infected who had been run over by the truck the night before. Both of its legs were fractured, mangled beyond repair, one almost torn off. It was pulling itself away from the light, attempting to make the treeline and hide itself until nightfall. It had an impossible task as it had almost one hundred feet before it would reach the darkness. Dunkin' doubted it would make it.

He went back to the truck, placed the rifle on the seat in the cab, then found a small length of rope in the truck bed. He tied a noose as he walked towards the infected that was clawing its way to the forest. Dunkin' stood over it as it continued to scrape at the dirt, ignoring the man. Dunkin' dangled the noose in front of the infected and slid the rope around one of its wrists as it reached forward. With a quick tug the rope tightened, snaring the injured infected. Dunkin' held the other end of the rope tightly as he dragged the broken creature further away from the treeline towards a lone tree in the yard. The infected dug its nailed in the earth as he was being pulled away, the morning sun burning its eyes, its mouth open in a silent scream. At the tree, Dunkin' pulled the rope up to a low hanging branch, being cautious to keep his distance away from the infected who was more concerned about the light than about having its hand bound. He tied the rope tightly around the limb.

Dunkin' stood back. The infected, unable to stand on two broken legs, one arm secured high to a branch, used its free hand to cover its eyes. It made no noise, it just moved itself, attempting to shield itself from the sun. Unable to hide completely, it rolled away, twisting against the bindings that held it to the tree. It rolled back, looking at Dunkin'. For a moment, he thought it was human again; Dunkin' could see it pleading to end its life. He wanted to torture the captured infected for taking part in killing Taylor, but that would be like blaming the cat for killing a mouse for food. Despite his anger, compassion overruled. Dunkin' pulled the Ruger from his waistband, thumbed the hammer and pulled. One bullet to the head at close range.

Making his way to the front door of the house, Dunkin' was thankful he had closed it when he left, preventing the infected from gaining access. The house was as they had left it. He went inside, found a can of Spam, pulled back the lid and dumped it onto a plate making a loud plopping sound. He had always hated the salty, gelatinous formed meat, but his hunger won out. He had access to forks and knives but used his hands instead. He followed the Spam with an old can of Coke he had found in the pantry. It was warm, but sweet and wet. With his belly full, Dunkin' went to work for the next few hours and loaded every last item of food, clothing, cleaning supplies and tools he could fit into the back of the truck bed. A heavy blanket from the master bedroom served to cover the gear and he tied it in place. What couldn't fit into the truck was left on the front lawn for the next group of scavengers.

There was only one thing left to do.

Dunkin' walked to the cellar door at the back of the house. It was open, no doubt full of the remaining infected from the night before. Killing at a distance was easier than purposely torturing one of them. He tossed a rock down the cellar stairs. It struck something soft before landing on the concrete floor. The infected had returned after a night of hunting. Dunkin' closed the cellar door and braced a large branch against it.

He went back inside the house and systematically walked from bedroom-to-bedroom lighting curtains and bedspreads on fire. Dunkin' did the same on the main floor, then casually walked outside. He leaned against the truck as the flames spread, taking a firm hold of the structure, engulfing the entire house. He wasn't certain how many infected were in the basement, and destroying a perfectly good home seemed like a waste, but he had to do something to avenge the death of his best friend.

As the heat of the fire increased, the windows shattered, flames burst through the roof. Dunkin' casually looked on, watching the flames spread to all areas of the structure. A few minutes later, black smoke began to billow out of the basement windows. He wondered if the trapped infected would attempt to escape. He retrieved

Taylor's rifle, placed it on the hood of the truck in case. The flames continued to eat at the house, weakening the frame, and eventually the second floor collapsed onto the first floor in a bundle of unrecognizable materials. If there were any infected in the basement, the door was secure and would prevent them leaving.

Inside the basement, smoke filled the stone-walled room. Heat increased to a point where the infected moved away from the corner of the ceiling that was engulfed in flames. The bright light, heat and smoke made the basement intolerable, so they pushed towards the only exit they knew. The one closest to the exit arrived at the door and attempted to leave, its face slamming against the hardwood. If it had felt pain, it would have screamed. As others tried to leave in a panic, they stumbled, tripped, some walking over the ones on the earthen floor, no regard for others in their group. As the infected pushed their way to the door, they formed a mass of arms and legs and bodies, nails clawing at the wood door. The first one to arrive had been pushed down to the floor. Worn boots and shoes stepped on his head, eventually fracturing it, and his head split open. The door creaked at the weight pushing against it, attempting to break it open.

The flames caught the basement beams; fires raced along, dropping hot embers on the clothing of the infected. It wasn't the smoke or the heat that killed them, but the flames that burnt their bodies, cooking them. There was panic, caused by the unknown—yet they didn't scream. Flames eventually caught their clothing on fire, spreading from one infected to the next, burning them, as they died a second time. This time, they would remain dead.

Carrie pulled whatever vegetables were worth saving out of the garden, placing the edible ones in a moth-eaten towel she found in the cabin. John walked along the side of the patch, then without warning collapsed unconscious, falling face first into the dirt. She ran across the garden, jumping between furrows, to his side. John lay prone, motionless. Carrie was unable to determine if he was breathing. She rolled him over and laid his head on her lap. His eyes were closed. She brushed the dirt away from his face, noticing how pale his skin was. As she looked down on him, she saw that his wallet had fallen from his jacket, so she scooped it up, placed it in his hand and curled his fingers tightly around it. She didn't know how to determine if John was alive or not. Fumbling for a carotid pulse, she placed two fingers on the side of his neck. Carrie paused, waiting for a beat, something to show signs of life, if that was possible. Her fingers slid up and down his neck, trying to find a pulse. Then she felt it; it was soft, barely detectable, but it was there. She kept her fingers in place, waiting for it again. Finally, Carrie felt another pulse. Still uncertain how often his heart should beat, she kept her fingers in place. The pulse was slow but constant.

John remained unconscious, his head on Carrie's lap, his fingers still loosely grasping his wallet. With no clear idea how to treat him, she stroked his hair and kept him comfortable. Looking down upon the man, Carrie realized that she cared for him and was truly worried that the transition back to being human was killing him. She pulled him close, removed her jacket, draped it over him, and held him tightly.

John opened his eyes, forcing himself to roll off Carrie's lap, startling her. "Hey bud. How you feeling?"

He didn't answer. She didn't expect him to. Like a baby waking from a long nap, he had trouble opening his eyes, rubbing them with the back of his hand. Sitting in the dirt, he finally looked at Carrie. As tired and exhausted as she was, and despite his current condition, Carrie was able to notice how much more human he looked. Almost all indications of the infection were gone. John rubbed the side of his head; the signs of pain were evident. She recognized someone with a bad headache; her mother had been diagnosed with chronic migraines just after Carrie was born. John had the same exhausted look and heavy eyes, and he massaged his left temple.

John straightened himself, shielding his eyes from the sun. He pulled his knees in tight, heaved, then turned and vomited—a black, foul smelling, viscous fluid. Carrie jumped back to avoid getting any on her. John's wallet fell to the ground, and she quickly brushed it aside to keep it safe. When he finally stopped heaving, John wiped a little vomit from the corner of his mouth with the back of his hand and spit to clear the bitter taste. It was the most human thing Carrie had seen him do.

Looking like someone recovering from a long night of drinking, John's eyes closed. He began to breath deeply, heaved, paused, got on all fours, arched his back and vomited again. The vomit splashed in the dirt, leaving a large thick black puddle between his hands. He heaved again, opened his mouth, and coughed. John continued to arch his back and attempted to vomit, again but there was nothing left in his stomach.

Exhausted, John fell to the ground again, rolled on his back, moaned softly, then fell unconscious again. Startled, Carrie put her hand on his shoulder and shook him vigorously. John's head rolled back and forth from the forceful shaking.

"Stop," John mumbled, barely audible.

Stunned, Carrie fell backward, wide eyed.

Several hours later, the entire structure had collapsed upon itself, most of the building now lay in ruins in the basement. What little was left of the house was just a smoldering shell; hot spots still visible. Tiny flames licked at charred timbers in the pile, grey smoke swirled up high. Some of the house debris had fallen into the side yard where

Taylor had died, covering his body and those of his attackers. It was a fitting burial for the man as the fire continued to burn what was left of the bodies in the yard. Scavengers wouldn't have anything left to feast on.

Looking about, Dunkin' was happy he hadn't set the surrounding forest or houses ablaze. The heat he felt as the fire roared had diminished greatly. As he stood there, he scanned the neighbouring house. The more he thought about it, moving into it seemed like a good idea. He had enough food, clothing and supplies to last a year comfortably, or just winter in style without too much effort. And he hadn't inspected the other home yet. It might be just as well stocked as this one. Only, this time he would check the basement first, no more surprises. With the colder months arriving, the infected would hibernate through the winter and the threat of attack was limited to assaults from other human survivors just trying to stay alive. Since the houses hadn't been found in three years, he was fairly certain he would go unnoticed, but the fire and smoke might have attracted anyone close by. Yet the fire had been well worth the risk, if only to avenge the death of his friend.

Walking toward the other house, Dunkin' pulled his gun from his waistband and cocked the hammer back. He made his way to the right side, looking back over his shoulder, scanning the edge of the woods for any type of movement. Loose leaves blew across the lawn, the dried grass crunching under each step. He held the gun loosely by his side as he rounded the corner, watching for any activity from the house or the treeline. At the back of the house, the grass and weeds were knee high and the plastic tool shed in the corner of the yard was partially covered by tree branches that hadn't been trimmed since the event.

As he made his way through the yard, Dunkin' found the back

door with growth crawling its way up to the handle. He took the handle and gave it a twist. Locked. The door hadn't been opened in years. Looking up at the windows lining the second floor, he saw all were intact. Continuing to the opposite site, he rounded the corner and froze in his tracks as he drew his gun.

John sat up, rubbed his eyes, then lifted himself up beside Carrie, her jacket falling to the ground. She stood next to him, amazed at the abrupt change in her friend, still in shock after hearing him speak. Reaching down, she scooped up the wallet, stuffing it into his jacket pocket, and donned her jacket. Turning towards her, John glanced at her and his hand grazing hers as they passed over his pocket.

"Th—" John knew what he wanted to say, but the word failed him. His second attempt didn't prove any better. He couldn't form the word in his mouth. His lips and tongue were dry as dust.

Carrie turned to face him, held him by his shoulders. "You're welcome." She felt a sense of pride as she observed his progress, the transition from infected to human. Then, over John's shoulder, Carrie noticed black smoke slowly dissipating into the fall sky. She stepped past him to get a better look. He turned as well and stood close beside her, his arm gently pressing against hers. Carrie didn't notice; her attention was focused on the smoke. It was difficult to determine how far away the fire was. She kept her eyes on the smoke and for any noise in the distance that would provide a clue as to what was happening.

It was some time before the smoke vanished and gave way to clear skies. Anxiety grew as Carrie knew that the infected would be hidden for the day, so the fire had to have been set by humans; infected had never been able to master fire. And that fire was close, too close not to worry about how the fight could possibly make its way to her and John. Without realizing it, Carrie took John's hand

and squeezed it tightly; he squeezed back. They remained in place, watching until the smoke was completely gone, then a little longer for any sounds that might provide a clue as to the origin of the blaze.

As the pair stood watching the smoke over the treeline, John's head began to fill with images, faded reflections of his past life that flickered quickly in his mind, without cohesion or reason. They seemed random, but some of the figures seemed vaguely familiar. He tried to make sense of what he was remembering but his head still hurt. Looking down at Carrie, he smiled softly; this girl had spared his life. He felt grateful for her compassion.

As Dunkin' approached the corner, he raised his gun and walked heel to toe, each step slow and methodical until he had a clear shot. In the back section of the house, trees had overtaken the yard preventing sunlight from breaking through the canopy of thick branches and coloured, fall leaves. It was dark enough to confuse them into believing it was still night.

There were several infected, feasting on the carcass of a deer, burying their faces deep in the flesh, devouring chunks of meat. They weren't aware they had been discovered or even cared. They continued to eat as Dunkin' aimed and fired. The closest one to him was hit in the shoulder, unaffected. It turned to look at Dunkin' with a large chunk of raw meat between its teeth, the lower half of its face covered in fresh blood. It didn't look at Dunkin' with fear, rather it regarded him as a potential meal. As it stood, getting ready to attack, Dunkin' took aim and hit it above the left ear, killing it. One of the remaining three turned from the deer to their dead group member and began to gnaw at the open head wound.

Stepping closer, Dunkin' aimed at the female who had started to eat his first kill and pulled the trigger. Her head kicked back, her long dirty hair fell away as a skull fragment broke loose. The two remaining males rose quickly and turned towards Dunkin'. He fired twice, one was hit in the shoulder, the second shot missed. The infected barely noticed being shot and continued his assault towards Dunkin'. With a steady hand, he fired again. This time, the bullet struck the right side of its head, it fell backward, still alive but unable to walk.

The remaining infected was now less than ten feet away. Dunkin' raised the gun and waited until it got closer. When it was within arms reach, he pulled the trigger and the bullet struck him in the jaw, exiting through the back of the neck, shattering the cervical spine, dropping the infected mid-stride. This one too was still alive, but paralyzed from the neck down.

Carefully approaching the disabled infected, he kept his gun high and his sights on the edge of the woods for any movement. One of the infected Dunkin' had taken for dead moved slightly, the head wound apparently not fatal, and attempted to stand. It planted its hands on the ground with great effort, pushing itself up. From close range, Dunkin' aimed for another head shot and pulled the trigger. The infected fell over, twitched several times startling Dunkin'. He went to the second male with the jaw and neck wound, its spine severed; he looked directly at Dunkin', his damaged mouth opening and closing, in a grotesque visual of flesh and bone. Dunkin' took aim again, pulled the trigger once, twice and didn't stop until he was out of bullets. Even then, he pulled the trigger several more times despite the gun being empty.

Softly, Dunkin' whispered, "Why couldn't you just die like the rest of them?" Killing was not in his DNA; he had never wanted any part in it. He was tired of the killing, even if the infected were already considered dead. He looked down, pitied them, wondered if they felt any pain before they died a second time. He quickly scanned the area before making his way inside the house. At the front door, Dunkin' grasped the door handle and twisted. Locked. Checking the windows to the right and left, he found one of the windows had been left slightly ajar. Before entering, he reloaded his handgun then holstered it. Using a knife to slice the screen, he squeezed his fingers under the frame forcing the window up, then crawled into the house and started to carefully check for anything that might be hiding inside.

By the front door, a half dozen jackets hung on hooks, and on the floor below were boots, running shoes and flip-flops haphazardly tossed one upon the other. On the dusty hardwood, mouse tracks left behind by the home's tenants indicated their movements for the past three years. This house wasn't as clean as the last, with dishes piled in the sink, plates stacked on the kitchen counter and pots still on the stove. The cabinets were filled with canned goods; cases of pop and water were stacked in the hall closet. There was more food here than in the first house.

This place looked lived in, a home for a happy family, at least that's what Dunkin' wanted to believe. In the living room, an aquarium was almost completely dry, the contents evaporated, the occupants long dead. A laptop lay open, still plugged into the wall. He ran his fingers over the keyboard, holding down the power button, but it failed to wake the sleeping computer; the battery was long dead. Dunkin' recognized the unopened blue and silver can that sat beside the computer. Wiping the dust from the top, he flipped the pull tab of the Red Bull energy drink and heard the familiar sound of a carbonated drink. Tilting the can back, he guzzled the contents and waited for the rush of caffeine that would hit him in a few minutes. It was sweet and delicious, a familiar taste from his days in college. Placing the can back in the clean spot on the dusty table, he went to case the rest of the house.

By the time he finished checking the entire home, the caffeine rush had hit him hard, causing a pounding headache—a minor inconvenience for such a delicious treat.

Dunkin' had loaded up the truck with the contents from the first house, but he decided to unload and place it all in the living room. The wind had picked up, a chill hung in the air, frost would most certainly arrive soon.

When he was done, he cracked open a can of Coke, took stock of the inventory and fell into the sofa, causing a large plume of dust to rise into the air. Dunkin' placed a musty pillow behind his head and fell asleep before he finished his drink.

John was alone in the bathroom, looking in the mirror. It was a face he now recognized. He ran his fingers along his chin and cheeks; he needed a shave. He hadn't seen himself in years and he thought he looked older, tired. Despite looking at himself, he had a difficult time understanding who he was.

Removing all his clothing, he ran his hands over every inch of his body, finding the bullet wound in his abdomen and the chunk of skin that was missing from his hand from when he attacked the family in the cabin. He was thin, recalling he used to have a belly, now he had folds of skin where his belly had been. His skin had weathered. He thought it had the feeling of worn leather. That stopped him. John realized he remembered what leather felt like. His memories were coming back, but those memories were jumbled, out of order.

Few memories remained of his time as an infected, but the images he could see disturbed him. They were flashes, brief moments of things he had done, or his other self had done. He never would have done those things if he had been himself. Images of his former life blended with his life when he was infected, making John wonder if it had all been a dream or some side effect of bad drugs.

He moved his jaw back and forth, stretching the facial muscles, looking at his plaque-covered teeth. He had always had strong, white teeth, now he wanted to see a dentist. He laughed at himself, paused, he laughed again. He remembered how to laugh. Things were looking up.

Still gazing into the mirror, his palms resting on the sink edge, he quietly went through the alphabet and counted to one hundred. Basic childhood skills, but he needed to start life over again.

He had been in the bathroom for over an hour before Carrie gently tapped on the door, "You OK in there?" she asked softly.

Still naked, John opened the door. Carrie turned away, laughing. "Cover up, will ya."

John pulled up his pants and put on a shirt, stepping into the main room. "Sorry," he said apologetically. "I'm still not myself." He has a soft smile, but his eyes look old and tired.

"It's really nice to hear you talking. Do you remember anything of the past few days?"

John walked over to a chair, pulled it out and sat. "I don't remember much. What I do know, is that I don't like what I did. I mean, did I really do those things?"

"I don't know if you did what you remember, I just know what you've done since you saved my life. Do you remember that?"

He shook his head, unable to look at Carrie. "I've done some horrible things, things that I feel horrible about. I can't imagine why I would have hurt people, if that's what I did. I don't know, I mean did I—or was this, is this, all a dream? Am I hallucinating?"

Carrie knelt before him. "You can't hold yourself responsible for what you did after you became infected."

"Infected?" John looked truly puzzled.

Carrie pulled a chair and sat facing him. "What is the last thing you recall? Think hard, try to picture your life the way it was before you got sick." She picked up his hand and held it.

John kept his head down, attempting to recall what his life was before the event. He let his mind go blank as images raced quickly before him, like flash bulbs going off in his brain. He saw cities, towns, places he knew were not in North America, cities in other countries, people dressed in odd clothes. He put his hand to his forehead, pulling down, rubbed his eyes, then wiped the corners of his mouth.

"This can't be all me." John voice was scared. "I'm seeing people from all over the world, places I've never been. The things I'm seeing are horrible, sickening."

"You don't know anything about the event, do you, or when the meteor crashed into the earth" she asked.

Without raising his head, "No."

"Not everyone was infected at the same time. You may be recalling scenes on television. The infection started in Europe and spread to America and Canada. Rumour has it, the Australians may have stopped the infection before it hit there, but no one knows for sure. We heard a lot of stuff over the years."

"Can you tell me what happened?" John straightened himself in the chair; he had been crying.

With her thumb, Carrie wiped away his tears, "No one really knows for certain, but what we do know is that some type of virus started making people sick. Those that got sick died—but didn't die. It was as if every system had slowed, no heartbeat, no blood flow, they didn't age. It was like they were awake in suspended animation. Everything changed physically. When you were sick John, you couldn't tolerate cold or light; you hid from the light. At first it was easy to stop the infected, we just shone a bight flashlight in their eyes.

We blinded them, then we could kill them—until we ran out of batteries for the flashlights."

"But you said we were already dead; how did you kill us?" He corrected himself. "Or them?"

Carrie paused, "The infection made it difficult. A wound that would have been fatal for a human barely stops an infected, so we have to shoot them in the head, destroy the brain. That's pretty much the only way to do it."

"How many people became infected? Are there more of us, or them, or you?" John fumbled with his words.

"We think—we don't know—but we think most of the world became infected, only a small number were immune from the disease. Those of us that had natural immunities banded together at first, then when food and gas ran out we began to fight. We broke off into smaller bands. It's been a hard three years."

"Three years!" he cried. "I've been one of those things for three years. And you've had to fight and kill us or them to stay alive?"

"You did what you had to do to stay alive and we did what we had to do. It's survival, John."

"But I saved you? Why?"

"I don't know." Carrie stood and walked around the room. "You saved me from an infected fox. You killed it and didn't kill me. So, we stuck together. I still don't know exactly why." She chuckled. "I saw something in you that I couldn't just dismiss. I saw beyond the infection."

"You saved me."

Carrie nodded. "We saved each other. More than once. Do you understand?"

"Not really. I'm waking up from a nightmare and I've lost so much time."

Carrie took the chair again. "Do you realize, you may be the first person to turn human again. Maybe the virus has run its course; maybe the billions of people who are infected will become human again. Maybe life will get back to something familiar again."

"Familiar? Do we have a familiar anymore?" John laughed.

"Hey. You laughed. That's a start."

John got up and walked around the room. "I feel like I've been in a coma for three years and now that I'm awake, everything's gone." He had a sudden realization and looked around. "My wallet, have you seen my wallet?"

"Check you jacket pocket. I put it there earlier," Carrie tapped her own left breast, indicating where it was placed. He pulled the wallet from his jacket and carefully retrieved his picture and stared at it. "There's no way to track people down is there?"

Carrie stood beside him, glancing at the picture, "Your daughter?"

"My life." He ran a finger down the side of the image, "I can't even begin to imagine what she's gone through. Do you think she's one of those infected?"

"Since you turned, there's a good chance she did too."

John seemed scared. He turned, walked slowly into the bathroom and closed the door, leaving Carrie alone.

Dunkin' had inventoried all the gear from the two houses, placing the canned goods in the kitchen, survival gear in the living room, and clothing on the dining room table. All the medications were arranged in the bathroom along with cleaning supplies.

Standing back, he admired his collection. Alone, he had enough stock to last two years if his luck continued. However, Dunkin' no longer wanted to be alone. He had lost the will to fight.

He found a school workbook and colouring pencils in one of the children's packs, cleared room on the dinning room table, and made notes of the stock he had accumulated. He sipped from a water bottle as he wrote, missing his family and Taylor. Being alone was his worst fear, now come true. Securing each sheet of paper on the respective piles, he went to the bathroom, found the bottle he was looking for and pocketed it. He checked all the windows and doors, making certain they were secured before leaving. He locked the door behind him when he left.

Outside, he walked around the yard, located a large tree with strong limbs, slung the rope over one shoulder and began to climb. Dunkin' continued the accent as far up as the trunk would support his weight, located a horizontal perch and sat down. After years of climbing trees and securing himself, he was certain this would hold his weight.

He lashed the ropes around his legs to the tree branch then secured his body to the trunk. Pulling the bottle of valium from his pocket, he swallowed a few at a time with a mouthful of water until the pill bottle was empty. Finishing the water, he let both bottles fall to the ground, zipped up his jacket high and tucked his hands in his pocket.

Dunkin' faced the house he had burnt down that morning, knowing his best friend was under the smoldering rubble, a thought he just couldn't tolerate any longer. His family and all his friends were gone, he was alone and scared. It was his time, he decided.

Most of the leaves had turned or had fallen to the ground. Dunkin' had doubts if anyone would ever find his body. The one thing that scared him most of all was his body being food for the infected. This high up, once he fell asleep and died his body would rot before they could eat him. It was the only way.

The area was beautiful, peaceful he thought, a good place for a final resting place. It was better to choose the time and place of his death than to die at the hands of someone else. This way was painless, and the choice had been his. Soon, he thought, soon he would see his family again—if there was a god—and that god permitted a murderer to see his family—the family he had killed out of mercy. "Mercy," he thought. Then again, if there was a god, would he have orchestrated pandemic that killed most of the world's population?

It took longer than he thought before the drowsy feeling overtook him. Dunkin' didn't fight it, his eyes became heavy, his muscles lost all their strength. He felt the cold more than he ever had, but he welcomed the feeling.

Dunkin's right hand slipped out of the jacket pocket. He tried to put his hand back, but strength fail him. His head bobbed up and down, his chin fell to his chest, his breathing slowed until it was shallow. He took one last look at where Taylor was buried and fell asleep.

Night had fallen by the time the bathroom door opened; John slowly entered the main section of the cabin to the smell of mashed potatoes and sweet carrots. He quietly sat down at the table and waited for Carrie to join him.

"You know something, I don't think I could smell before." He tapped the plate. "This smells really good. Thank you."

Carrie smiled. "I'm still in shock to hear you talking. Freaks me out. I can't even tell anymore that you were infected. I'm so hopeful this means everyone who turned will get better." Carrie sat down at the table across from him, "We still don't have much, but I added spices to make it more, palatable, I guess. I found some dried onion flakes, garlic powder, salt and pepper. I hope it's OK?"

"It's gonna be great. Thank you." John picked up a fork, scooped up some mashed potatoes then a few carrots. "I'd be OK never having meat again," he chuckled.

They began to eat in silence. Their meal was almost done before Carrie asked, "Do you remember your life? What you did? Married? Friends?" She laughed, "Sorry, I'm throwing a lot at you."

John politely smiled. "It's all right. I worked in an office, I think. It fuzzy, blurry, I recall bits and pieces but not a lot. One thing I do remember is that I hated wearing a suit. And when I changed, I was stuck for three years wearing the same suit and tie. I'll tell ya, I'm never wearing a suit again."

Carrie laughed. "Try and find a new suit right now. Not exactly survival gear." She paused. "Are you ashamed of what you did?"

John shook his head, finished his mouthful. "Anything I did, I did because of the infection. I had no control over it. I'm scared thinking about what may have happened to Katie. I called her Katie. She hated being called Katie; it was Katherine. She wanted to be all grown up and mature."

"How old was she?"

John savoured the sweet taste of brown sugar on his carrots. Without looking up, he said, "Eight, last I time I saw her. It feels like yesterday. You say it's been three years, so eleven now—if she's still alive."

"Where did she live? We can go back and look for her?" Carrie offered.

"Does it matter? An eight-year-old left alone in Philadelphia; if she wasn't infected, how could she survive alone in this world. I shudder at the thought of what might've happened to her by some of the gangs. Chances are, since she was my daughter, she would have turned too. Basically, it's kill, or be killed."

Carrie thought about what John had said and agreed there could be a hundred scenarios of what might have happened, but not trying to find her was worse than doing nothing at all. She moved in close.

"Then we go to Philly and look for her. If you reverted back, she could have turned back too. We owe it to her to go, don't we?"

Carrie took a mouthful, watching John carefully. He looked human and terribly sad at the loss of his daughter. "Winter is coming," she said. "You know, once it's cold enough, the infected will hibernate. With any luck, we only have to worry about other humans. We can pack up all the gear we can carry, start heading west and be there in less than a month. I can check the cell phone, it should have GPS, we might be able to find a faster way to get there. If the satellites are still working that is. I have my doubts."

John felt a lump in his throat. "Thank you. But it's too dangerous. I'm not sure I'm up to something like that. I still don't feel all that great." He laughed. "I don't remember what I'm supposed to feel like. My body aches, my muscles feel like I ran a marathon." John stood with his plate and helped himself to another half serving. He added a little more to Carrie's plate without asking her if she wanted any. "My head is still fuzzy and my bones hurt, if that makes sense, and I keep having these flashes of, something, things that I can't place."

Carrie thanked him and ate even though she wasn't hungry. "Those are probably repressed human memories coming back to the surface and blending with infected memories. Can you tell the difference between the two?"

John swirled the mashed potatoes into the brown sugar and carrots. "I can't tell. It's like a throwing all your ingredients in a food blender, whipping them up, pouring it into a bowl and then trying to dissect what's in the slurry," he explained, as his free hand swirled a finger in the air. "I can see quick flashes of things I don't comprehend or understand."

Carrie finished the rest of her plate, picked up John's as well and took them both to the sink. Turning to John, she said, "I don't think any of that matters, we need to find …"

"Katherine. Katie," John said with a smile. "She thought Katherine was too formal.

There was quite a bit of food left in the pot as she emptied everything onto a clean plate. "We should pack up our gear and head out as soon as day breaks to search for Katie. What do you say? If we wait until the snow falls, it will make travelling that much more difficult." Carrie paused, "Difficult but safer. What do you think?"

John stood, cleaning the table without looking at her, "Let's discuss this in the morning. I need to feel one hundred percent before starting on a month-long journey in this weather. Maybe my body is still getting used to the change. And eating so much. It's a lot for me to go through; my memories may come back over night, and I may remember more about Katie in the morning. Let's re-visit this tomorrow. OK?"

Carrie shrugged and smiled. Nodded in agreement, she went back to cleaning up the kitchen area.

Not long after, she double-checked the lock on the door, brushed her teeth, something she missed doing daily, then helped set up John's bed in the tub with extra blankets and a pillow. "You gonna be OK in the tub?" she asked, watching him wiggle in, trying to get comfortable.

Climbing out of the tub, he smiled. "I think I'll try the bathroom floor."

"You don't wanna sleep on the floor in the main room?"

As John set up the blankets on the bathroom floor, he looked Carrie square in the eyes. "It's still too early for you to trust me that much. I'll stay in the bathroom where you can lock me in if things go awry."

Carrie agreed and wished John a good night as she closed the door. She thought it best that he wasn't aware she still slept with a handgun under her pillow.

Hours after bedding down, John shifted back and forth on the floor, pulling the blankets up high, then kicking them off. Sleep was not easy to come by. The room was dark, as dark as when he used to bury his head in the dirt like an ostrich to protect his eyes from light. Now, the darkness scared him, terrified him; all he wanted was light. The room was black, as black as anything he had ever seen; there wasn't any light, not a sliver beaming through a crack in the wood, nothing. Standing, he blindly felt his way to the door and gently pushed on it. It was locked, tightly secured. For the first time in a long time, John feared the very darkness he used to live in. Laying back down, he felt trapped in the room but would not let his anxiety overtake him. Despite not being able to see anything, he still turned his head back and forth, looking into the darkness for something that might be lurking. It was irrational thinking, he knew that, there wasn't anything in the room, but it felt like a million thoughts were inside his head, talking to him. He let his body go limp, emptied his mind and took in a few deep breaths. Then he began to relax.

Every time he would drift off, images filled his head, images that he didn't recognize or understand, places he thought he knew but he could have seen on television or in movies during a time when those things existed. Images began to flash in and out so fast, it became impossible to know for certain what they were or where they were from.

Forcing his eyes shut, John pulled the blanket up high around his neck, took in a deep breath and held it for several seconds, then exhaled. He repeated this several times, thinking about Katie, forcing any other image away, far away. With his breathing under control, he focused on his daughter, attempting to remember when he last saw her, what she was doing, what she wore, where they were. He began to recall work, small fragments of his life, Katie's birthdays, and outings with her. In his mind, he watched her grow up, then the visions of Katie disappeared in a haze. He felt when the infection took hold, felt his body change, sensed the pain of the transformation. He could see his body gradually alter, his mind slowly going blank, then nothing until the re-awakening. Now, John was being flooded with images of so many things, he couldn't possibly comprehend what he was seeing.

The images came cascading in, flashing so quickly he wasn't able to view them, they seem to be coming from all around, people, places and events; he couldn't have done all the things or have been to all the places he was seeing in his mind. He forced his eyes shut hard and covered them with his hands, but the images kept coming. He saw a large group of infected walking, some held up in a building's basement. In the darkness, they huddled around for warmth, bodies bumping into each other; he could see their faces and they scared him. He had been like that once and instinctively he knew what they were doing. He saw their faces, as they parted way, allowing John to pass them all until he came to Katie. John's head began to hurt so much that he was certain he was having a stroke and would die. Then, silence. All the strength left him, his arms dropped to his sides and he passed out.

Day 924

Carrie woke that morning wondering what the day would bring. Slipping out from under the covers, she felt the chill in the air. The temperature had dropped overnight and she was happy she hadn't been tied up in a tree. Despite feeling comfortable in her new tiny cabin, she had promised John that they could go to Philadelphia and search for Katie, and she would live up to that promise.

As her feet hit the floor, she heard tapping on the bathroom door. "Are you awake yet?" John asked quietly.

Carrie wrapped herself in an oversized sweater, unlatched the door and greeted him. "Morning roomie," she said, turning towards the kitchen to make herself something warm to drink. But before she could pump the water, John sat at the table and asked her to join him. She went to the wood stove, stoked the embers and added a few logs before sitting down.

For the first time, Carrie noticed how very handsome John was, even though his was looking rather serious, almost ominous. She crossed her legs under the chair and tucked her hands inside the sleeves. "What's up?"

"Do you remember when you thought I was the first of my kind to change back to being human?" John asked. Before Carrie could answer, he pressed on. "Turns out, I'm not. There are thousands of us. And there will be more."

Carrie paused, shocked at what she was hearing, "That's good news. That means the infection has run its course and people are recovering."

Without saying a word, John stared at Carrie, unblinking, his eyes clear and focused, "No. This is something different, something better."

"Better?" she questioned him. "What do you mean, better? What are you talking about?" She was confused by his sudden change and direct comments.

John had a sincere expression on his face. "What we've become is not human; we're more than human, and for me, the infection has completed its final phase."

Carrie sat back in her chair and with an inquisitive look, she stared at him. "Thousands? There are thousands just like you? What do you mean final phase?" She felt her stomach twist into knots; she swallowed. "And, not human?"

"Katie is still infected, but she isn't dead. I saw her last night and she told me where she is. I told her I would go to her. She's waiting for me."

Fear overtook Carrie, her pulse quickened, inside the sweater sleeves her hands clenched into fists ready to fight. Looking up at her bed in the loft, she knew where her handgun was. John stood between her and the weapon. "K, you're scaring the shit outta me. Let's take a step back and why don't you explain what the fuck is going on?"

With a calmness that Carrie had never seen in him, John stood and walked about the room. Carrie kept her guard up for anything that might happen.

"Last night, I heard hundreds of thousands, if not millions of voices calling me. It was silent communication; we can't talk in the transition phase, but I could hear them in my head. And I can speak to them and understand the others just like me. They are all over the world, every corner, every country. They told me what we are destined to be."

Carrie immediately knew the danger she was in, stood and circled the room, keeping her distance from John, slowly making her way toward the loft. "Destined for what?" She already knew the answer but had to stall. “Destined for world domination? An attempt at a new world order?”

“We are the next stage in evolution. Each one of us has within us to evolve into what I’ve become, what those before me have become. The transition is scary, but worth it.” John stretched his arms out. “I feel strong, alive. I can feel my heart beating. I have a pulse again.”

Carrie made her way around the table and was close to the bed in the loft, keeping her focus on John, hoping his attention remained on her and not on her movement. She paused behind a chair, placing her hands on the back, grasping it tightly. If he attempted anything, she could swing the chair to protect herself. “Explain ‘worth it.’”

John adjusted himself in the chair, crossing his legs, a move making him look human, unaware of her intentions. “Last night, I heard from people like me who have already made the transition. What I discovered is that we are so much more than human; we are the next stage, and once we’ve all fully transitioned, we’ll be stronger, more intelligent, disease free—and we will all stop aging.” He leaned forward on the table and locked fingers. “Be honest, wouldn’t you prefer to be like this? Like me?”

Carrie saw her chance, she turned and casually moved closer to the loft “No, absolutely not. The cost to become like you is too high. You killed your own kind and those that were uninfected. Is that what you call progress? Because honestly, what you did was horrible and disgusting. Is this how you justify your existence? You reached a higher plane and those you’ve killed along the way don’t matter.” She backed up to the edge of the loft and climbed the ladder, pretending to adjust the blanket as they spoke, ready to reach under the pillow for the gun and kill John if she had to.

“You’re right. It’s cliché, but sometimes there are casualties along the way. If it wasn't for you, I wouldn't be here, so I could never hurt you. You know that, right? At least, I couldn't hurt you, but those who are making the transition still aren't sentient and they don't know the difference between right and wrong. They are simply trying to survive."

Backing away slightly from the bed, Carrie relaxed when John admitted he couldn't hurt her, but she remained vigilant to the possible risks. John continued to explain that each of the infected that evolved like himself were leaders of a region and would have hundreds or thousands of drones beneath them until they themselves evolved. John was the first of his type in this region. As a leader developed, the drones would follow, and the leaders would co-ordinate matters from long distances.

"So, what happens when you all evolve, and the process is complete. There won't be any more drones. Do you fight for supremacy? This is what you want?" Carrie asked.

"It's not what I want, it's what I've become. And what I am is what you see before you," John offered.

"And me? What about me? And what about the rest of humanity?"

John paused, knowing that the answer would not be what Carrie wanted to hear. "We are now the dominant species on the planet. History has always shown that when a new dominant species arrives, it displaces the old. I'm sorry, that's evolution. You know it."

Carrie knew at that moment that she had to stop John and the others. Before he could react, she pulled the gun from under the pillow, cocked the hammer and pointed it at him. Her aim never left John as she stepped from the ladder.

Looking down the barrel of the gun, she addressed him. "So, you're saying that eventually, you and your kind will kill the rest of humanity?"

John wasn't surprised by Carrie's reaction. "I'm saying that mankind has shown by example what has been done in the past. We can learn from your mistakes, become better."

"You and your kind are no different than humans were only hundreds of years ago. They fought, killing each other for land and food. Look at what your drones are doing now; they eat themselves if they have to. No different than human history."

John thought for a moment. "True, but we are stronger. We are disease free and still evolving. It's evolution. There can't be two dominant species on one planet. You and your kind have to be," John thought for moment, "eliminated."

Anger welled up inside Carrie. She pulled the trigger, a section of wood exploded behind John. She purposely aimed just to the left of his head. "Next shot won't miss."

John laughed. "Why would you give me a warning shot? You know I have to do this. It's not just who I am; it's what I am. You may as well just shoot me now because I won't stop—we won't stop—but I'm not going to kill you. I owe you that much. But you won't make it out of the cabin if you do shoot me."

Confused, she asked, "Who's gonna stop me if you're dead? I assume you can be killed."

"Of course I can be killed. But you don't have enough bullets for all of them." John held his hands up slowly. "May I?" Carrie nodded.

Slowly, John walked to the cabin door, unlocked it, and with purpose and effect, pulled it open. Outside, hundreds of infected stood in the morning light. Stunned, Carrie stumbled backwards, horrified at what she had just seen. Her heart beating wildly in her chest. She had never seen infected in the bright daylight, but there they were, scraps of material wrapped around their eyes to protect their vision. They stood perfectly motionless, all facing her, looking through their makeshift sunglasses.

John closed the door, turning to Carrie. "You are only alive because I'm alive. Kill me. They kill you. It's your choice."

Carrie lowered the gun, "What now?"

John grabbed Carrie's backpack and tossed it at her. She let it hit her and fall to the floor. "Fill it with whatever you want. Take anything you can carry and leave. I've already told them that you've got free passage, and no one is to touch you. I owe you that much at least."

"You told them I've got free passage? To where?" she screamed. "What if I blow your fucking head off right now? They're a bunch of mindless drones. They don't know what's going on." She raised the gun, aiming it his head.

John seemed unphased by her sudden burst of anger. "I die. But I've already been dead. I'm not afraid to die again. I told them, if I'm dead, kill the girl. It's simple. If you don't believe me, shoot." He offered himself, stepping closer to the end of the gun barrel so Carrie couldn't miss.

The gun was held high, aimed directly at John's head. Their eyes locked onto each other; no further words were spoken for several minutes as Carrie weighed her options. Eventually she lowered the gun but continued to hold it at the ready. Despite what she was seeing, Carrie had feelings for John, and she couldn't simply kill him. Emotions swirled inside her, instinct fighting reason—what she knew she should do versus what she could do.

Without taking her eyes off him, Carrie picked up the backpack and placed it on the table. "How long do I have?"

John took a seat, and offered the chair opposite to him; Carrie sat. "Take as long as you need. Find what you need—food, clothing, any medications, whatever—you can have as much as you can carry. But make no mistake, do anything stupid and you will be stopped."

Picking up the backpack, she unzipped it, dumped the contents onto the table then rummaged through them, picking and choosing what she wanted. Quickly, she pulled food from the cabinets, finding items that would be light enough to carry—a few bottles of medication, the phone and solar charger. Once her pack was full of clothing, food and ammunition, she put on warm layers and a heavy jacket, jamming the handgun into one of the pockets and zipping it closed.

It took less time than she thought to pack her gear. Carrie didn't want to be around John any longer than she had to. Slinging her pack over her shoulder, she picked up the rifle, checked the clip and made her way to the door.

"I will find you and kill you. That's a promise." Carrie's stared at John, never wavering.

Like a gentleman, he opened the door to reveal the hundreds of infected, standing guard outside the cabin. They remained motionless; their eyes covered with their makeshift shields to protect them from daylight. As Carrie stood at the door, they slowly parted to create a narrow path that led out beyond the edge of the woods.

Glancing over her shoulder, Carrie noticed John standing proudly as he gazed at his group of disciples. Carrie was filled with fright at the thought of having to walk past hundreds of infected, wondering if they would obey John and simply let her slip away. She looked out into the crowd, a gathering of young and old, men, women, and children in tattered clothing, with grey skin and the stench of decay and waste. Before taking her first step, she looked back at John, the man she'd saved and considered a friend, "This isn't over," she stated through clenched teeth.

John laughed as if he had just heard the funniest joke ever told. "Over …" He laughed a little more, then composed himself. "Over. Of course, it's not over. We've barely begun."

Carrie wanted nothing more than to stuff the barrel of her gun down his throat and pull the trigger over and over until she ran out of bullets. Instead, she took one step outside the cabin, and waited to see if the infected would pounce on her. Instead, they parted slightly further, and watched as she started to make her way through the crowd. To intimidate her, some would get too close and forcibly bump her, causing her to stumble into the infected on the opposite side. She despised even touching them as the intense odour reminded her of rotting flesh. Her anxiety grew as she walked carefully between them. She moved her right hand down to the handle of the stock and rested her index finger on the trigger.

Carrie paused for a moment, turned, and saw John standing in the doorway, watching her walk away. She wondered if she had been played all along, or if he'd really had a sudden realization of who he truly was the night before. When she finally made it beyond the group of infected surrounding the cabin, Carrie walked another twenty feet before turning again to see John still standing in the doorway, ensuring that she leave as ordered.

"Is this a 'till we meet again' moment—or the end?" Carrie shouted.

"We will meet again," John said, "there's no question of that."

Even from fifty feet away, Carrie could see him slowly smile.

"After all, I've been told your family and Noah are also uninfected—and I know where they are."

In one motion, she raised the rifle, and without taking aim—fired.

NOT THE END